P9-BAW-385

MR. FAHRENHEIT

T. MICHAEL MARTIN

Balzer + Bray
An Imprint of HarperCollins*Publishers*

For my grandparents

Balzer + Bray is an imprint of HarperCollins Publishers.

Mr. Fahrenheit
Copyright © 2016 by T. Michael Martin
All rights reserved. Printed in the United States of America.
No part of this book may be used or reproduced in any manner whatsoever without written permission except in the case of brief quotations embodied in critical articles and reviews. For information address HarperCollins Children's Books, a division of HarperCollins Publishers, 195 Broadway, New York, NY 10007.
www.epicreads.com

Library of Congress Control Number: 2015951287
ISBN 978-0-06-220183-6

Typography by Ray Shappell
16 17 18 19 20 PC/RRDH 10 9 8 7 6 5 4 3 2 1
❖
First Edition

AUTHOR'S NOTE

Mr. Fahrenheit is a work of fiction containing some nonfiction elements that have been altered slightly to fit the story. For instance, Captain Thomas Mantell really did die tragically in pursuit of a UFO in 1948, but the conversation between him and the control tower in *Mr. Fahrenheit* is my invention. Similarly, some details about the "Roswell Incident" have been rearranged and may not match the real-life accounts of the events . . . though whether those accounts are "fiction" themselves is a matter of opinion, I guess.

The bands and lyrics featured in *Mr. Fahrenheit* are also made up. If you're interested in learning more about the history of early rock 'n' roll, particularly doo-wop, I highly recommend *Doo Wop: The Music, the Times, the Era* by Bruce Morrow and Rich Maloof.

The world is nearly all parceled out, and
what there is left of it is being divided up, conquered, and
colonized. To think of these stars that you see overhead at
night, these vast worlds which we can never reach. I would
annex the planets if I could; I often think of that.
It makes me sad to see them so clear and yet so far.
—Cecil Rhodes, *The Last Will and Testament
of Cecil John Rhodes*

◖○○

But the true voyagers are those who leave
For the sake of leaving; hearts light, like balloons,
They never swerve from their destinies,
And without knowing why, they say always,"We must go!"
—Charles Baudelaire, "The Voyage"

PROLOGUE

FIRELIGHT OF THE VANISHING SUMMER

Without something to wonder at
we should find life scarcely worth living.
—Harry Houdini

He is just a boy, that's all, just a child walking through the fire-light of the vanishing summer's last sunset. He walks with his nerve endings ignited like constellations. The air tastes dark and electric on the back of his mouth; sweat molds his hair into sharp broomstraw points on his brow; a wind slips by and the witch-grass hisses, and dead leaves grasp his naked calves, like hands begging him to go back. *No,* he tells himself. But it doesn't quite steel him, so he adds: *Ellie.* And when the boy feels his hands still shaking, he slips them into his deep hip pockets, where he carries magic in the same fashion a gunslinger hauls his iron firepower. The boy won't be held back. Not tonight, and never again.

He steps into the shadow of the haunted home.

His name is Benji Lightman. He is eleven years old. He lives in Bedford Falls, Indiana. And he is walking toward this ancient front door so he can perform his ultimate trick:

On the night before middle school begins, Benji will make himself disappear.

The house—which is "the House," capital *H*, like Hell—has loomed on this hill forever. Benji cranes his neck to take it in, dwarfed by the ghost fortress, which shoots skyward like a jagged arrow fired into the brighter heavens. Benji knows the legends: A crazy hook-handed doctor lives inside the House; Satanic warlocks meet here every full moon to sacrifice stray dogs. The stories aren't true, though. (They *almost definitely* aren't true.) He asked Papaw (who has loomed above Benji forever, too), and Papaw said the stories were "comprised of the same material that falls out of a bull's ass." Which sounded more convincing this morning, at home. In the sunlight. With Froot Loops.

Now Benji pauses before the porch step, steals a last glance over his shoulder, and sees his friends a world away across the wild yard. Zeeko, the shorter of them, scrunches his dark face toward the sky, glasses flashing, shoulders hitching with each breath, lips moving with prayer. He is nervous and does not want to throw up (which he will, in fact, soon do). A few eighth-grade giants stand beside him, long-shadowed and stubbled like cacti, and epic in every way Benji is not.

But that is not what Benji will remember most.

What he will remember is this: Christopher Robin Noland, looking back at him in that blazing August light . . . and bursting into applause.

Christopher Robin Noland, the new kid next door; Christopher Robin, rail skinny and homeschooled; Christopher, who always looks like an unmade bed but is the only real friend Benji has ever made since meeting Zeeko in preschool.

"YEAH, BENJI! AW-RIGHT! LET'S DOOO THIS, BAY-BUH!" he crows. "WAHOO, BANJO! WAHOOOO!"

The eighth graders, who brought them here, stare at Christopher as if he's an alien.

But there is something in that admittedly awkward shout that Benji loves with his whole heart: an unembarrassed joy. It is the sound of someone who is certain something astonishing is coming.

Ellie, Benji thinks. He'd hoped she would be here, and maybe she'll still show up.

Shaun Spinney, most gigantic of the older kids, shouts, "What, Lightman, you forget your tampon?" Benji has no clue what that is. He doesn't let on. "Don't you wanna join our frat? Hey, if you don't, we can go back!"

Benji steps onto the porch, feeling the old wood shudder and cry out through the sole of his sneaker.

But he won't be held back.

Because he knows that behind this red and rotting door, destiny is waiting. From his pocket Benji draws out his black wand, the great one with the glowing LED tip, and he wants to say *"Lumos,"* the way Harry Potter does when he ignites his own wand. *Those stories are comprised of the same material that falls out of a bull's ass.*

"Lumos," Benji whispers.

The wand lights the brass doorknob with a hundred star points, and when Benji's palm meets the metal, the door opens a shrieking inch, almost all by itself. The smell of the House is like darkness and decay and bad memories, but it does not frighten him. He's dreamed every night this summer—almost every night of his *life*—of something coming for him, something from beyond the rusting silos and gas-mining equipment and corn-fields on Bedford Falls's horizon, some flawless moment in this perfect summer that will make him disappear (*presto!*), undergo a metamorphosis, and vanish any memory of the "weird kid" he's always been.

In this dusk light, at the nexus of his life, Benji is about to do it.

He really believes that. With his whole heart.

Benji Lightman opens the door.

And the ghosts begin to scream.

PART ONE
WATCH THE SKIES

Many years ago, the great British explorer George
Mallory, who was to die on Mount Everest, was asked
why did he want to climb it. He said, "Because it is
there." Well, space is there, and we're going to climb it.
—President John F. Kennedy (1962)

Magic reminds us that the universe is a huge,
capital-M Mystery.
—from the documentary *Make Believe*

1

Benji opened the door and strode with the Bedford Falls High School football team into the locker room.

He put on his uniform piece by piece: the gloves he always wore on cold game nights, the shoes with special spikes. The cinder-block walls glowed white in the fluorescent lights as the room filled with the electric anticipation of pregame.

After the team dressed in their blue-and-gold uniforms, they gathered in a semicircle around Coach Nicewarner, who began to tattoo a dry-erase board with X's and O's. Coach looked a lot older than his fortyish years right now, which made sense given everyone's stratospheric expectations for the team this year: Led by the greatest athlete in the school's history, Bedford Falls was on their way to their first undefeated season in decades.

"Make no mistake, fellas," Nicewarner shouted in a nasal, farm-boy accent, "we're going to have to fight tonight. Nobody rest for a single play. Not one single play!"

The team responded, "YES, SIR."

"Don't you dare think of this game as a 'warm-up' for next week. This is their field. You match 'em on it hit for hit, gut for gut. You will not let them take down your team—or your town."

"NO, SIR."

"We will win or lose as a damn team. No single player can do it all, y'understand?" Coach said, though this wasn't entirely true.

"YES, SIR."

Coach Nicewarner capped his dry-erase marker, tossed it to an assistant, and addressed the team, now in a much more sincere voice.

"It's a cold night out there, gentlemen, so you do what you always do: You give your hometown the sun. Show the other team what Magic football means. It means one good, unforgettable ass-bustin'! Okay, let us pray!" Coach looked Benji's way. "Captain, you want to lead us?"

The team's captain, the brilliant Bedford Falls quarterback—who was standing beside Benji—nodded and stepped forward. The team collectively took a knee and bowed their heads.

And as the Our Father filled the room, Benji finished buttoning his tuxedo, put on his top hat, and left.

This field house's hallway was decorated in the style of every field house hallway in the charted galaxies. Teams from years past stared down somberly from photos on the walls. Stenciled between them were words of generic manly wisdom (*You 4GET your PAIN, You REMEMBER your GLORY!*). Benji wove through the parents hovering outside the locker rooms, and he could hear the home team's own pregame pep talk, which was identical to Coach Nicewarner's in its God-praisin' and ass-bustin' themes. It was just a game night, that was all, and Benji had attended almost every game night for four years. They'd lost their novelty for him a long time ago.

But as he opened the door at the end of the hall and stepped toward the familiarly chaotic night, his insides backflipped with nervous excitement. Time and experience might dampen most miracles, but the sight of genuine beauty was not among them.

She was standing at the end of the tunnel.

The concrete tunnel ran beneath the bleachers before shooting onto the field. Benji could feel the stomping game-night mania of countless fans inches above his head; on the field, the Bedford Falls band blistered the air with their brassy rendition of the school fight song, which would momentarily summon Benji into the lights.

But it was the sight of the familiar silhouette at the other end of the tunnel, and nothing else, that made his heart skip a beat.

"Hey!" he called.

Ellie Holmes turned. "Benji Lightman! When did you become so dapper? Does James Bond know you raided his wardrobe?"

Huh? Benji thought, then remembered: The school had just bought him a new "Magic Mascot" tux. "Also, Batman's wardrobe," he said. He pulled a string on his shoulder; a black cape unfurled all the way to his ankles.

"Holy fashion icon." Ellie grinned.

By the time Benji reached her, she'd turned away, aiming the Media Department's expensive video camera toward the Bedford Falls fans in the bleachers across the field. She looked miserable, for some reason.

"What's up?" he asked.

"Nothing. Okay, well, not that it's a gigantic deal, Benji Lightman, but the apocalypse is upon us." She thumbed the camera's Zoom button; the lens whirred as the Bedford Falls crowd grew larger on the LCD screen. "And lo, the skies were opened," she said, speaking loudly as the band crescendoed, "and the seven plagues burst forth, and the first among those plagues was this:

11

a swarm of innumerable FIGs returning to torment us even though homecoming isn't until next week, damn you!"

Benji burst out laughing. FIG was code: "Forgot I Graduated," a term applied to people who had technically completed high school but didn't quite seem *finished* with it. There were a ton of Bedford Falls–based FIGs, of course—depressing fixtures of the local high school party scene. Bedford Falls's FIG population always exploded during Homecoming Week, but it did seem like this year's migration had begun earlier than usual. Maybe this was partly because tonight's game had been delayed by a snowstorm and was taking place a day late, on a Saturday. But it was probably mostly because everyone wanted to get an extra look at the Magic quarterback.

Still staring at the camera, Ellie shook her head and sighed, a never-ending stream of her breath (which smelled like cinnamon) rising in front of her green eyes. If she was trying to look like the world's cutest dragon, well, she did. Benji made an effort to look away.

When she finished and glanced up, her forehead was creased a little in something approaching fear. "Promise me you'll never let me do that after I leave next year," she said.

"Not for all the gold in Gotham."

Ellie chuckled. "Wait, promise on camera. Pics or it didn't happen!"

"On my honor as a double-oh agent," he said when she raised the camera to him, "I swear I won't let you do that after we leave next year."

"Fabulous. Now say Something Profoundly Profound to your future self."

"Ummm."

"Slightly more profound, please."

"Congrats on becoming the greatest magician since ever."

"And in spite of all your successes, Mr. Lightman, have you ever forgotten where you came from?"

"Oh, yeah. I purposely forgot, like, pretty much immediately."

Ellie laughed. "Good man. Oh! That reminds me: How's the application to the Magic Lantern coming?"

Benji's smile faltered, just a bit. Then the marching band blasted its final note, which was his cue.

"How do I look?" he asked.

Ellie gave him a once-over, then reached up and tilted his top hat a little to the left, her soft wrist touching his cheek for an infinitesimal moment. "Poifect," she said, and Benji didn't know what Coach Nicewarner had been talking about: The night didn't feel cold at all.

The moment when he emerged onto the field was, as always, vaguely fantastic.

The field lights, which climbed high and silver on spindly poles, tossed a white illuminative bubble above the stadium. Under the dome of light, the chalked yardlines appeared ignited. The bleachers on both sides of the field were packed to capacity, eight thousand-ish people. As the final note of the fight song ("A Mighty Magic!") hung on the air, a deep voice resounded over the speakers.

"Bedford Falls fans, please welcome yourrrrr Bedford Falls Magic mascot: Bennnnnjiii BUH-LAZES!"

Half the crowd roared as Benji wove between members of the marching band now standing at attention. He knew this was just an Indiana high school football game, and that people weren't applauding for him so much as for the idea of the football team, the only positive and *pure* thing to come from Bedford Falls in years. But wow, did he love performing.

He stopped in the perfect center of the field, facing his crowd in the away bleachers. A microphone was clipped to his lapel. He cleared his throat, reached into his tuxedo pocket, and thumbed the mic on.

He said, "Who are we?"

His voice boomed from the arena speakers, amplified a thousand times (and always sounding slightly higher than he imagined it). The Bedford Falls crowd's roar, led by the cheerleaders, vocalized around one word:

"MAAAAGIC!"

Benji clapped his hands, which burst into instantaneous flame, courtesy of the pyrotechnic flash paper on the palms of his gloves. At the same moment, two cheerleaders fired T-shirt cannons: Cotton comets arced into the crowd, which said, *"Oooooo!"* (Their *"Oooo"* came in a more subdued volume than you'd probably expect from spontaneous combustion and free shirts, but they'd been seeing this trick all season.)

At the perfect instant, with smoke obscuring his hands, Benji twitched his wrist: A magic wand, loaded on a spring, ejected from his sleeve and flew into his hand.

"What do we do?" Benji asked. (Somewhere behind him, in the home crowd, a fan shouted, "SUCK!")

The Bedford Falls side disagreed: "MAAAGIC!" Now a volley of blue and gold sparks jetted forth from the wand's tip. Benji whirled on his heels, aiming his spell in the direction of the home stands, grinning like a perfectly friendly wizard nemesis.

He hurled the wand to the turf. It detonated between his feet, raising a great column of smoke. A few people in the home stands booed, but a couple of little kids, who hadn't yet learned to hate on command, shouted in delight.

Benji raised his hands with a flourish; playing cards, propelled by springs, flew from both sleeves like doves. He grabbed a card from each deck, displaying them to the audience: One card read *8*, the other *0*. His team's undefeated record.

Benji reeled back like Bedford Falls's famed quarterback, preparing to slam both explosive cards to the ground. He shouted his final line: "Let's make it *nine* and—"

A squeal of feedback screeched over the speaker system. Benji flinched, thrown off his rhythm.

There was a kind of rumbling sound, like someone was wrestling over the microphone in the press box. Then, a voice: "Lightman puts flash paper on his gloves to make the fire. You can get it on Amazon for three bucks a sheet."

The voice wasn't the announcer's. It sounded like a teenage guy.

"The wand's a Sparkler Stick. Twelve bucks," the guy said, starting to laugh. "Bedford Falls, you suck, you bunch of rednecks! Have fun tonight, 'cause Newporte's gonna kick alllll your asses next week! Benji Lightman, you suck, Bedford Falls you suck, NEWPORTE HIGH SCHOOL FOOTBALL FOREVER!"

The Bedford Falls crowd booed. Some in the home crowd started laughing. A grown man's voice, off mic, said, "Kid, you get the heck away from that!"

After what sounded like a scuffle for control of the mic, the younger voice spouted one final sentence.

"Hey, Lightman, don't set yourself on fire again."

Benji's cheeks flared. In his mind, he pictured an old red door.

He cut the thought off, shouting, "Let's make it nine and zero!"

He hurled the cards to the earth: two bangs of light and smoke, this time in the school colors of blue and gold. The marching band blared to life and the Bedford Falls Magic football team erupted out of the stadium tunnel, a rushing stream of shoulder pads and shining helmets, splitting around Benji like they were a river and he a stone.

He was almost back to the tunnel when a Bedford Falls player grabbed his bicep. The player's fingertips bore white rings of athletic tape, the better to grip the ball on cold nights.

"Wrong way, sexy," he said. The voice echoed through the stadium; Benji realized his lapel mic was still broadcasting and switched it off.

"Whatever you're thinking of doing," Benji told him, "let's do the other thing." But he was already resigned to the fact that protesting was useless, because he recognized the expression on the player's face: laser-guided rage. It was the same focused fury, familiar from four years of football game nights, that had made this quarterback the most singular and legendary athlete in the history of Bedford Falls High School.

Quarterback Christopher Robin "CR" Noland said, "Nobody puts my Banjo in a corner."

The marching band departed the field in formation. The teams were stationed on the sidelines; the only people on the field now were each team's offensive captain and the referee waiting on the fifty-yard line. CR was Bedford Falls's captain. A lean mountain who towered over Benji by six inches, CR had hit puberty early and hard: Shortly after moving to town during the vanishing summer before sixth grade, he'd sprouted like a kid christened by comic-book radiation.

Nearing the (bewildered) referee, CR stuck two fingers through his helmet's face mask and whistled in the direction of the Bedford Falls sidelines. "Zeeko, this is a party of three!" he called.

Zeeko—the team's trainer and one of the few African Americans on the sidelines—looked uncertainly at Coach Nicewarner, who, after a moment's indecision, motioned for him to join CR.

"Jesus, help us," Zeeko muttered as he caught up with Benji and CR, his eyes enormous behind his thick glasses. But there was a laugh in his voice.

As they reached the fifty-yard line, the other team's captain glared at CR. "Son," the ref said to CR, confused, "this is a captains-only, no-mascots type deal."

"Hell, sir, you think I don't know that?" CR said earnestly. "These good-looking studs *are* captains."

"Love of God, son, they don't even have uniforms," said the ref. As if Benji's tuxedo wasn't enough, Zeeko was wearing the plaid hoodie and boxy Kmart jeans that had earned him his (affectionate) nickname, "Dad Clothes."

CR grinned, this huge smile that was absurd on his face, but it was precisely that goofiness that made it the sort of smile you just had to believe. *C'mon, now, would I lie?* "They're injured," he said. "Special teams."

"More like special ed," the other team's captain muttered.

"You'll want to watch that mouth, kid!" CR growled. The captain visibly recoiled. It was not CR's normal voice: It was his Quarterback Voice. *Talk about magic*, Benji thought.

"Sir, I sure don't want to tell you how to ref," CR said, normal-voiced, "but I think our crowd's kinda ticked about that little prank on the speakers. Am I saying that maybe, just maybe, somebody in your press box let those Newporte players in? Nope! That, I am not doing! But how about we let these fine young Americans stay here for the coin toss, just to call it even?"

The ref paused, tallying the calculus of pros and cons. "Well . . ." he said, "let's not make a habit of this."

"Great, thanks a ton!" Then CR turned to the sidelines again and shouted, "Eleanor, come get a close-up!"

The ref looked like he wanted to object as Ellie walked toward them with her camera in tow and a rueful smile on her face. But she stopped about fifteen feet away, which was apparently an acceptable distance, and the ref seemed to decide it was time to rip the Band-Aid off.

He flipped the coin, the floating disc twirling and flashing in the field lights. He caught it and slapped it onto his wrist. "Call it, Bedford Falls."

"Heads," CR replied.

The ref took his hand off the coin. Tails. "We choose to receive the kickoff," the other captain said.

Benji looked at CR, wondering if he might be upset by this not-so-awesome turn of events. CR just stage-whispered, "Benji, turn your mic on."

As Benji did so, CR did something strange: He slammed his fist on the chest of his filthy jersey, which he'd refused to wash since their victory the week before. (The Bedford Falls football field, he said, was the place in the world that most felt like his home.)

A thin trickle of dirt tumbled off the jersey. CR caught it in his hand and said, "We're gonna need more. Zeek, Banjo, put your hands out."

Confused, they held their open hands palms up in front of him.

CR proceeded to beat his chest like Donkey Kong until their palms were sprinkled with dirt.

He nodded, satisfied.

CR (to the captain, but amplified for the rest of the stadium): "Do you know what that is?"

The captain: "Dirt . . . ?"

CR: "That's our field. That's Bedford Falls."

CR nodded to Benji and Zeeko, who suddenly understood. They tipped their hands, letting the earth tumble to the field, like they were baptizing it.

"So now this is *our* field," CR said, and then shouted directly into the mic, so his Quarterback Voice boomed through the universe like something vast and ancient. "You're in our house, fellas!"

Following the call of his performer's instinct, Benji snapped his fingers, the pyrotechnic sheets momentarily flaring the moment with magical light as CR finished:

"You are *IN. OUR. HOUSE!*"

And the Bedford Falls fans surged to their feet, their roar cracking like a joyous lightning electrifying every atom of the night. Benji, CR, and Zeeko turned from the stupefied captain and referee, Ellie following with the camera capturing everything: four friends who had become the unlikely center of the universe striding together toward their sideline. It was just a game night, that was all, but amid that happy mayhem, nothing in all the world could have felt more enchanted.

Nothing else on planet Earth.

2

The Bedford Falls victory was as spectacular as it was assured. Final score: 59 to 3, and their opponents only got on the scoreboard because CR let his second-string quarterback (a wide-eyed junior nicknamed Charlie Brown) take over near the end.

A post-game party was assured, too, but its location wound up surprising Benji. And when he looked back on this night later, he wondered if "surprising" was the wrong word. "Inevitable" was better, maybe.

Or "destined."

After the game, Benji hung his tuxedo and top hat in a garment bag, tugged on two hoodies and a pair of jeans, then, very cautiously, peeked through the door into the hall outside the locker room.

The instant the door cracked, a solid wall of media people—photographers and writers and TV reporters with logos on their microphones—swarmed forward.

Benji smiled apologetically, said, "Players and sorcerers only," and closed the door.

"Christ on a friggin' cracker, Banjo," CR said, toweling his hair in front of a locker, "how many people are out there?"

"All of them, I think," Benji said. CR gave a dry chuckle. "Like, twenty. Mostly local, but there's TV people from Chicago. Want to do an interview?"

He already knew what CR's answer would be, of course: *Hellll no.* The reporters in that hall would have donated a kidney to a terrorist in exchange for a few minutes with CR. In their minds, he was CR Noland, the Number One College Recruit in the Midwest. But the instant CR stepped off the football field and removed the cocoon of his helmet and pads, the attention usually made him a type of uncomfortable that verged on panicky. It wasn't something Benji ever brought up, though.

"This TV reporter," CR said, pulling on boxers under his towel, "is she hot?"

"*He's* wearing a wedding ring."

"Double whammy!"

Zeeko and his dad burst out laughing at the mini medical station on the other side of the locker room. Zeeko's dad, Dr. Eustice, was a doctor from Sierra Leone who volunteered as the team's medical guy during games. Zeeko had inherited a lot from his dad (Zeeko's dream was to be a doctor in Bedford Falls), and one of those things was Dr. Eustice's easy, wonderfully booming laugh.

The locker room filled with more players from the showers, their celebratory shouts thunderclapping in the cinder-block cavern. CR accepted a series of fist bumps, but didn't look away from Benji. "Text Ellie to meet us at my truck behind the field house, okay?" CR said. "We'll sneak out the back . . . Shit, wait, there might be some reporters out there."

Benji thought about that, then said, "How 'bout this: I'll tell the reporters you're gonna have a quick press conference out on the field."

"Ha! I like it."

"Misdirection is useful, I'm telling ya. BTW, where's the party?"

"Charlie Brown's house." CR smiled, tying his shoes. "The kid still can't believe he got to touch the football."

Benji was almost to the door when CR called, "Oh, hey, Banjo. I liked how you exploded the wand tonight. I know it's not a new trick, but—new 'illusion,' sorry—but you threw it real good."

"Thanks, man," Benji said, honestly touched.

CR waved: *no biggie.*

After sending the reporters out of the hall, Benji headed toward an exit. He texted CR:

All clear

As he opened the door, someone quite large bumped into him.

"The field is that way," Benji began, then looked up. "O-oh. Hi, Mr. Noland."

The middle-aged man's face bore a resemblance to CR's, but only a blurry one. They shared the same broad mouth, the same sky-blue eyes. But CR's father's eyes always seemed narrowed, as if in some kind of ambient, low-level disgust. *Disgust with what?* Benji used to wonder. He'd decided the answer was "nothing in particular," which was of course another way of saying "everything." And you got the feeling that if that mouth had ever smiled, it had been by accident.

Mr. Noland stormed past Benji and toward the locker room, leaving Benji thinking, *I hope you're hurrying out of there already, CR.*

Benji stepped out through a side door in the field house, grateful, after the cramped hallways, for the wide-open space and cold air of the Indiana November night. The stadium was to his left, maybe a hundred feet away, and as he watched, the towering lights that ringed the stadium powered down one by one. There was a growing chorus of protest from the reporters on the field. Just before the last light went black, the announcer came over the speakers: "The stadium is *closed*. Everyone off the field."

Benji chuckled and pulled a deck of cards from his pocket, raising his gaze (still hazy from the field lights) to the sky, practicing complex card flourishes without looking at his hands—

An eye opened in the sky.

A few cards startled from his fingers. A globe of light, a strange and bright green light, pulsed in the clouds. It flickered, almost like heat lightning, except this was winter, and in the center of the pulse was a dark circle, like a pupil.

Benji blinked. And it was gone.

He turned when he heard CR's truck skid to a halt behind him. Zeeko opened the passenger door, hopped out, and whispered to Benji, "Be gentle. Our friend has come down with a mild case of *'I'm gonna kill my father.'*"

Uh-oh, Benji thought.

"My dad," CR said, "is a dick."

"In other news, the earth is round," Zeeko said.

"Ha-ha-ha," CR said sarcastically, then grinned. "That was sorta funny, actually." Benji got in, sardining himself between CR and Zeeko.

"What'd your dad say?" Benji asked.

CR seemed to weigh whether or not to tell him. "Just . . . whatever, it doesn't matter," he said, although clearly it did. "He hates me. He doesn't need a reason. He just needs an excuse to remind me. It's like he's jackin' off with sandpaper. Whatever, I don't care anymore. It's game night, Banjo, let's make my sobriety disappear."

"So, we're going to Charlie Brown's house, then?"

"Nope," CR said. "I just decided the party's gonna be somewhere else."

The old quarry, outside Bedford Falls, belonged to CR's dad. Getting there required enduring several miles of teeth-chattering forest roads, and then you were greeted by fences topped with rusting hoops of barbed wire, and a locked gate with a sign assuring you *TRESPASSERS WILL BE SHOT.* Inside the fences, you found a couple of acres that had once been a successful extraction point for natural gas and a quarry for granite and shale; they'd actually used some of the granite from here for the floor in the first Apple Store in Chicago. But nothing remained of that pre-Recession hot streak except a few Noland Natural Resources trucks and the enormous quarry pit, which had long since filled with water and become a frozen lake. This land was just a junkyard, mostly, home to abandoned cars, refrigerators, and ambitions.

Within an hour, the open space in the middle of the junkyard filled with a crowd of three hundred people, which was double the usual post-game party attendance. There was way more alcohol than usual, too. Both surpluses sprang from the same phenomenon: a Homecoming Week FIG invasion. Benji recognized some of the FIGs from when he was a freshman, plus or minus beer bellies. *More FIGs than a Newton factory,* he thought as he directed traffic with CR and Zeeko, and made a mental note to tell Ellie the joke when she got here. Somebody hooked their phone to a car stereo and whammed the night with distorted hip-hop; a few defensive linemen lit a bonfire that belched orange constellations of ash into the wild wind (which struck Benji as a fairly unwise decision, given that the quarry was surrounded by several miles of trees).

"Okay," CR said, "Banjo and Dad Clothes, y'guys babysit me, okay? I'm gonna get beertarded."

So Benji and Zeeko followed CR toward the crowd, the bonfire, and the nexus of everything awful about high school. And Benji did what he always did to survive the hot mess of makeouts, beer, and breakups: He pulled out a deck of cards.

He took off his gloves, even though he knew his cold fingers would fumble a few complex flourishes. Drunk people were a *very* easy audience. He walked the crowd, approaching people with a handy cheesy line ("How much does a polar bear weigh? Enough to break the ice. Heyo! Pick a card"). An hour passed and the party blasted, but those things seemed to happen just outside the searchlight of his awareness. The act of magic *cocooned* him, made him feel lighter with a kind of time-free joy. And that was why he wanted so badly to leave Bedford Falls, to move to Chicago and try to land an apprenticeship at the famous Magic Lantern Theatre and Shoppe.

After several orbits around the bonfire, Benji felt his phone buzz in his coat. He pulled it out, clicking the button so the screen lit up. A text from Ellie:

Help me, Benji Lightman, I am fake-texting to avoid FIG encounters! (near the front gate)

Benji texted back:

En route

He spotted her on the outskirts of the bonfire crowd, sitting on the hood of an old truck with a huge magnetic winch for towing cars. He was about thirty feet away when his phone buzzed again:

Stay there.

Shaun Spinney, 12 o'clock.

SHAUN SPINNEY?!

Benji looked at the crowd, now purposely focusing on the individual people, his heart thundering weirdly. He didn't recognize anyone.

Ellie texted:

Retreating hairline. Ambitious but unsuccessful goatee.

His gaze landed on a particularly heavyset FIG in a Colts jacket, who was drunkenly yanking people into embraces with a fervor that suggested bro-hugs were about to be outlawed.

Benji gasped so loudly that it drew a snort-laugh from Ellie. He felt a happy voltage, a current conducted through the medium of their texts. He looked at her from the side of his eye. She had taken off her knit cap and tucked her long, deep blond hair behind her ears, which he knew she hated because they were pointy. But God, she looked adorable lit up over there by the bonfire light.

Ellie texted:

We're talking to Shaun. Now. That is a thing we're going to do.

"I cannot believe my life right now!" she shouted before Benji could text back. "Is that Shaun Spinney? Is that *the* Shaun Spinney?"

Spinney turned and raised his hand in the tentative wave that is the universal sign for "I'm not sure who this person is."

"Ellie Holmes and Benji Lightman," Ellie explained as they reached him.

Recognition lit Spinney's drunk features. "What's up, bitches!" he cried happily. He yanked Benji into a bro-hug. Benji's eyes popped wide. Over Spinney's shoulder, he saw Ellie do a face-palm.

Spinney released him. "What the hell you been up to, cutie?" he asked Ellie.

Ellie began to answer, then suddenly glanced down at her

phone. "Oh, no! This is sad and inconvenient: I just received a very important text. Would you boys excuse me?" Benji shot her a look as she winked and walked a few feet away.

"So how you been, man?" Spinney asked, oblivious.

Benji had no clue what to say. He hadn't seen Spinney since Spinney graduated a couple of years ago. He'd been the quarterback himself then, a kind of mini god who CR looked up to, although he knew Spinney was a capital-D Douche-canoe. Benji hadn't *spoken* with him since the summer before middle school, and their last encounter hadn't exactly been a friendly one. But Spinney seemed genuinely thrilled to see him now.

"Not bad," Benji said.

"Yeah? You gettin' any?"

Thankfully, Benji's phone buzzed. He looked down. Ellie, who was still only a few feet away, had texted him:

U should congratulate him for being on the cutting edge of 2001's facial hair style.

Benji grinned tightly.

"You should be gettin' some like *crazy*," Spinney said. "Enjoy high school, Billy. Enjoy the shit out of it."

Ellie texted him:

Seriously tell him I'm super excited about the reunion tour w/ him and the rest of the Backstreet Boys

"So how's college?" Benji asked, biting the inside of his cheek.

Spinney hesitated, then waved his hand dismissively. "Ahh, it—it's gay." *Oh, good. So we're doing homophobia now, too.* "The girls are all stuck up 'n' shit. Screw that, man. I'm taking a year off, is what I'm doing."

And then—this surprised Benji—something painful flickered in Spinney's eyes.

"I'm not kidding. Enjoy high school. Best damn years of your life. You can't be young and dumb forever."

Ellie texted:

Well, he's half right.

Benji couldn't quite suppress his laugh this time. When he looked up, he saw that Spinney had been staring at the phone. Spinney must have read the text, because anger flashed across his face.

"Hey," Spinney said, "you know what else is funny? It was so damn funny at the game, huh, when those guys from Newporte got on the speakers."

Benji blushed. "Uh, yeah." He decided to play it off. "Well, I guess everybody who was there knows how I do a couple tricks then, huh?"

Spinney looked confused. "I wasn't at the game. It was all over Facebook."

"O-oh."

Someone closer to the bonfire shouted for Spinney. He headed back into the crowd.

Ellie approached Benji and said, "Quite a specimen, that boy. He was wearing his high school class ring. How does he not know how tragic that is?"

"Ignorance is bliss?" Benji said, face still hot after what Spinney had said.

"Then he is the blissiest man alive," Ellie said, getting a laugh from Benji. "Hey, it's super pretty down by the lake. Why don't we continue this convo down there?"

"Sure." After a moment, he added, "Want me to grab Zeeko, too? I think CR's having too much fun with the crowd to want to leave."

Ellie was already down the embankment to the shore of the lake when she replied, "Yeah, whoever." He thought (but couldn't be sure) he detected a note of terseness in her voice.

And it only occurred to him then that maybe she hadn't wanted anyone else to come.

He and Zeeko met Ellie on the trash-strewn shore of the quarry's brightly iced-over, acres-large lake. There were a few rusted beach chairs on the shore. The moment Zeeko spotted them, he picked one up, stomped the ice to make sure it was solid, then broke into a jog across the lake. Still running, he slammed the chair onto the ice and sat down: an improvised chair-sled. "That," Ellie said, "is a pretty damn fabulous idea."

She and Benji followed Zeeko's lead, gliding out there across the lake-frost. Benji made a snowball and threw it at Zeeko, the loose dust trailing behind it like the tail of a meteor. He missed by several miles, and Zeeko shouted, "A for effort!" They all sledded for a while, snow-battling and ice-capading, and Benji had the weird sensation of being nostalgic for the present, because he knew he'd remember this moment for a long time. The quarry was beautiful if you could ignore the trash and focus on the fun of riding the frozen world.

But Benji *couldn't* quite do that. He was too distracted. He hadn't realized it until talking with Spinney, but what had happened at the field tonight—those asshats from Bedford Falls's rival, Newporte High in Indianapolis, telling the stadium how his illusions worked—had broken his heart a little.

It reminded him of this birthday party he'd done a couple of months ago. After his performance, the eight-year-old birthday girl had come up and asked him where he learned his tricks. He told her he'd gotten them from Santa, and the girl got this unspeakably sad look on her face and said, "Santa isn't real." When Benji tried to insist otherwise, the girl interrupted with solemn finality: "I googled it."

Magicians are in the business of wonder, but the truth is,

most illusions depend on unextraordinary items. Thread. A rubber band. Smoke and mirrors. People always talk about "misdirection," but in Benji's opinion, a more accurate way of describing what a magician does was just "direction." He directs your gaze toward the apparently impossible so he can steal your heart, and give it back to you, enlarged. And by doing that for you, he can do it to himself, too.

But only if you let him.

"What happened to him?" Benji asked as he and Ellie stopped in their chairs but Zeeko continued to sled.

"Who?" she replied.

"Spinney."

"I would say he just ran the hell out of *maybes*," Ellie said. "Like, when you're a kid, you're just this adorable mass of—"

"I'm still adorable," Zeeko called, chair-zooming by.

"Don't I know it. Date me, stud."

"Sorry, dahling, my parents are strict: They don't want me to date until I'm married," Zeeko said as he glided away.

"Anyway," she said, "kids are adorable little *maybes*: Maybe they'll be president, or walk on Mars, or maybe they'll cure cancer or write the great American novel or run a three-minute mile. But the older you get, honey, the fewer *maybes* you got. So you wake up one day, and hot damn, you've used all yours up, and you're not 'a potential.' You're not what you might be. You're just what you are." She shrugged. She might have been explaining gravity.

"What I like about you is, you're always so positive," Benji said.

Ellie smiled, playfully punching his shoulder, which didn't hurt at all. "Just a realist, my friend." After a moment, the smile faded, replaced with an un-Ellie-like fear. "I shouldn't be so bitchy about him. I'm probably worried I'll end up like him, honestly. I'm still working on that short film for my application to the film program at Northwestern. I've got some okay footage around town, but I can't get the narration written. The movie's message leaves something to be desired. Specifically, a message, ha-ha."

"I'm sure it's awesome."

"That's sweet. That's very sweet. But no, it's emphatically unawesome. I just have this feeling, like this emotion crushing my windpipe sometimes, that the things I want to do with my life are not going to happen for me, that I'm going to be a cautionary tale instead of a success story. What if the people at Northwestern hate my stuff, you know? People say you should make what you love, but when you do and people reject it, they're saying that what you love is stupid, that your love *itself* is stupid. Just, ugh. Life is not supposed to be this complicated, Benji Lightman!"

Benji laughed. "I don't think it *is* that complicated, though," he said. "I don't accept that Spinney did anything except give up. At some point, there had to be a moment when things could have gone either way for him, when he could have made whatever life he wanted. Like, your life might look like this huge, roving landscape, but only a handful of pinpoints actually *matter*. I've believed that since I was a kid. Spinney had to become the kind of person who deserved that life, though. Maybe the moment was that he could have chosen to work harder or just drop out. I don't know. It sucks for him that he didn't live up to that moment, but that's his own fault."

Ellie thought about it a little. "Do you think everyone has one? A moment that changes everything?" she said.

"Yeah."

"Even you, Benji Lightman?"

For a moment, an image of the front door of the House flashed through his mind. As always, he shook it out of his head, refusing to think about it. And then he noticed something.

Without Benji quite realizing it, his and Ellie's voices had softened to whispers, white breath lacing together and upward between them. His heartbeat was suddenly very *insistent*, drumming in his fingertips. The shouts of the party dimmed like a song ending, and was he imagining it or did Ellie lean a subtle millimeter toward him just now, some other question in her bonfire-lit eyes?

"GUESS WHO'S BAAAACK?" CR sang directly into Benji's right eardrum. Having somehow made his way from the shore without them seeing, CR now answered his own question by slipping and dropping on his ass directly between Benji and Ellie. It looked painful. CR just chuckled. "Oh man, I love you guys. Are you having FUN?"

"What the actual hell?" Benji said, ear ringing like a school bell.

CR looked up at him. "You wanna go to Dairy Queen?"

"They're closed, big guy," Zeeko said, gliding to a stop beside them.

"And also it's a little cold for ice cream, Christopher Robin," Ellie said, sounding unamused.

"Why do restaurants gotta close?" CR said philosophically. "Like, *hello*, my stomach is open twenty-four seven. This is America! Let's go to Wendy's." Several slipping/skating seconds later, he got to his feet.

"CR, keys," Benji said, following him to the shore and up the embankment.

"I'm okay to drive."

As Ellie caught up with them, an idea came to Benji. "Wait, didn't you give me your keys earlier?" he said.

"'Course I didn't," CR replied, and displayed a gloved palm

with a half-dozen keys on a metallic ring. Benji, with a wink Ellie's way, quickly glided his own palm above CR's. A satisfying *tink* as the keys hovered into Benji's handheld magnet, then the keys were gone, zipping up Benji's sleeve on a retractable string in the blink of an eye.

CR didn't notice the trick. "I swore I had 'em!" he said. "Do you have 'em?"

Ellie tried not to laugh as Benji turned out his pants pockets.

"Aw, shit and no," CR said. "We have to find 'em. Banjo, we *haaave* to. My dad'll be so pissed. . . ." His face crumpled, like a little kid who's lost something important and knows full well how much trouble he's going to be in.

Aww, dude, it's okay, Benji thought, feeling sort of bad. "Hey, why don't we clear the party out, look for the keys, lock up the quarry, then go get some food? It's getting late anyway."

CR brightened and, on the second try, successfully gave Benji a thank-you high five.

Ellie suggested CR go look around his truck. As he walked away, she said to Benji, "That boy's a *charmer* when he's inebriated. I wonder why he and I ever broke up." She scratched her head like a confused cartoon character, though Benji had a notion: When she and CR had dated a couple of years ago, they'd fought more or less constantly. "Speaking of breakups, let's end this shindig, Benji Lightman."

He and Ellie recruited Zeeko to help relay the bad news to the partiers (it was impossible to get angry at that guy), then the three of them split up to clear the crowd faster. It took them a while to get the party to break up, the nucleus near the bonfire splintering into subgroups of people loudly looking for their rides and debating where to go next.

The whole time, Benji kept thinking about when Ellie had asked him if everyone had a moment that changes everything. *Did she want me to lean toward her—like, maybe, kiss her or some-thing?* For a split second he had thought so. . . . But he doubted it now. Anyway, the truth was, he'd been completely wrong about his "moment" before. During that summer a billion years ago, he'd gone into the House electrified by hope and a kid's sense of destiny that were soon shattered (with assistance from Spinney), because he'd been so sure it was his great life-changing moment. Now the memory just always made him wince.

You don't really believe that things can change like that, do you, Benjamin? Or hey, maybe it was your moment, and you didn't live up to it? said Papaw's voice in his head. *You need to just accept that you're going to Bedford Falls Community Col-lege. You know the difference between a dream and a bucket of bullshit? The bucket.*

That's not true, Benji said back.

Then why did he feel pressure in his solar plexus, why hadn't he told anyone that he still hadn't applied for the Magic Lantern apprenticeship even though the deadline was coming up? Chicago was a magic city, it was where David Copperfield got his start, and Copperfield and other famed magicians came to the Magic Lantern all the time. Benji always assumed that sometime in the future, like when he became an adult, he'd be worthy of being part of that amazing place. But he was running out of future. He was terrified that he wasn't good enough, that if they said no, his hopes of "moments" would vanish, and he'd wind up staying in Bedford Falls forever.

It'll work out, Benji told himself.

The quarry was now deserted, the roaring bonfire reduced to a diminutive crimson pyramid, logs popping with final, feeble light. He headed back toward CR's truck to announce that he'd "found" the keys.

CR wasn't at the truck, though. Benji looked around and

spotted Zeeko and Ellie about thirty feet away. They sat on the hood of Ellie's ancient Subaru station wagon, aka the Rust-Rocket, which was held together with duct tape and prayer. Ellie was drawing Zeeko in her sketchbook. He'd taken off his thick glasses (they were on top of Ellie's head) and was posing in an awkward-family-photo pose: toothy smile, eyes closed, chin propped on fist.

Benji heard someone muttering down on the lakeshore. It was CR, who was struggling to open a long, thin duffel bag.

"Hey, CR, guess what I found?" Benji said, walking to him.

CR shrugged, unzipped the oblong duffel bag, and pulled out a hunting rifle.

"Do you know what he told me?" CR fumed, then caught on to Benji's nervous expression and said, "Relax, it's just twenty-two caliber. Buck season starts this week, hellooo?

"After the game, you know what my dad says?" CR went on, pivoting toward the lake, flicking the lens cap off the rifle's scope. "Dick looks me right in the eye, goes, 'Very smart move with that showboating at the coin toss, Chrissy. Say there were college recruiters there tonight—do you truly believe that it would improve your scholarship prospects? Jesus. If brains were TNT, you couldn't blow your nose.'"

BANG—CR fired. Ellie and Zeeko yelled in surprise as the bullet flew across the lake, slamming into the sheered face of the granite wall on the far edge of the quarry.

Benji stepped forward. "Heyyy, maybe not so much shooting guns while drunk?"

CR said, "Yeah," but fired off two more thunderclapping shots. "We should prank the Newporte guys back, man. That's the tradition, pranking each other. I know it's against the rules now and we could get suspended and blah blah."

"If you get suspended, you're not eligible for scholarships."

"Only if we get caught, Banjo. I just want to *do* it. The quarterback is *supposed* to do it. It's what I always thought I'd do. And my dad makes me feel like garbage because I'm going after the only future I ever wanted."

CR dropped the rifle to the ground. Shoulders sunken, eyes listless, he looked like all the most helpless parts of a small kid and an old man. For all his vaunted athletic power, CR could be brought to his knees by his dad so easily.

It really wasn't fair. After the fateful day at the House, CR had transformed from the awkward, homeschooled new kid in town into that rarest of middle school creatures: a very kind, popular guy. It would have been easy for him to stop saving Benji and Zeeko seats every lunch period at the Cool Kids' Table, but he never did, not even after enough time had passed for him to learn about the social food chain. Eventually, a couple of guys insisted Benji and Zeeko sit elsewhere. "Yeah, that's hilarious, 'cause I think so, too," CR had said. He picked up his tray and led Benji and Zeeko to the only available seats, which were at a small table where kids with special needs sat with their aides. CR ate lunch there with Benji and Zeeko that day and every day for the rest of middle school. Occasionally, some of the nicer cool kids visited there, too. Almost unconsciously, CR had issued the edict that being an asshat was not synonymous with being awesome. He was like a hyperactive superhero who used his powers for good—for mischief, sometimes, but mostly for good. And it always broke Benji's heart a little when his best friend got a dose of Kryptonite.

"Let's travel through time for a second," Benji said. "A year from now, will you give a crap what your dad thinks?"

"What?"

"Will what he says matter? Will *anything* from Bedford Falls matter?"

CR didn't smile, but he came close. "No."

"*Hell* no," Benji said. "'Cause we're getting out of here."

"Right," CR said. "*Adios*, I'm getting out. Thanks, Banjo. You know just what to say to make a girl feel better." He clapped Benji on the shoulder.

Watching CR clamber up the shore, Benji stood still, feeling a pang of resentment he didn't like. *I said* we're *getting out of here*, he thought.

What a weird night.

He didn't mean anything by it.

What a weirdly depressing night.

A gust of wind pulled past Benji, moving his shadow as it stirred the sky. He cast a last glance toward the lake, looking up to watch the moon glow through the patchwork clouds, in that lovely way it always does.

But the sky's reaction was wrong.

The clouds in front of the moon hadn't turned white. They'd become green.

"Banjo?" CR called. "What's up?"

"Good question," Benji murmured.

And then, while Benji watched, a cluster of clouds separated from the rest. The cluster was high in the heavens, thousands of feet above him, but now it began to descend, like the clouds were in a controlled dive, piloting themselves toward the quarry.

Benji's brain jabbered a string of explanations, but only for a moment before his whole head was filled with silence.

The green light saturating the detached cluster intensified. By the time it was a few hundred feet above Earth, the color neared neon. In the perfect center of the clouds was a nucleus, brighter than everything around it. Witchy veins of light webbed outward from it.

It looks like an eye, Benji thought, and remembered seeing something similar outside the field house. *Like an eye, opening up.*

He was conscious of Ellie, and Zeeko and CR, sounding surprised and concerned up on the embankment. But they were far away, voices at the other end of a tunnel. Benji was just watching the sky, mesmerized by that cloud and whatever was inside it—

The beach chair on the shore beside him levitated.

He let out a shocked shout. The chair rose up in the windless air, then whiplashed forward as if wrenched by an imperceptible tether. It shot end over end across the lake like a stone, skipping on ice with sparks of frost, then dematerialized into the cloud, which had now journeyed into the quarry and kissed the face of the ice itself.

"What was that?" Zeeko said shakily somewhere behind Benji. "Ellie, I can't see anything, bring back my glasses!"

"Benji Lightman," said Ellie, coming down the embankment, "I don't love this."

What is "this"? Benji started to say.

But the junkyard spoke before he could.

Up there in the dark beyond their cars, colossal pipes began to vibrate, to issue musical tones like harmonic ghosts.

CR's truck throttled to life, its headlights igniting, the light beams spearing across the lake, striking the ancient torpedo-shaped gas tanks on the opposite shore.

The barrel of CR's rifle lifted from the ground beside Benji, looking like a finger trying to scrape the sky. Then, as the chair had done, the gun flung itself into the air toward the lake.

With an athletic instinct alien to him, Benji raised his hand and snatched the rifle in mid-flight. He looked back to CR and Ellie, who had come down to the shore and were watching in confused fear. "You see that?" was all Benji could say, heart surging with wonder.

The cloud had grown, obscuring the sides of the quarry. The gas tanks, which had glittered on the far shore, were all but invisible.

It's not "growing," he thought. *It's just coming closer. It's coming at us.*

That's stupid. Clouds don't do that.

Clouds don't glow, *either—*

At that moment, the cloud-light winked out.

It happened all at once, like when someone trips on a cord and unplugs the Christmas tree. The junkyard became still and silent; the truck's headlights snapped off.

A horizontal seam opened in the fog.

Slowly, a silhouette clarified from the mist.

"What the ass is that . . . ?" whispered CR beside Benji.

Goose bumps flew across Benji's whole body, and a wild memory flared through his mind.

As a boy, he'd loved the Wizard of Oz. Not the book or even the movie, but the Wizard himself, that titanic head that floated in space. Benji hadn't seen the whole movie until he was older, only the scene when Dorothy met the Wizard, so for years he didn't know there was "a man behind the curtain"; to him, the Wizard and his sorcery were real. And right now, gazing from the abandoned lakeshore as the silhouetted shape emerged and took charge of the night, the Wizard was what lit up in Benji's mind. He thought of that dreadful, enchanted face. He thought of the Great and Terrible.

"That's a flying saucer," Benji said.

The disc.

The disc.

The disc whirled fifty yards from the shore. It spun in the

bright and soundless night above the false starscape of the lake. Lights, trillions of eerily beautiful green lights, blinked on the underbody of the craft. They illuminated its shape, which looked for all the world like two silver Frisbees whose lips had been fused.

Benji felt a hand on his shoulder, heard CR say, "Leaving, holy shit, we're leaving, let's leave!" Ellie nodded and began retreating up the shore.

A portal opened on the bottom of the saucer. A circular beam of atomic-green light blazed out and hit the lake. It had the effect of lightning: The ice glowed, then shattered with a sound like a thunderclap. Shards of ice floated upward in the light.

Tractor beam.

"Oh my God!" Zeeko cried. "What is that? Ellie, *please*, give me my glasses!"

Suddenly, as if realizing it was not alone, the saucer's portal closed, cutting off the beam. The ice crashed down into the freshly opened crater in the lake.

And the saucer began approaching the shore.

"Benji— CR— Get up here!" Ellie shouted, her voice shaking.

Thirty feet out now, the portal on the saucer's belly opened again. Benji took a step backward, stumbled over his bootlaces, fell on his butt. CR lifted him to his feet, saying in the most frightened voice Benji had ever heard him use, "Christ on a friggin' cracker, man, I said let's go."

"No," Benji murmured, eyes still drawn to the disc.

"What?"

Benji understood he should be terrified, too. And on some level, he was. But fear and awe battled inside him, and wonder won the war.

Twenty feet away, the saucer eclipsed the moon. Its portal

opened. The hypnotic light shot out, again rupturing the ice.

It's gonna take us up into the saucer.

CR grabbed Benji's arm; Benji yanked it free.

"God*damm*it, what are you doing?!" CR said.

At first, Benji did not quite know. He was raising his arm, not sure why he was doing it, just suffused with an inexplicable and absolute certainty that he *should* do it. He was raising CR's rifle.

Which was normally so rusted and rickety-looking. But in that instant, as Benji curled his finger on the trigger, the rifle with its black slender barrel and moonlit sights seemed to undergo a metamorphosis.

Benji pulled the trigger, and the magic wand blazed.

The bullet screamed over the misted face of the lake and found its target on the far shore: the cluster of propane gas tanks. CR and Zeeko and Ellie shouted in time with the *BOOM* as the bullet's impact ignited the tanks' flammable payload. *BOOM BOOM*, and a pair of tanks jetted straight up, missiles ripping skyward with rooster tails of red fire. A chain reaction—*BOOMBOOMBOOMBOOM*—animated a half-dozen more rockets, but Benji's gaze didn't trail them to the stars.

The last of the tanks, like an improvised torpedo, came caroming over the surface of the lake toward the saucer's beam.

The portal began to seal but the saucer had reacted too late: The flaming tank touched the rim of the tractor beam and screamed up into the ship.

Benji spun away, shouting, as the detonation bloomed. Air displaced and threw him to the shore, the heat and light rippling his clothes like a storm. He looked back as the saucer nosedived perhaps fifty feet away. Fire and silver smoke bellowed through a breach in the hull as it crashed through the ice.

The gun dropped from Benji's quaking grip. His ears rang.

His vision was imprinted with the afterimage of the saucer's explosion.

Ho.

Lee.

Shit.

A weak red glow streamed from the impact crater in the ice. The pair of propane tanks that had rocketed into the sky now clanked, malformed, onto the lake.

The light from the lake bottom flickered off, on, off . . . off.

And then Benji was stepping onto the lake, heading toward the crater.

Through the ringing in his ears, he dimly heard CR shout for him to come back, that Benji was out of his mind, that the ice was going to crack underneath him. Benji stomped on the ice ahead of him. Solid.

When he reached the crater, he went to his knees, looking into the water. It bubbled like a cauldron.

Someone arrived next to him. He looked over, and was surprised to see Ellie.

"What the ass has just happened here, Benji Lightman?" Ellie's voice shook, and her green eyes filled with . . . not fear, but for a millisecond something purer. Higher. Was it awe? "What exactly did you just do?"

I don't know, Benji thought, pulse slamming in his temples. *Oh my God, I've got no idea.*

"How deep you think the lake is?" Benji asked her, and CR shouted from the shore, "Deep? What does that matter?"

Benji said, "Where's Zeeko?"

Zeeko, who had thrown up beside Ellie's car, stood up and croaked, "Here."

"Are you guys okay?" Benji asked.

CR said, "Compared to *what?*"

Benji's gaze returned to the water, which was now as seamless as black glass. All he could see was his reflection. "It's too dark," he said, mostly to himself.

"Haul ass outta here, that's what we've gotta do. Right? 'C-cause what if more come?" CR shouted, his characteristic confidence gone. "*Oh, no!*" he cried suddenly.

"What?" Benji said.

"We don't have my keys, y'guys!"

"Do you have a flashlight in your car?" Benji asked Ellie, then answered himself, "Wait, never mind, I've got something." He reached into his coat and pulled out a fistful of flash paper. The combustible sheets might have failed to wow the audience tonight, but flash paper was phosphorescent, and could burn underwater.

Benji grabbed a softball-size chunk of ice, wrapping the flash papers around it and twisting them tightly on both ends. He pulled out his magic act "FireFingers": striking pads affixed to the fingertips of his gloves. He had to snap three times before he got the spark, then he dropped the ignited papers into the lake like a message in a bottle.

A few sheets separated from the center and spread as they sank, making a glowing jellyfish canopy. The descent took eternities. The light began to dim, and still Benji saw nothing, and he felt an overpowering fear: He hadn't just done what he thought he'd done, all of this was imaginary . . .

. . . and something glimmered through the deep dark like chromium.

The light went out.

"Who do you call about something like this?" he heard CR say.

Call?

"The fire department! Yeah, that's right!" CR said. Ellie

laughed weakly, and CR replied, in an embarrassed and defensive tone, "Well, *I* don't know! It was sure-shit on fire!"

And Benji, staring into his reflection and the velvet abyss beyond, said to himself and to Ellie:

"I think we should keep it a secret."

3

Benji stared into the crater, waiting for her to say anything.

He lifted his gaze.

Ellie looked straight back into him.

Her eyes stayed locked with his, the bright green irises electrified. Despite the ice, a pleasant warmth rippled through Benji's body.

"How about airplane people?" CR called.

Reluctantly, Benji looked back to the shore. "What?"

"The dudes that make planes go. The FBA, that's their name! What's their number?" CR prospected his phone from one of his pockets.

"Uh-oh," Ellie said.

Benji shot to his feet. "CR, wait a second! I don't think we should call anyone yet!" He helped Ellie up, then speed-walked toward the shore.

Zeeko was coming down the embankment now. Just as Benji reached the shore, Zeeko pointed past him, shouting, "Look!"

Benji flinched, spinning back toward the ice. But he didn't see anything. "Look at what, Zeeko?"

"The—under the ice, there was light for a second. Blue light."

There wasn't, though. *Zeeko is so freaked out that he literally threw up. And he doesn't have his glasses. Maybe he didn't see anything?*

"Well, I thought there was," Zeeko said. "Benji, what was that thing? Ellie, please, give me my glasses."

They were still tangled in Ellie's hair. She removed them and handed them to Zeeko, who thrust them onto his face.

"Or nine-one-one," CR said. "Hey, we can just call the sheriff!"

Benji snatched the phone from CR's hand. "Dude, *wait*. Did you hear what I said?"

"You want to keep it a secret," CR said. "That's—actually, that's a good idea. The best idea! Okay? We never talk about it or come back here again. We forget it."

"Forget it? That's not what I meant." Benji shook his head incredulously. "CR, do you know what that was?"

"Yes." CR fixed him with a serious stare. "Bro, you just shot the shit out of a government drone."

Looking relieved, Zeeko snapped and pointed at CR: *Bingo!*

"A drone?" Benji not-quite-guffawed. "Why would there be a drone here? Is Bedford Falls the new target in the War on Terror?"

"That's what I'm afraid of right now."

"How would a drone shoot, like, an antigravity ray?"

"Science, probably!"

Ellie glanced at Benji, subtly rolled her eyes.

"Whatever that was, wherever it's from," Benji said, "shooting it down is not something we can just forget. If I live to be a billion years old, I'll never forget this. CR, that thing in the bottom of the lake could be the biggest thing to happen since . . . ever. Not just in Bedford Falls—*anywhere*." Benji felt his hands shake and goose bumps shiver over his skin; he was not cold.

"Guys, I'm freaked out, but don't you see how amazing this is? How could you possibly want to walk away from that?"

"Wait," Ellie said. Benji could actually see the adrenaline and shock draining from her face. "We might have just killed something. You might have just killed something. That's seriously screwed up. That's just *serious*."

"The saucer was coming toward us. I reacted."

"So it was self-defense?"

"I guess. I don't know." He felt a pang of guilt or uncertainty, but only fleetingly. "I don't know if anything bad would have happened. But I felt like I had to. I'm sure it was the right thing to do. Anyway, I don't think that's the important thing, Ellie."

She frowned. "Then what is?"

"The future. We have to figure out how to handle this perfectly." His stomach churning with nerves and excitement, his mind pinballed from one possibility to the next. Should they hold a press conference? Put it online themselves? (*Hashtag WTFlyingSaucer*, he thought.) He had no idea. He was in a quarry filled with garbage, but he felt the touch of infinity. He had to live up to this.

Ellie still looked upset. "Can we just slow this train down, please?"

"There is no choo-choo train here!" CR shouted. "We're not going to tell anybody! For one thing, I'm drunk. And I'm trespassing. I'm a drunk trespasser! Do you even know how pissed my dad'll be? If I'm lucky, best-case scenario, he murders me. Worst-case scenario, he won't let me play in the game this week."

"I'm talking about the discovery of the millennium," Benji said, exasperated but smiling, "and you're worried about chucking a leather ball through the air. Dude, there might not even *be* a game. Probably won't be. This thing could change the whole wor—"

47

"Did I say I was done talking, Benji?"

Benji flinched. It wasn't that CR had raised his voice. In fact, he had lowered it. But he hadn't spoken so much as *growled*. It was his Quarterback Voice, engineered for express intimidation, and he'd never used it against Benji before.

"There's going to be a game," CR said, "because I *said* there's going to be a game. We're telling nobody about this. Do you understand that?"

"Hey, hey," Zeeko said gently, "let's not be a-holes to each other for a minute, okay?"

Benji tried to catch Ellie's gaze, but she walked a few feet away, hands tense on the back of her neck, obviously still trying to process what had happened.

"I love that plan," Benji said to CR.

"What?" said CR.

"Your plan: Don't tell anyone about this until after the game on Friday." Benji smacked himself on the forehead. "Why didn't I think of that?"

He *had* thought of it, of course.

But there is this concept called "the Magician's Force," when the magician asks the spectator to pick a card, any card, from the deck, and then forces them, *very* subtly, to select the one card the magician wants. The magician directs their destiny, in other words, only if the audience believes they have free will.

Smacking oneself on the forehead was nobody's idea of "subtle." But if Benji thought CR would be an easier audience because CR was drunk, well, he was right.

"So . . . we're on the same page, plan-wise?" CR said, distinctly less growly.

"Totally."

"Okay. Okay, great. Awesome. Yeah." You could almost hear the competitive machinery in CR's head powering down as he gave a sheepish half smile. "Sorry I was an asshole a second ago."

Benji waved it off: *no big deal.* Which it wasn't.

Not now.

And then they were all silent for a long, long time. By now, even the embers and the firefly ash of the bonfire were gone, so the only light came from the moon and stars peppering the sky.

"So after we wait," CR finally said, just above a whisper, "what then?"

Benji walked to where Ellie stood, a few feet away, and said to her, gently but openly hopeful, "What do you think? I could use your help." But she just shook her head, still overwhelmed. Nevertheless, he turned back toward the lake. The water in the ice crater remained calm, an eerily beautiful mirror reflecting the heavens, like Benji Lightman had somehow tossed a net over the whole of the night sky and reeled it to Bedford Falls.

"We've got a lot of *maybes*," he said.

4

The Lightman family house had been passed down, father to son, for the better part of a century. Bedford Falls had originally built it to be the city-owned home for whoever they elected sheriff, but after a few decades of Lightmans comfortably holding that office, the city simply sold it to the family. And so the house—smallish but well maintained, built of bricks and ringed by a picket fence—had been owned by several generations of men who uncovered secrets for a living. One day, Papaw often said, Benji would own "this good ol' house."

The house didn't look ol' now. In fact, the house and everything around it looked sparklingly brand-new and full of possibilities to Benji.

He'd driven himself, CR, and Zeeko home from the quarry in CR's truck. (The three of them lived on the same street; Ellie, who lived across town, drove home by herself.) The drive back had been silent. After the quarry, there wasn't much to say.

Walking up the flagstone path to his porch, Benji was a little surprised to see that Papaw's bedroom light upstairs was turned off. Benji was out well past his (ludicrous) eleven p.m.

curfew. He'd expected Papaw to be waiting up, eager to hand out a few choice words.

Apparently, he thought, with a private joy buzzing in his head as he unlocked the door, *this is my lucky night.*

There was nothing in the foyer but the dark and the familiar Papaw-smells of shoe polish and chewing tobacco. Benji noticed a hot-pink line of light glowing under the door to Papaw's den down the hall. Voices, whispering musical voices, came from inside. *Jukebox*, he thought.

He quietly kicked off his shoes, then started down the hallway, one hand on the wall to steady himself. He passed the coatrack, the gun cabinet, and a picture of his dad in an army uniform, sitting in front of an American flag. Then he eased open the door and peeked inside the den.

Papaw sat in his recliner, his head tilted to one side. The light and the music radiated from his old jukebox in the corner; air bubbles floated upward through the water in the jukebox's neon piping, throwing quavers of light around the room. People always said Benji looked like Papaw, even though there really wasn't any resemblance at all. More than anything, Papaw looked like a seventy-something version of Richard Nixon, to the extent that Benji had once seen pictures of the former president in his first-grade history book and asked his teacher why nobody had told him his grandpa had been the leader of the free world. Papaw looked a little younger than his years now, in the jukebox glow.

Benji didn't recognize the song that was playing, but the bit he heard before the record ended was pretty good (if admittedly generic). *"Put us three young men together, hey, and what are our jobs?"* sang a guy's voice. *"To move your soul with rock 'n' roll! We're the Atomic Bobs!"*

Benji thought about waking Papaw, who sometimes complained

about a bad back whenever he fell asleep in his chair. But Papaw seemed okay there, his breathing steady and deep. Benji was intimately familiar with the sounds of Papaw's sleeping breaths, which had whispered through the vents between their bedrooms for as long as he could remember. Those breaths were calming in a way an awakened Papaw never was. Sometimes they'd carry Benji, tidelike, to sleep.

Benji noticed a light on in the kitchen, farther down the hall. Papaw had left a handwritten note on their small, worn kitchen table. He did that a lot. Notes were pretty much their major form of communication. *Text messages*, Benji thought, *from the pre-smartphone century.*

The note read,

BENJAMIN—
WE'LL TALK A LOT TMRW. GET SOME SLEEP.
—SHERIFF R. LIGHTMAN (PAPAW)

But Benji didn't think he was going to get much sleep at all.

Quoth the Internet Oracle (Wikipedia):

A flying saucer *is a type of supposed flying craft with a saucer-shaped body. The term was coined in 1947, shortly after the first reported sighting. Saucer sightings were once very common, to such an extent that "flying saucer" was a synonym for UFOs (Unidentified Flying Objects) through the early 1960s . . .*

But after the early 1960s, Benji read on, saucer sightings inexplicably ended. UFOs were still reported, but the new sightings were literally and figuratively edgier and darker: jet-black, triangular crafts that inspired feelings of dread, which somehow made him doubt that they were real.

'Cause I didn't feel that way when I saw the saucer. Why didn't

I, though? He didn't know. He didn't even quite understand the overpowering impulse to keep it, nor what he wanted to do with it. Maybe, if he would just learn more about saucers . . .

On his secondhand Dell laptop, he went to YouTube next, and found these old black-and-white newsreels about saucers. Somebody had remixed them with old doo-wop songs about aliens. Benji had always *endured* doo-wop (an early variety of rock 'n' roll where people's voices not only sang the melody but also sometimes added nonsense words like "shoop-shee-doo-wop" that mimicked instrument sounds), since it was one of the only kinds of music Papaw ever listened to. But Benji found himself really sort of liking it now. The melodies were simple, but damn, were they catchy. Also, there wasn't any Auto-Tune, so the singers sounded like humans instead of cyborgs.

And the era the songs came from just seemed so much friendlier and *simple*. The lyrics had this wonderstruck feeling, too, like I AM IN LOVE AND THIS IS THE MOST SIGNIFICANT EVENT IN ALL OF HUMAN HISTORY. They didn't try to over-explain their feelings, and that was good, because that was how love actually was: You realize you love someone, and you only understand *why* later on.

Heart first, brain second.

It was kind of like magic that way. Benji understood why people wanted to know how tricks were done, but he knew from experience that when you try to dissect something amazing, you never find what you're looking for.

Still eager for more information, he clicked onward.

Which led to clips of 1950s sci-fi movies. In the movies, the cardboard saucers wobbled on fishing lines, police were always oblivious and inept (Benji did not mind this at all), and teenagers were the Only Ones Who Can Save Civilization as We Know It. He spent more than an hour watching the clips. They weren't precisely educational programming, but he liked how all the younger characters seemed supremely *sure* of themselves, how they were so certain that they were the ones destined to rescue the world. It reminded Benji of this period in elementary school when he'd been obsessed with self-improvement experiments: trying to teach himself piano or speed-reading or baseball grips or computer chess, all in the vague (and vaguely embarrassing) hope that he'd one day discover he was a prodigy at something. There was a central flaw to the self-improvement projects, though: He never felt like he had a "self" to be improved. He suspected sometimes that he'd been out sick the day everyone received their manual for how to be a person.

He thought again about the moment he'd pulled the trigger. Why had he done it?

Because I felt like I was meant *to,* said something warm opening in his chest.

And maybe he was. As a little kid, he had always assumed something miraculous would happen to him. He'd get super-powers, maybe, or a letter from Hogwarts, or he'd spend summer break getting really buff and come in on the first day of school wearing only swimming trunks, and maybe he'd flex a couple of times in front of the class and borrow the teacher's hairbrush to comb his mustache. Something subtle like that.

His assumption of magic was the reason he'd walked into the House all those years ago. In his mind, he built the summer between elementary school and middle school into an enchanted slice of time. If he could just do something amazing, something *cool*, he could make the memory of his former unamazing, uncool self vanish. When Shaun Spinney told him that if he spent two minutes in the House, Benji could join Spinney's middle school frat (*Good Lord*, Benji thought, *how did I even believe that existed?*), he jumped at the chance. And something *had* happened in the House that had changed his and his friends' lives, of course. It just hadn't been what he'd planned, and it was something he'd spent a long time trying to forget.

Whatever was going to happen now with the saucer, Benji felt (or at least hoped) he had some central role to play. Things like magic and Ellie gave him joy, but he'd never really known what his purpose in life was supposed to be.

So, saucers aside, that was why the old movies were awesome: Everyone had a role and a quest, and you knew that if they just lived up to each moment, things would turn out basically okay. In more ways than one, everything was black and white.

5

Two loud knocks on his door awoke Benji. He startled, and blinked gummily. His room was still dark.

"Benjamin, it's that time," Papaw said softly, and opened the door. Light from the hallway crashed in.

Benji blocked the light with a hand and squinted. The red blinking display of his alarm clock read *4:49*. "Time for what, sir?"

Even in his semiblindness, Benji sensed his grandfather's reaction: It was like the literal air in the room sharpened, turning brittle on the edges. Papaw grew quiet, but Benji was fluent in Papaw's silences: Somehow, Benji had just disappointed him. This was not a rare phenomenon, but Benji normally at least knew what he'd done.

So he was surprised when Papaw spoke with a smile pasted onto his soft voice. "Stay up too late, did'ja? Rockin' around the clock, weren't ya?" In fact, Benji did feel like he'd been asleep for seven entire seconds. He'd wrenched himself from the internet around three thirty, then lain in bed and dreamed. Mostly with his eyes open.

"Hey, let's get our rears in gears, Benjamin." Papaw walked to the bed, already wearing his work shoes, polished bright and sharp as gavels on the floorboards. His hand came out, hovered a moment, and then awkwardly patted Benji's foot through the quilt. "That carnival ain't gonna open its own self."

The Homecoming Week Carnival. Of course.

After Papaw left, Benji toppled back onto his pillow, his pulse slamming behind his eyes so his ceiling's glow-stars winked like the sky's real ones. The Homecoming Week Carnival! Spared from Papaw's wrath by the Lightmans' one and only tradition! Huzzah, random sentimentality!

Benji whispered the simple truth: "*Wow*, do I not want to go, though."

Traditions are gravity, Papaw liked to say. They kept you connected to something bigger than yourself. So making an excuse to avoid going to the carnival would wipe away Papaw's good spirits. Just as important, it would activate the astounding mental machinery that allowed Benji's sheriff grandfather to apparently X-ray his brain. Which was not number one on the list of things you want when you're deciding what to do with a downed spaceship.

Maybe Ellie and CR and Zeeko can come by the carnival. The thought adrenalized him. He got up and thumbed a quick group text:

Morning! Going to set up the carnival.

Not much else going on in my life.

Pretty bored, TBH.

U?

Then a smiley emoji, lifting its sunglasses to wink.

After he pressed Send and got dressed (wearing an older, beat-up winter coat, because these carnival mornings were often messy), he felt like someone had synthesized the buzz of every Christmas morning ever and mainlined it into his brain cells. He still had no clue what to do about the saucer. But in a way, that was part of the joy. The future was an utter enigma, and for the first time Benji could remember, the unfathomableness didn't frighten him.

Papaw stood at the front door buttoning his navy policeman overcoat. "'S'actually not too cold this mornin'," he said, just above a whisper. Always soft-voiced on these mornings. "Why they scheduled homecoming so late this year, I'll never understand. Typical government screw-u—" He stopped short of his rant, though. And then promptly went into another: "Why're you wearin' *that* coat, Benjamin? You make it look like we can't afford—" Stopped again. As if in apology, he said, "How about breakfast on the go, bud?" and handed Benji a brown bag turning translucent from the greasy sandwiches inside. Benji caught the smell of Robert Lightman's Breakfast Special (Papaw's accent made it *"Brake-fist Spay-shul"*), made only once a year: a jumble of eggs and green peppers and bacon. Benji was surprised to feel a thin dart of nostalgia pierce his chest.

"Sounds good, sir," he replied.

"And *tastes* even better." Papaw winked.

He opened the door and stepped into the night-colored morning.

There had been a time when Benji loved going to the fairgrounds with Papaw, helping the carnival workers fit their attractions into assigned places, like pieces of a wonderful puzzle. That era had come to a close the year Benji had discovered (with a combination of embarrassment and pride) the first sprigs of dark hair in his armpits. Truth be told, he had stopped loving these mornings when he realized he did not love them so much as the *idea* of them, the way the imagining and dreaming of them made him feel.

They felt like church.

The gentle quality of predawn sound and light helped form that sense of sacred space, though that wasn't the most important element. Silence was common in the Lightman household, after all. But the particular silence on these mornings had once seemed to take on the shape of a door, a door that was shut and locked between Benji and his grandpa every other day of the year. *Keep your eyes open, wide open, Benji, and Papaw will share something precious with you.* And so Benji would stay still and expectant, feeling something that was precisely like pain but wasn't pain expand against his ribs. The un-pain, Benji supposed, was a feeling of *connection* to Papaw, which was the closest he and Papaw could ever come to simply loving each other. It was a feeling that a candle was about to be lit, and if Benji just listened and looked close enough, he would be able to truly see Papaw, to *know* Papaw, to not have the feeling that he slightly misunderstood everything Sheriff Robert Lightman was trying to say.

It didn't happen this year? Benji would think, because all he ever experienced was the ever-present feeling of not knowing how to please Papaw, or even if Papaw wanted him to try. *That's . . . well, that's okay. Just keep that feeling inside you, Benji, like fireflies in a jar. Maybe next year will be the year.*

He stopped believing that, of course. He grew up.

And so here was the insanity of it all:

Even now, something about walking with Papaw in this certain slant of predawn light (strong enough to see their shadows, black shapes moving over the lawn kissed silver by the snow) hooked Benji momentarily back into the inescapable gravity of nostalgia. He closed his eyes, exhaling as he opened the door to Papaw's police cruiser, breathing out his un-pain.

As the engine growled to life, old rock 'n' roll blared over the car speakers. Papaw grimaced and turned off the broadcast.

"I kinda like the quiet of a mornin'. Makes things prettier, ain't that so?" It wasn't a request for an answer (Papaw's questions never were); it was a pause to let you nod in agreement. "I think we're gonna have a good day, Benjamin. As we always do." Papaw, who loved to say he found liars for a living, was the tradition's great pretender.

The county fairgrounds lay on a few acres of hillside just past the east end of Bedford Falls. To get there, you took these lunar county roads and drove through infinite miles of untended cornfields and granite refineries disintegrating where they stood. Once upon a time, they'd both been the lifeblood and treasure of Bedford Falls, but that was before (according to Papaw) globalization and NAFTA and a historic streak of incompetent presidencies ground their bootheels on the little places of the world. *At some point,* Papaw would say, *people in this country decided they'd rather pay less for their goodies than earn a wage decent enough to buy 'em. Mary and Joseph above!* Going through the fields was usually depressing as all hell, like a trip in a semifunctional time machine that would let you glimpse— but not reenter—A Time Many Years Ago When (Trust Us on This, Young People) Everything Was Better.

Now, Benji caught his reflection in the window smiling as the cornfields flowed by. He was looking at the sky instead.

By the time Papaw parked the cruiser in the gravel lot in front of the fairgrounds, a dozen big-rig trucks sat idling at the front gate. Their payload was a portable joyland: all the disassembled segments of roller coasters and games and carousels. Daytime would come and make them look cheap, but they were gorgeous in the fine rose of dawn.

As Benji and Papaw got out of the cruiser, a man who

resembled a mustachioed oval hopped out of the lead big rig. "Young fella, how are you this blessed mornin'?" Papaw smiled, extending his hand. "As for me, I'm better than I deserve. Sheriff Robert Lightman; glad to meet'cha." His voice was warm, like they were old friends (in fact, they'd never met; the carnival staff was a rotating cast of characters).

Papaw actually waited for the guy to answer.

The man ignored the offered handshake. "Tell the truth, we'd be a lot better if you weren't half an hour late," he said. Benji winced from his hot breath. The man held up a "hold on a second" finger, turned his head away, and spat a loogie in the gravel. *Classy*, Benji thought.

"Am I *that* late?" Papaw replied, sounding slightly horrified. "I'm sure sorry for that. Where abouts y'all drive in from?"

Of course, Papaw had never been late to anything, and was not late now. (Either way, it wouldn't really matter: The carnival wouldn't actually open until the homecoming game later that week.) The mistake belonged to Mr. Mustache, who smelled like he gargled beer. Mr. Mustache wouldn't be on the receiving end of any of Papaw's arctic stares or silences, though, because he wasn't *talking* with "Papaw": He was meeting Sheriff Robert Lightman, Bedford Falls's folksy, charming, "hey hey your begonias sure look fine" lawman. Seeing other people connect with this version of Papaw had always made Benji feel jealous, and weirdly inadequate. There was still the slightest sting of that now. But mostly, after last night, nothing could have bothered him less.

His attention snapped back when Papaw clapped Mr. Mustache on the shoulder and said, "Well, of all the places y'all take yer wonderful carnival, I'm sure you'll find Bedford Falls the friendliest. Now, let's get this gate open for ya." The man grunted and got back into his truck.

Benji followed Papaw to the fairground's padlocked gate, which was the centerpiece of the rusted chain-link fence in front of the grounds. The fence surrounded the entire fairgrounds; a hundred feet to the left and right, it brushed against the untended cornfields that were threatening to reclaim the carnival land.

"Mary and Joseph, what a sorry state of affairs that man is," Papaw said under his breath as he worked the key into the lock. "You know why he's like that, Benjamin? Men like that, they turn to seed for one reason: They got no home. They had one once, but then they up and left, thinkin' they could find somethin' out in the wide world, thinkin' they're gonna light this earth on fire. But what's out there? Heartache, that's what. Lonesomeness and disappointment. There's nothin' more important than knowing your place in this world. You understand that, don't you, Benjamin?"

Benji decided to try an experiment, and just shrugged in response.

"I knew you would. I'm glad we had this talk," Papaw said, oblivious, and shouldered the gate open.

They spent a few hours walking the fairgrounds and waving their arms like conductors, directing each of the carnival big rigs toward their designated spaces on the fairgrounds. It was the worst kind of work: boring *and* stressful. In the few spare moments when Benji wasn't supervising the movement of several tons of steel (his favorite attraction was the genuinely impressive Ferris wheel, named the Starlight Express, which made a gigantic, eye-like silhouette against the sky), his mind whirled to the saucer. Not so much because he was trying to come up with answers, but because the questions themselves were so intoxicating.

Incredibly and wonderfully, it really seemed possible that Benji was the first person to ever witness a genuine UFO crash. The most famous crashed-spaceship story was "the Roswell Flying Saucer Incident," when the US military supposedly recovered a saucer and then told the public, "Heh-heh, funny story: It turns out it was just a weather balloon!" The weather balloon story was a cover-up, but not for a saucer. As was later revealed, the military was covering up the crash of a top-secret balloon designed to detect atomic bomb tests by those pesky Soviets.

Has anyone else ever just seen real UFOs?

The answer was yes . . . but it occurred to Benji that this was the wrong question to ask. People always equated "UFO" with "alien spacecraft," but that definition was inaccurate: UFO meant *un*identified flying object. It meant something you couldn't explain soared through the sky. The term "UFO" was the equivalent of a large question mark, but weirdly, people used the term to essentially say, "There's no mystery. I'll tell you *exactly* what I saw. Period."

What are we going to do with the saucer? Benji thought. *And then what happens when we do?*

In his head, the smiley emoji lifted its sunglasses and winked.

Benji checked his phone throughout the morning, but nobody had responded to his text. The silence was easy to shrug off early in the day (after all, few rational humans voluntarily rise before the sun does), but when he clicked the screen on just after eleven, a notification read *Message Seen 10:31 AM.*

For the first time, the day's inner smile wavered.

He thumbed another text:

taps microphone

is this thing on? :]

Almost immediately after he hit Send, an empty speech balloon inflated next to Ellie's name. The balloon expanded as she typed a response. (The one in his chest did the same.)

Then, all at once, the animation next to Ellie's name disappeared. Benji checked to see if his (secondhand) phone had dropped out of network. He had full bars.

Benji stared at his phone for a few seconds. But the balloon wouldn't reinflate.

He was slipping the phone back in his pocket when it started vibrating. The screen lit up with a selfie CR had taken with Benji's phone: CR, sitting on the toilet, grimacing like he was in the midst of an apocalyptic dump.

Benji tried to keep the disappointment out of his voice as he answered, "Hey."

"Can you talk?" CR said quickly in a hushed tone. "Like, privacy-wise?"

Benji looked around. He was in the heart of the fairgrounds: the central midway, a wide walking path surrounded by the most popular rides. About a hundred feet away, Papaw shouted at a big-rig driver who was trying to back the haunted house into its slot between the mirror mansion and carousel: "Cut 'er left, now. *Hard* left. No, Mary and Joseph, hard *left!*"

Just to be sure nobody would hear him, Benji left the midway and went to the chain-link fence that separated the cornfield from the fairgrounds, sitting down on a big gas-powered generator. "Yeah, I can talk," he said. "What's up?"

"We're butt-screwed, that's what," CR said. "There are pictures online from last night."

Benji's stomach sank. "What?" How was that possible?

"I *told* everyone the party was a no-pic zone, but there are pictures every-goddamn-where."

Oh, thank God. It's just pictures of the party.

"And half of them are location-tagged! LOCATION-TAGGED, BANJO! What is wrong with, like, our generation?!"

Even over the phone, Benji could hear CR's breath speed and shorten; it became a thin, reedy whistle. *He's going to have a panic attack*, Benji realized, startled. When CR first moved to Bedford Falls in the summer before sixth grade, he'd had panic attacks every couple of weeks (mostly when he was in cramped spaces, though Benji's backyard tree house was an exception). But CR hadn't had one in years.

"Buddy, just take a breath," Benji said gently. After a few moments, he heard CR's breath slow and steady. "If they're just pictures of the party, what's the problem?"

"My dad, obviously," CR said, sounding marginally in control.

"Has he seen them?"

"I'm still alive, so no. He's sleeping off a hangover. Probably won't even come out of his room until tomorrow. But they're on Facebook, and he's on Facebook, because old people love Facebook. Look, if he sees the pics, he'll go out to the quarry and he'll see the hole in the damn ice. *Maybe* he'd let the party slide, but not shooting down a drone on his property. I looked it up: Shooting down a drone is illegal. IT IS SUPER NOT-LEGAL."

Benji's chest tightened. An image popped into his mind: adults swooping in, stringing yellow *DO NOT ENTER* tape around the quarry. What if Mr. Noland called the police or the FBI, and the saucer got taken away before Benji even got to learn more about it?

"Even if my dad doesn't see the pics, though," CR said, breath quickening again, "what if—what if there's a GPS on the drone, and the government tracks it to the quarry? If I get arrested, man, I'm ineligible for scholarships. We have to *do* something. Please, okay? ASAP. Now. Tonight."

"Do what?"

"I don't know! Pull it outta the lake, break the GPS, blow it up, light the damn thing on fire. *Something*, okay?"

Benji thought about that. He would *love* to pull the saucer out of the lake. Even if they waited until after the homecoming game to decide what to do, they would have to retrieve it from the ice first anyway. Then they would have the chance to get a closer look at the saucer, inspect it, and once CR and Zeeko saw that it wasn't a drone, they wouldn't just want to turn it over without discovering whatever secrets might hide within that chromium-colored mystery.

That can still happen, Benji tried to tell himself. *Once we pull it out, we can all figure out what to do, together.*

But how in the hell, said Papaw's voice, *do you plan to pull it out?*

Benji suddenly felt light-headed. He closed his eyes, thinking. . . .

And when his eyes opened, he saw something strange.

Way at the far end of the midway, the front face of the carnival haunted house seemed to be flying into the sky, like Dorothy's home riding the twister to Oz. A moment passed before Benji understood the illusion.

A crane. It's being lifted by a crane.

"CR, can you get everyone to delete the pictures before your dad gets online?"

"I—I don't know. Maybe. Probably. But what if that thing has a GPS?"

"You know that big tow truck at the quarry?" Benji said. "The one with a magnetic winch, by the gate?" CR grunted impatiently in the affirmative. "Does it still work?" Benji asked.

"I guess. Why?"

Benji smiled. "Because I think I've got a plan."

6

Benji rode his bike to the Bedford Falls High School football stadium that afternoon after he and Papaw finished at the carnival. CR had practice, which Ellie and Zeeko (as the class videographer and team trainer) would be attending, too.

Benji cut through "downtown" Bedford Falls to get there, pedaling past the liquor stores and pawnshop and soaped-over storefront windows and fast-food drive-throughs. A ghost moon was rising in the late-afternoon sky, and it brought back a random memory: He was in the backseat of Papaw's cruiser at night, staring at nothing in particular with his forehead cool against the window, when all of a sudden he gasped, "PAPAW," in the awestruck voice of every six-year-old kid who ever stumbled upon a discovery of historic dimensions. "THE MOON IS FOLLOWING OUR CAR."

Papaw, of course, laughed his ass off. And Benji had realized something: The most beautiful ideas are the most fragile, and the most dangerous. If they shatter, they cut you.

As you get older, you retreat into the safety of shutting up. You stop sharing your hazardous hopes with anyone . . . even yourself, eventually. To Benji, the really terrifying thing about growing up wasn't that it seemed hard, but that it seemed so *easy*, so effortless to make the hundreds of compromises that slippery-slope you into a quietly desperate life.

Maybe that's what happened to Bedford Falls, he thought now, feeling he understood something important about his hometown for the first time. Bedford Falls had once been a boomtown for a handful of industries, most recently natural gas, but now it felt futureless. And when people don't have a future, they get nostalgic instead. Now Bedford Falls was just what (generous) people might call "a sleepy town."

Sleepy's okay. But the sleepiness here seems so dreamless.

But Benji smiled as he zoomed through the stadium's parking lot, which was jam-packed because of all the FIGs and reporters here to watch CR. What was going to happen to Bedford Falls now that the saucer had been shot down?

Whatever it is, this place sure isn't going to be dreamless anymore.

Not after tonight.

The football practice felt a week long. Benji sat waiting on the turnstiles just outside the stadium, hearing the crowd in the bleachers applaud CR's passes under the hot field lights. Maybe CR had been hurtfully oblivious last night when they were talking about leaving Bedford Falls, but that didn't matter. Benji felt proud of his best friend, and happy for him.

When Coach Nicewarner called the end of practice and the crowd started dispersing, Benji's phone buzzed. Ellie had texted him.

Can we talk? I'm parked in the gravel lot.

Benji tapped a response:

En route!

She was sitting cross-legged on the hood of her RustRocket station wagon in the crappy spillover lot behind the stadium. *How is it possible that she makes everything around her look both better and worse?* He didn't know, but it had been that way since the first time he'd met her in fifth grade.

Benji's dad had died in Afghanistan just before Easter that year. His convoy had hit an explosive device on a bridge, and he drowned when his Humvee fell into the river. If Benji was sad about his dad's death, it was mainly that he'd always felt *insufficiently sad* about it. He didn't even really remember him (nor did he remember his mom, who died of ovarian cancer when he was a toddler). His dad had always been deployed or stationed at a base in England.

On the day it happened, Benji got off the bus, the loops of his backpack straps cutting into his shoulders because he had a double load of books; Zeeko had been sick, and Benji was taking his makeup work to him. Benji was thinking about going on YouTube and watching videos of David Copperfield's recent performance at the Magic Lantern in Chicago, but then he saw a big black SUV in his driveway, and his first thought was that Papaw had bought an awesome new car and maybe he'd let Benji sit on his lap, steering the steering wheel while Papaw worked the gas pedal, like they'd done in the police station parking lot on Benji's tenth birthday. There was a gap in Benji's memory here. On the other side of the gap, a priest and a guy in an army uniform were standing in the corner of the living room, and Papaw, whose eyes looked dark and deeper in his face than normal, like raisins pushed in bread dough, sat on the couch with Benji, asking him if he understood what Papaw had just told him. Benji said, *Uh-huh*, his body sort of tingling like when his foot would fall asleep. *I just, I gotta go give Zeeko his homework.*

From there, Benji's memories were still frames from a movie.

He's kicking a rock as he crosses the road. The Eustices are hugging him, Dr. Eustice's chest hair feeling like springy coils under his polo shirt. Benji is standing by a coffin with a flag on it, and he sniffs a few times, and Papaw looks at him like he's relieved that Benji is finally crying. But he's not crying: A lot of ladies are wearing different perfumes, and the smell is gross.

As the months pass, Benji kind of realizes Papaw isn't the only one who stares at him when they think he's not looking, like they're confused by his reaction. Benji tries smiling at them, which seems to make it worse. He feels weird—weirder than normal, even. But he doesn't know to feel anything other than what he's feeling.

Then he gets this idea: Summer is coming up and there's going to be a countywide fifth-grade talent show in the new high school auditorium, and what could be better than a magic show to make the memory of the old him disappear?

The day of the talent show, he's seated between Zeeko and a girl from the other elementary school in town. The girl has blond-almost-brown hair and bright green eyes, and she is so beautiful that Benji feels embarrassed to be next to her. He's *noticed* girls before, of course; he's even liked a couple In That Way, the feelings like flickers of heat lightning in his belly. But this girl makes his blood glow.

"Badass tuxedo," she says, and inexplicably doesn't seem to be making fun of him. "Is that for the show? I'm gonna draw something on the overhead projector; I don't even know what yet," she says, talking rapid-fire, leaning in, like she's sharing something urgent and secret, "but I think it'll be good—Oh my God, is that a *top hat*?"

She grabs the hat, which he's been turning over in his hands, and puts it on. "Do I look dumb?" she says. In fact, nothing in history has ever looked less dumb. "Can I wear it when I go on?

I *super* swear I'll give it back. Hey, what's your name?"

"Benji Lightman."

She smiles so wide that the skin at the edges of her eyes crinkles. With a clarity of thought and emotion he's never felt in his life, Benji thinks: *I love you.*

"I'm Ellie. I'll tell you my last name if I can borrow the hat after you're done, Benji Lightman. Deal?"

It was. He gave a flawless performance that day because of how good and special she had made him feel. That was their perfect beginning. How could it not have a happy ending?

"Hey, Ellie Holmes," he said as he reached the RustRocket.

With a jerky nervousness, she glanced up from her phone, then brushed her bangs off her brow. Her forehead was wrinkled in a way that let Benji see what she would look like when she got a little older. She was going to look great.

"How's life?" Benji said. He couldn't quite suppress anymore the giddiness he'd tamped down most of the day. "Read any good books lately? See any good movies? Shoot down any good flying saucers?"

Usually his bad jokes got her to smile. But not now.

"You okay?" Benji said.

"Umm, well, that remains to be seen."

"You still want to go to the quarry, right?"

"CR and Zeeko said to meet them at the front gate," she replied, which didn't really answer the question. As she had at the quarry last night, Ellie seemed so uncharacteristically uneasy. He waited for her to go on.

Finally, she said, "I'm not exactly sure we're up to this task, Benji."

"What? Why?"

"I'm not trying to be mean, but . . . Look, it's because of you.

You're worrying me a bit. Last night, you just seemed . . . it was like you didn't understand how ridiculously serious this whole thing is."

"No. Ellie, I'm taking this extremely seriously."

"Then why aren't you freaking out?" She half laughed.

"Because . . ." No words came. "It's hard to explain. Here." He lay back on the hood, pointing his index finger skyward. "Do you ever lie on your back outside when it's snowing at night, and the snow just looks like white streaks zooming past, and even though it's sort of silly, you pretend they're stars and you're flying at light speed?"

After a moment, Ellie leaned back, too, and looked up. "Yeah, of course," she said. She put her hand close to his on the hood.

"And you know how the night sky feels like . . . like pure possibility?" Benji said. "Just totally beautiful, like anything can happen. And you look at the stars and it's like your past doesn't define you. It feels like you are looking at The Future. Like the sky is a time machine."

"Well, when I was a kid, anyway."

That made Benji uncomfortable for a reason he didn't quite understand, but he went on. "Ellie, I'm scared, but only a little, because the saucer makes me feel like the sky does. Everything feels big and possible, and I just don't accept that that is a *bad* thing."

Ellie was quiet a long time before she said, "Benji Lightman, you know what I think? I think that may be bullshit, but it's the most beautiful bullshit in this world."

"I don't know if that's a compliment."

"That makes two of us." She grinned. "I wish I could be that sure. I'm still kinda terrified to give myself to this fully. I trust *you*, but I don't trust *this situation*. Part of me just wants to walk away.

"If this is going to work, you and I have to do it together. We're different from CR and Zeeko, Benji. You know that, don't you?"

Benji felt warmth spread in his chest. He nodded.

"We won't joke about what is happening," Ellie said. "Or deny it because it's scary. And the one thing we *absolutely* will not do is forget. We won't forget that that there is no instruction manual for the impossible. We have to swear to be absurdly careful and totally honest with each other, Benji Lightman, okay?"

"Of course," Benji said. "I swear."

She seemed to search his face. She must have liked what she found there, because she extended her hand, which he shook. "I got the school's camera," she said. "So I guess let's go record history or *what*ever. Pics or it didn't happen, am I right?"

7

As they drove through the night toward the quarry, Benji thought about the House.

The House's rusty front door had shrieked like a demon as it opened. He walked down the hall; creatures skittered within the walls. Spinney had said he had to spend two minutes alone in the living room. Benji stood as still as possible in that casket-dark room, counting *one-Mississippi*s, his LED wand quivering in his hand—

A door across the room banged open and an actual ghost came roaring toward him.

"COME TO THE BASEMENT, LIGHTMAN!" it moaned. "COME STAY WITH ME FOREVERRRR!"

Benji, of course, freaked. He tried to flee but tripped on his own feet, falling down on his beloved wand, snapping it in two.

The ghost began to laugh. It raised its hand. Which held an iPhone.

"You are such a *woman*," Shaun Spinney said, pulling the sheet off his head. He kept the phone pointed at Benji.

He's recording me, Benji thought. He sprinted into the hall, but Spinney's friends stood in the front doorway, trapping him, their laughter booming. CR, Zeeko, and Ellie raced in behind them, their faces matted with dirt (Spinney's friends had pinned them to the ground). Ellie had said she would try to make it, and it turned out she had.

"I'm so sorry, Benji," Zeeko said, about to cry. "I tried to scream, I really tried."

"You dickwads," Ellie said furiously. "Screw *you*! You hear me? Go to hell!"

And CR, this homeschooled kid who was always so awkward and timid and kind, glared at Spinney with a look like black ice.

"What are you doing?" CR said.

"Uploading your little friend, is what I'm doing," Spinney said, grinning with half his mouth. "Lightman, you're gonna be one viral-ass video."

It was over. Benji would be a loser forever. The internet does not forget.

"Put the damn phone down," growled CR.

And Benji noticed something: CR had a stone in his hand.

CR's arm cocked fiercely back, like the hammer of a gun. His whole body hauled forward with frightening power and grace, launching the stone down the hallway with a song of wind. The stone hit its mark, smashing into the center of the phone's screen. The phone flipped from Spinney's fingers, then vanished into a black hole in one of the rotting floorboards.

The world went silent with amazement.

Spinney blinked at his hand. Spinney's friends blinked at him.

CR's huge eyes echoed the same awe and fear Benji felt.

How. Did you. Do that? Benji silently asked.

CR, with one shoulder, shrugged: *I. Got no. Idea.*

"What the ass just happened?" Ellie whispered, shaky-voiced.

Spinney seemed to decide his phone wasn't going to teleport back into his hand. He raised his gaze to Benji and his friends, and the compressed rage on his face made Zeeko actually whimper.

"Shit," Spinney said philosophically, "I guess I'm gonna destroy you guys. You first, Little Lightman." He stepped toward them.

CR snatched up another stone.

Spinney, seeing this, stopped.

"That's not his name," CR said. "Banjo, you tell this guy your real name, man."

All at once, everything inside of Benji, all the anxiety and terror that normally formed the shape of him, rushed away with a flood of wind and light. He reached for the magic in his pockets.

"My name," he said, "is Benji . . ."

His palms reemerged, bearing two tiny squares of flash paper.

". . . Freakin' . . ."

With all his strength, Benji collided his hands above his head. A flash of heat and all at once he was bearing a bouquet of flame. He said, ". . . *BLAZE*—"

But he never got to finish. His small fireball had inexplicably transformed into a tower of flame that rocketed heavenward. Shouting, he looked up and saw something horridly amazing. The cobwebs overhead had caught fire. The flames spiraled upward, greedily consuming the cobweb, and once they kissed the ceiling, the blaze *fwoosh*ed, fanning across the bone-dry ceiling and walls.

"WHAT THE EFF-WORD? WHAT THE EFF-WORD?" Zeeko screamed.

Smoke flooded the hallway with almost supernatural speed. Shaun Spinney, that great and noble soul, plowed into Benji, shrieking, "Let me out, bitches!" Spinney's cohorts likewise trampled Benji, disorienting him in the smoke.

"This way," CR coughed somewhere behind him.

Benji followed the voice. After a few moments, he staggered out the front door into the blessedly cool air of dusk. CR and Zeeko were just ahead of him on the porch. (Spinney and company were fleeing across the lawn like they thought the House was about to explode.)

"C-call nine-one-one, Zeeko," CR said as he ran down the porch steps. "B-Banjo, what're you doing?"

Benji was still on the porch, staring at the front door. Over the roar of the inferno, he could hear someone gasping for oxygen inside.

Ellie.

He dashed back into the House. An invisible wave of heat seemed to singe his throat and lungs. He stumbled down the gray vortex of the hall, calling her name, his head swimming from the smoke. *I'm going to pass out*, he thought, then four magical words from school flew into his head: *Stop, Drop, and Roll.*

The lower air was marginally clearer. He crawled in the direction of a weak cough, and found Ellie facedown on the floor in the living room. She *had* passed out.

"Ellie!" he said, shaking her. "Hey, Ellie, come on!" Her eyelids flickered open briefly, her gaze glassy and confused. Groaning with exertion, Benji put her rag doll–limp arm over his shoulder and stood.

But the House suddenly gave a great screaming *BOOM!* The floor beneath Benji quaked. To his left, floorboards flew upward like a volcanic blast. Authorities later theorized that the fire had lit some kind of natural gas pocket under the house.

Benji half ran, half dragged Ellie back into the front hall, where the smoke had changed from gray to flame orange. *Which way is the door?* He gambled on going left, speeding now, coughing so hard his throat seemed to rip. He reached out blindly ahead of him, found a hard round surface. *Doorknob!* he thought, and tugged the door open.

Despite the blaze, he went cold with terror.

He'd opened the door to the cellar. He could see the rotting stairway, could see the crater down there in the earthen floor where the explosion had occurred. Emerging from that crater, Benji saw what could only have been a horrid hallucination in his last moments of consciousness: a real ghost, a silhouette like a man but twisted and malformed and hideous. The dark man reached for him. . . .

A funnel of black smoke spiraled out of the cellar. Benji swooned, darkness encroaching at the edges of his vision. The next thing he knew, CR was dragging him and Ellie across the porch and onto the front lawn, telling him the fire department and Papaw were on their way. Benji gave a thumbs-up, said, "'Kay," and knew no more.

Now, driving with Ellie, the memory didn't bother him anymore.

He'd always told himself that the embarrassment was just a prologue to something wonderful. Part of him had whispered that all that dreams-come-true talk was kids' bullshit, and that Benji was being selfish for even wanting it to be true. But now he felt that maybe, just maybe, it had been carrying him to *this*, to the saucer.

When they arrived at the quarry, CR (who had driven his own truck here) went to get the tow truck at the front gate. He was jumpy and not eager to talk. Ellie popped a fresh memory card into the camera and said, "I'm going to go find the best spot to film." She headed up a nearby slope that rose to a summit twenty feet above the lake; from the top, she'd have a panoramic view of the quarry.

For a minute, Zeeko and Benji were alone, looking over the frozen lake. It looked exactly the same as it had last night, the hole the same size and everything. Benji glanced over and noticed that Zeeko seemed uncharacteristically tightly wound, too.

"Hey," Benji said, "you know this is going to be great, right?"

"Maybe. It's pretty scary. I want to help you guys, I love you, but messing with drones is serious biz."

"It's not a drone, Zeek. You're the smartest guy I know. You have to know how ridiculous that is."

Zeeko looked at the ground. "Yeah. Perhaps, Benji." He met Benji's gaze, his eyes filled with a kind of solemnity that made him look older. "The Bible talks about chariots of fire in the sky, you know. They're called angels in the Bible, but some people— mostly crazy people on cable TV—think those passages refer to aliens. Look, my faith in God is big enough to allow for the possibility of alien life. None of this changes the really important things about my life. But if that thingy down there really is from another world, I just hope everyone else is ready for it. If you make people get rid of one belief, you better have another one to replace it."

"People will believe that life is capable of beautiful and amazing things, right? This is like a miracle fell out of heaven."

"Well, I wouldn't say 'it fell' so much as 'it was blown up,'" Zeeko said, grinning a little.

The tow truck pulled up behind them. Benji gave Zeeko a pat on the shoulder and directed CR to back up to the end of the hill just above the shore. CR turned off the ignition, hopped out, and grabbed something out of the bed of his own pickup.

"What's that?" Benji asked.

"It's you, Banjo," CR replied. Actually, of all things, it was a wooden Radio Flyer sled.

CR set the sled on the edge of the frozen lake and then fetched a huge stack of disc-shaped lead weights from his truck, the kind you put on bench-press bars. The words *BEDFORD FALLS FIELD HOUSE* were stamped on the rims of the weights. "How much you weigh?" CR asked.

"One-thirty-something. Why?"

As CR loaded 130-something pounds of weight onto the sled, Benji understood. The sled was going to test the strength of the ice before Benji ventured out onto it himself. "Dude!" he exclaimed, genuinely touched by CR's concerned forethought. "That's super smart, man! Thanks!"

Something seemed to flit over CR's face like a dark cloud. CR shrugged. "Had to be smart eventually, I guess!" he said with a laugh. He produced several bungee cords from his jacket, which he proceeded to loop around the weights and the sled, tethering them together. Then he attached the big metal hook from the tow truck to the back of the sled.

It was almost time. Benji turned to face the overlook. "Ellie?" he called.

"Benji Lightman?" Ellie replied.

He raised a make-believe camera in his hand. "Action."

CR kicked the loaded Radio Flyer out onto the lake.

The sled glided, its runners making ice-skate sounds. The tow truck's long metallic cord, which ran from the truck's winch to the hook attached to the sled, unspooled as the Radio Flyer traveled. When the sled was a few feet from the crater where the saucer had gone down in the center of the lake, CR pulled a lever on the winch, stopping the sled just short of the lip of the crater. There was the faintest crackle sound, and Benji tensed, fearing the ice was about to give way and send the sled plunging.

But it didn't. "Phew!" Ellie said from the summit.

As they reeled the Radio Flyer back toward the shore, Zeeko said, "You're sure about this, right?"

"Absolutely," Benji replied.

"We got no choice, Zeek," CR said.

Once the Radio Flyer was back, CR handed Benji the hook, which was so heavy Benji had to suppress an *oof!* "Okay, Banjo, if you can get the hook to actually snag the drone, great. But as long as you can just get the hook to *touch* it, we'll still be okay, I think. Once I throw the switch back here, the electromagnetic power will turn on, and the hook'll connect to the drone and we'll be able to drag it out."

"Got it," Benji said. He became aware of a considerable number of butterflies in his stomach.

He turned toward the lake. He'd spent so much of the day anticipating this moment, but now that it was at hand, he was surprised by a momentary urge to delay. *It's just nerves. And excitement. And nerves.* He exhaled forcefully, cheeks puffed, pushing out some of the anxiety.

The ice crackled under his boot as he stepped onto the lake. For the first few yards, he moved with eggshell caution.

The area surrounding the crater was webbed with cracks. Benji decided to set the magnet on the ice and kick it ahead of him, just to be safe. The ice crackled as the magnet skidded across it . . . and then, *ploop*, the hook fell into the dark water of the crater. The metallic cord attached to the magnet sped as it descended to the depths, and Benji had a crazy and bizarrely hilarious image of an astounded Inuit fisherman pulling his fishing line from an ice hole and finding a flying saucer hooked to the end of it.

There was a dull metallic *clank!* sound below. The cord stopped moving.

Stepping more gingerly than ever, Benji approached the crater and peered down. Except for a reflected sky, the water was completely black. He pulled out a flashlight CR had brought, ignited it, and looked into the water.

His heart leaped as a flash of the saucer glimmered in the murk. By rather awesome luck (or fate), the saucer looked like it really had been hooked: The hook had gone just slightly inside the hole in the hull.

"What's going on?" CR shouted, so loud that Benji startled.

"It's down there!" Benji called. "I think we hooked it!"

"Are you ready for me to turn on the magnet?"

Benji glanced up at Ellie on the summit. "Are we rolling, Ellie?"

"Yep!"

"Okay, Banjo," CR said, "back up a couple steps, I'm throwing the switch! Three! Two! One!"

A moment of universal stillness, everything inside and outside Benji seeming to float suspended. The metallic cord twitched like a nerve, and he heard the thrumming crescendoing buzz of something powerful charging up. The cord swished in the water, stirring the stars out of their constellations.

Benji whirled to the shore. "You guys, it's working!"

When the saucer and the hook touched this time, the sound was not a muffled *clank!* It was more like a cannon blasting underwater. Benji whipped back toward the crater, caught off guard by the violent sound.

The ice shuddered underfoot. He stepped backward, suddenly frightened. From the lake bottom, he saw a brief but blinding pulse of blue light, which painted a strange series of concentric circles on the ice around him. Ellie shouted in surprise. The circles vanished.

The water within the crater surged back and forth.

Benji could hear hectic movement on the lake bottom: the saucer shifting, bucking.

Around the crater, the ice began to split apart seismically.

Benji backed away faster now, faster—

"OH GOD, BENJI, LOOK OUT!" Zeeko cried.

Something was shrieking toward Benji across the face of the ice. The Radio Flyer. He was halfway to the shore, thirty feet out, and had to leap to the side to avoid the sled, which was moving across the lake apparently under its own power, like a twin-bladed missile. It shot straight past him and vanished into the ice crater, as if drawn to it magnetically.

"The junkyard!" he heard Ellie shout; she was running down the slope to the shore where Zeeko and CR stood.

"What?" CR replied.

"The junkyard's going apeshit like last night!"

She was right. The trash heaps moaned and shuddered.

Under the ice, the saucer continued to whirl, to buck.

"BANJO, GET BACK HERE *NOW*!" CR said, and finally Benji headed back to the shore.

"CR, turn the winch on! Pull the saucer up! Let's do this!"

"Are you sure?"

Not at all! "Definitely!"

"I've got a bad feeling about this," CR muttered. He threw the switch.

The lake caught on fire.

Or that was how it seemed. The instant the winch engaged, Benji could see it turn the saucer over, and the entire surface of the lake was seared with green light from below. The ice grumbled.

Spellbound, Benji stopped twenty feet from the shore.

And the saucer's blinding tractor beam blazed into the sky.

For one stupefied moment, Benji gaped at the beam, which shot toward the moon like a beanstalk. A group of bats had been flying overhead and got caught in the light. They spiraled down toward the crater, shrieking.

As if from another world, he heard CR scream, "What is—is that a *plane*?!"

The ice was fracturing in every direction, pieces of the frozen plain collapsing into the black water as a whirlpool formed around the tractor beam. Benji fled for the shore as the whirlpool spread, feeling like a kid who has just pulled the bathtub plug and is horrified to his bones that he is going to be sucked down the pipe.

Where's all the water going? If it's going into the saucer, there's no way it can hold it—

The saucer exploded.

The explosion sent water and metallic debris geysering high and hard out of the hole in the ice. Shock waves flew across the lake, fracturing the frozen lake completely once and for all; chunks of ice surged toward the shore. Benji had to scramble up the slope to outrun them.

The sky over the quarry was filled with thin molten streaks as the debris screamed into the woods around the quarry.

A twisted piece of silver metal, a few inches long and shaped a little like a question mark, fell to the earth beside Benji. He picked it up, looking at it numbly.

Gone, he thought. *The saucer's gone.*

"Look out!"

Benji turned. CR was sprinting toward him, pointing overhead.

"BENJI, BENJI, LOOK OUT!"

Benji saw it coming: a final streak of light from the sky,

screaming toward him with a meteor whistle. CR caught him by the waist, tackling him to the ground. CR landed on top and stayed there, shielding Benji as the fire thing slammed into the ground behind the tow truck. Benji felt the impact buzz through his whole skeleton as the truck rocked violently on its shocks. Clods of dirt rained down.

The instant CR rolled off him, Benji raced behind the truck.

Collision dust hovered like mist, so at first Benji saw the fallen object only as a shadow shape, like a silhouette behind a curtain.

The object, ejected by the saucer's detonation and fallen from the sky, had embedded in the earth vertically. It stood just slightly higher than Benji's waist, glowing red with explosion heat, like a weapon forged in a fantasy story.

"What the ass is that?" he heard Ellie say; she'd run down the slope.

A faint smile flickered over Benji's face. "It looks like . . . a pod," he said.

The glow faded a bit, revealing the egg-shaped object's true color: quicksilver. With a gloved hand, Benji touched it. Even through the glove, he could tell the metal was cool to the touch: The heat had dissipated with amazing speed.

He took off his glove, placing his whole bare hand on the pod.

And as he did, the world seemed to zoom back, to fade far away. For a moment he felt a supremely pleasant, light electricity tingle his skin and brain. And then—he couldn't explain it—crisp and eerily beautiful images filled his mind. He thought of endless starfields, and old black-and-white movies; he kept thinking of when he had shot the saucer down, just replaying that over and over. He felt confused, but also had a sense that he was on the verge of discovery. . . .

He only let go when Zeeko grabbed his sleeve and pulled him back. Benji would have been happy to keep touching it, forever.

"Guys," said Zeeko, "something's coming."

And something *was* coming: police sirens.

8

Benji said, "That must be every cop in Bedford Falls."

Ellie tightened her grip on the wheel of the RustRocket. They were barreling down spindly Old Route 62, the only road connecting the quarry to Bedford Falls. Trees blurred by like black whips on the roadside. Back at the quarry, when they'd first heard the sirens, everyone, even CR, had frozen, but for a reason Benji couldn't really name, he had felt *calm*. He took control. There wasn't time for debate. There was only time to do what Benji said: load the pod-shaped debris into Ellie's trunk and drive toward Bedford Falls, with the hope that they could find a place to hide on the side of the road while the cops were headed for the quarry. Unfortunately, this road barely had a shoulder, let alone any convenient secret passages to Not-Get-Arrested Town.

"The cops might not even be coming for *us*," Benji said now, trying to help. "It could be something else."

"Not to be a doubting Tommy but in what POSSIBLE scenario could they NOT be coming for US?" said Zeeko, uncharacteristically bombastic. He propelled himself forward from the backseat, jutting his face between Ellie and Benji to peer out the windshield. He accidentally struck Ellie's shoulder; the steering wheel jerked and the right-side tires slipped from the road, spraying loose gravel into the treeline. She wrenched the Rocket back onto the road. Following behind them in his truck, CR punched his horn four times, as if to say:

KNOCK! THAT! SHIT! OFF!

"Benji, what if it *is* for us? What are we going to say?" Zeeko said. "Oh, God, please—"

"Wait a second . . ." Benji said. He leaned forward, narrowing his eyes. A half mile ahead, around a curve, he could see silhouetted trees painted with the fire and ice of the police flashers. But something was off.

The sirens.

Growing up in the police station, Benji could recognize different cruisers' sirens like they were people's voices. If it hadn't been for everyone's panic back at the quarry, he would have realized what was off immediately after Zeeko alerted them to the sirens.

Those sirens aren't *coming closer. And they're not just cop sirens.*

"There're fire trucks up there," Benji said. "And ambulances. The ones the city got last year, I think?"

He was right. The RustRocket rounded the bend and the road ahead was filled with motion and light; police cruisers and fire trucks and ambulances formed a barricade that blocked the road.

"Oh, Gaaaawd," Zeeko moaned.

"Zeek, dear, please don't you dare throw up in my car."

"No, you guys, I actually think we're okay," Benji said. "Ellie, just slow down a little." She glanced over. "You're speeding."

She replied with a look that said, *Right, because obviously getting a ticket is the hugest of our concerns right now.*

Parallel lines of safety flares hissed along the sides of the road. As the Rocket approached the barricade, Benji counted a half-dozen police cars, and a pair each of fire trucks and ambulances.

The emergency responders didn't even pay attention to the Rocket's arrival: All the firemen and deputies were running toward something in the forest to the left, though Benji couldn't see what.

"Holy Jesus, this *isn't* for us," Ellie said shakily over the wail of the sirens. She brought the Rocket to a stop at the sawhorses that formed the barricade.

Benji's eyes adjusted to the beachhead of light. He spotted a break in the treeline on the roadside to the left, and he realized the emergency workers hadn't actually been running into the forest. The break was the entrance road to Deedan's Eden, an organic dairy farm run by a hippie-ish guy. Everyone at school sort of suspected he also grew organic marijuana. Maybe this was a police raid?

Ellie gasped. "Is that a *plane crash?*"

Benji's stomach jolted. Ellie was right: A small, single-propeller plane had crashed down there in the middle of the farm's pasture. He could see the trail the unplanned touch-down had ripped into the soil, an erratic line punctuated by mangled metal and pools of fire. The cockpit seemed mostly intact, though it looked like a wing had been torn off. A dozen first responders swarmed around the plane, so he couldn't get a clear view.

"What're they saying?" Ellie said, mostly to herself. She tried to hand-crank her window down but it got stuck. She got out of the Rocket; Benji did the same. Over the sirens, they could hear overlapping shouts from the field.

"—stretcher, bring—"

"—no good—"

"—blood, Dorinda, get those gloves!—"

Two medics lifted a figure out of the wreckage and onto a stretcher that they loaded into the ambulance. A moment later, the ambulance's flashers ignited ("In the trade, we call flashers 'gumballs,'" Papaw had once said). Siren keening, the ambulance peeled out toward Bedford Falls.

"Your grandpa, Benji," Ellie said, hurrying back to the Rocket.

Papaw's familiar silhouette strode out of all the lights, hands on his hips. He was speaking with this sweet deputy named Wally, who always let Benji eat the Peanut M&M's he kept on his desk at the station. Before Benji could get back into the Rocket, Papaw spotted him.

"Benjamin?" he said, walking toward him. Because of the blockade's backlight, Benji couldn't see Papaw's face, but he didn't sound super thrilled. "What exactly in the hell're you doin' out here?"

"Hi, Sheriff!" This from Ellie, who abandoned her attempt to vanish into the Rocket and stepped out from behind Benji.

Papaw looked surprised to see her. He'd always liked Ellie. The first time he met her, when Benji was in middle school, she'd complimented him on the six-shooter he carried in his gunbelt, telling him that .357s were her favorite, too.

Now, why would a pretty young lady like you be interested in a mean old gun? he'd asked.

Sheriff, she'd said, *you're being sexist.*

Papaw had guffawed, and after Ellie explained that her (amiably redneck-y) dad sometimes took her deer hunting, Papaw said, *Well, I'll be.*

You'll be what? Ellie replied, grinning her firecracker grin.

*I'll be hopin' to see you again real soon. You're what I call
'a classy, old-time country gal.' Don't ever change that, sweetie.
Benjamin, you hang on to this one.*

"I'm sorry, Sheriff," Ellie said now. "I sort of kidnapped
your grandson earlier this evening. He was helping me with
calculus."

"Out here?"

"Well, you know. Calculus gets old. We were just cruising."

The term seemed to amuse Papaw. His eyebrows went up.
"'Cruising'? Did'ja make an appearance at the sock hop, too?
How 'bout the malt shop?"

From the backseat of the car, way too enthusiastically, Zeeko
went, "Hahahahahaha!"

"Howdy to you, too, Zeeko," Papaw said, grinning a little.

"Is anybody hurt?" Benji asked.

"No. Well, nothin' too serious bad. That pilot—somebody
said he's a surgeon from over 'n Indianapolis—he got the plane
set down pretty good. Took out some of Deedan's livestock,
though. That fella's raisin' holy hell about his 'mutilated cat-
tle.' Word from the ambulance is the pilot'll be fine. Worst-case
prognosis, he's got a concussion. He was talkin' some nonsense
when they pulled him out."

Ellie glanced at Benji, obviously thinking the same thing he
was: *What* kind *of "nonsense," exactly?*

"How'd the crash happen?" Ellie asked.

"I would reckon that it was because the doctor had a copilot
by the name of Jack Daniels. Found booze spilt all over the cockpit. Don't tell anyone that, mind," he added, and then sighed.
"Though God knows it'll probably get around this town, anyhow."

"Sheriff!" Wally called.

Benji looked over. A civilian had come through the sawhorses on the Bedford Falls side of the blockade and was

standing in the middle of all the emergency vehicles. That happened around accidents all the time; Papaw and the guys at the station called them rubberneckers or lookie-loos.

Benji's eyes widened a little when he realized who this lookie-loo was. Shaun Spinney.

Ignoring Wally's commands to get back into his own car, Spinney was staring at the plane crash, and, weirdly, he was also waving one arm over his head.

"Young fella," Papaw called, "you'll want to get back in your vehicle *right now*."

Spinney looked over momentarily, nodded, then resumed his waving.

Except Benji realized he wasn't actually *waving*: He had a phone in his hand, and he was trying to get a better camera angle.

Papaw had the same realization. "Mary and Joseph above," he muttered. "Why would anyone want to *film* . . ." He clenched his fists, wrinkled knuckles reddening. He reached into his back pocket, pulled out tobacco—something he only used when he was angry—and put a pinch in his mouth.

Then he marched toward Spinney, purposeful and furious. There was none of the usual good-ol'-boy friendliness in the way he moved; he didn't look like the public version of Sheriff Robert Lightman. He looked like *Papaw*, and a pissed-off Papaw at that.

"Young man, I done asked you once," he said. "Now, let me see your little toy."

Spinney looked startled to find Papaw beside him. "Huh?"

"Give me that damn phone."

"Why?" Spinnie smirked. "Are phones illegal on public roads, Sheriff?"

"By God, you're right: They're still legal . . . although give

Congress a little time and I'll bet they'll take care of that. But this is an emergency scene, and that gives me a little thing called 'absolute authority.' So you're either gettin' off my road or into my cruiser. If you think you can act like King Turd of Shit Mountain just 'cause you used to be someone in this town, well, lemme tell ya, aren't *you* in for a surprise."

Spinney visibly flinched when Papaw said *used to be someone*. It seemed like Spinney was giving up the fight: He turned away from Papaw and walked back past the sawhorses that marked the perimeter of the emergency scene.

But then, in an attempt to salvage a bit of his self-respect, he turned back, sneered defiantly, and continued filming. "Still gonna arrest me?"

"Yup," Papaw replied, striding toward him, looking like a gunslinger.

"For *what*?"

And Papaw, reaching Spinney, replied, "For litterin'."

Papaw's hand whipped toward Spinney. It was so quick, the movement of a much younger man, that Spinney didn't even flinch until Papaw had already snatched his phone.

Papaw pivoted on his bootheels and threw the smartphone, underhand-style, into a small creek that ran alongside the road.

The creek said, *Ploop!*

Spinney said, "OLD MAN, WHAT THE HELL?!"

"Also for disobedience and obstruction in regards to the efficacy of an officer of this municipality," Papaw said. "Wally, cuff this fella for me. I don't like gettin' trash on my hands."

Spinney stood there, flustered, his cheeks as red as the gumball flasher atop Papaw's cruiser. He looked like he might cry. "I— You— I'll sue your ass off! This is brutality, bitches!" Spinney sputtered while a grinning Wally cuffed him. "Guess what? That video's already uploaded in the cloud! Joke's on you!"

"Naw," Papaw replied, "the joke *is* you."

"Your grandpa," Ellie said, delighted, "is the badassiest man alive."

Benji looked over, smiling with a pride that caught him a little off guard.

After Wally loaded Spinney into the back of Papaw's cruiser, Papaw instructed the deputy to clear a path for Ellie's car. Benji and Ellie got back into the Rocket as Papaw moved the sawhorses and waved them through. As Ellie shifted to drive, the Rocket gave its customary crazy-high *reeeee!*

When Ellie stopped the car beside Papaw, Benji lowered his window to say good-bye. But Papaw didn't even look at Benji. He just stared, hands on his hips, at his feet. "That sound was your fan belt, hon. You'll want to get it checked out ASAP. If it breaks or slips off when you're drivin', you'll be out of luck." Papaw spoke softly, almost sadly.

Ellie, as confused about Papaw's behavior as Benji, said, "Will do, Sheriff."

"Papaw, are you . . ." *Feeling okay?* Benji thought, but he couldn't quite bring himself to say it. He'd never talked about, like, *feelings* with Papaw, especially not Papaw's feelings. "Are you secretly practicing magic? That sleight of hand with the phone was pretty great, heh."

Papaw raised his head. And it was odd: He looked . . . Benji couldn't quite find the word.

"What I did was foolish as all hell, Benjamin. That boy's parents'll be in my office tomorrow morning with a lawsuit in their hands. Practically guarantee it. This isn't what you sign on to this job for, it surely is not. . . ."

"All clear!" Wally informed them.

Papaw headed back toward the relative dark of Eden Farms. He called over his shoulder, "Benjamin, I got a long night ahead of me. Don't be spooked if you hear the front door open in the middle of the night."

After they drove through the barricade and the lights faded at their backs, Zeeko let loose an explosive sigh. "We made it. And I didn't hurl. And people say there's no proof that God exists."

Ellie gave a shaky laugh.

Benji wanted to be relieved, but he was distracted. He'd been searching for the word to describe how Papaw had looked a moment ago; it finally occurred to him. And it was a word Benji had never, in his entire life, thought of in connection with his grandfather.

Old, Benji thought, with a cut of sadness and unaccountable fear. *Papaw looked really old.*

"Hey, I don't want to be the bad news bearer here," Ellie said as she parked in Benji's driveway, "but the camera stopped working back at the quarry."

Benji's heart sank. "Wait, so you didn't record anything?"

"I got everything until you guys turned the magnet on. The camera blinked off about five seconds after that. I only got that blue light, y'know, that hit the ice."

"It was just circles, though, wasn't it?"

"I guess? We can watch it to make sure."

"Oh. That's good," Benji replied, thinking it was not good at all. "We'll figure out something else to record, I guess?"

"Right, well, that's the other thing. If the camera, the *school's* camera, is broken—"

"I'll figure out a way to pay for it."

"Indeed you will. But it made the junkyard go bananas, right? Is it really safe to keep it in your house?"

"Tree house," Benji corrected her, pointing to his old tree

house beside the detached garage in his backyard. "And all that other stuff happened because of the saucer. The thing we've got is just a piece of shrapnel."

Ellie seemed to want to press the point, but CR's truck was pulling up behind them. They hopped out. After making sure nobody was at the windows of the neighbors' houses, Benji and CR pulled the pod, wrapped in an old picnic blanket, from Ellie's trunk and put it on the ground.

CR groaned and whispered, "Let's get this done. I got two-a-days tomorrow, for Christ's sake."

"Don't blaspheme, if you don't mind," Zeeko said, though without much heart.

"Dad Clothes, I love ya, but I can't handle any Holy Roller stuff right now," CR said testily.

"What's the matter?" Benji said.

"Nothing you guys would care about."

"Okay," Benji said, trying to not sound defensive. "Why don't you try me?"

"It's Spinney." CR spat the name like poison. "I know you don't care that much about football, which is fine. But seeing Spinney like that is so depressing. He just seemed pathetic, y'know, trying to be a big man with the sheriff. Spinney's a douche, but he was a good quarterback."

"Not *CR good*."

"Seriously, man, I don't know how that happened to him. Well, I do know. He tore his ACL and got kicked off the team at Indiana U." CR was quiet for a moment, and in the half-light of the night, Benji couldn't quite make out his expression. "You know, I can usually handle my dad's 'CR will never amount to anything blah blah blah' rants. And I want to leave Bedford Falls as much as y'all—well, as much as Ellie and Banjo. I bet

Spinney was excited to leave town, too. But he had no damn clue he was peaking early. He just thought he'd always be . . ." CR laughed a little, which was good to hear. "How did your grandpa put it?"

"King Turd of Shit Mountain," said Zeeko.

Benji, Ellie, and CR goggled at him.

"Zeeko, such language!" CR guffawed. "Where did *that* come from?"

"Outer space," Zeeko deadpanned, making them laugh. "It's a weird night, I guess."

"You guessed right."

"Hey, CR," Benji said, "don't worry about Spinney. You're better than that. You're better than any of the FIGs in town. Just kick ass at the homecoming game and everyone will see that. Truly."

CR's huge smile was visible even in the semidarkness. "I bet you say that to all the boys who help you hide busted 'flying saucers.'"

One tree house. Four friends. Eight hands wrapped around a blanket wrapped around a secret wrapped around a winter night in Bedford Falls, Indiana.

A wooden ramp spiraled around the pine tree to their tree house in the backyard. They'd been here a million times, but not for a million years. The lock on the tree house door was rusted. But Benji remembered the combination easily, because it was the date he'd first met Ellie. CR bumped his head on the doorframe coming into the tree house, and said, "That used to be a lot higher," and they set the pod down on the planks of the floor. And as they stood there, the air filled with the nostalgic smell of pine, the arthritic tree limbs chattered in the wind, making the pod glimmer in a fine lacing of shadow and light. The four friends stood there, in a den of childhood and on the edge of the future, and Benji pretended he had something in his eyes. He had begun to cry.

PART TWO
IT CAME FROM OUTER SPACE

And so I'll hold you close,
my darling, on graduation day.
You may forget what you learned in class,
but please remember what I say:
In all the dark,
Although we're apart,
I'm just a dream away.
—The Atomic Bobs

You are a special kind of people.
You have a certain gift, a special ability.
For you, nothing is impossible.
You can alter reality, and you can create
the laws of nature. You are magicians!
—Dag Lofalk

9

It was a dream date.

Benji sat in the front seat, the leather plush and shiny red beneath him. His window was just barely opened, and the forest around him whispered with a breeze cool and sweet on the summer air. In the valley beneath him, dozens of cars (Studebakers, Chevys, Furies, T-Birds) glittered in the reflected light of the drive-in movie screen before them. Its black-and-white story seemed to float fantastically in the dark. The sounds of the movie filled the car, broadcast from the drive-in onto his car's brand-new radio.

The girl beside him smelled like cinnamon.

Although the dream felt intensely detailed, Benji was aware on some level that he was asleep, so when he looked at the girl, he was surprised to see she wasn't *his* dream girl. With her long dark hair tied in a braided ponytail, the unfamiliar girl wore an outfit like a costume in any 1950s flying saucer movie: penny loafers, a poodle skirt, a short-sleeved sweater with *J* stitched across the chest. The *J* was slightly distorted by the girl's rather, ahh, prodigious bust. *Judy*, Benji knew. *Her name is Judy.*

Judy looked over. Benji, suddenly very aware how tight his pants were, dutifully snapped his gaze upward.

"Well, hello to you, too." She smiled.

A tense silence hung between them, lightly electrified. They were on Lover's Lookout, after all.

Time for some backseat bingo, Benji told himself. *Make your move, daddio.* In this dream world, he knew he'd been looking forward to this date for a long time—fantasizing about it, frankly, and boy, were his friends going to rag on him if nothing happened tonight.

"Something I can help you with?" Judy asked. He saw a small chip on one of her bottom teeth. It was somehow lovely.

Her face tilted infinitesimally toward him.

"Tell ya what, I'd sure love some popcorn!" Benji stammered. His voice sounded strange, more country-accented than normal, but its awkwardness was very familiar.

"Oh," replied Judy, gamely hiding disappointment as she handed him the candy-cane-striped box of popcorn. He took a cold, buttery handful, and she turned back to the drive-in screen.

Cursing his lack of courage, Benji tried to watch the movie. It was called *I Was a Teenage Werewolf,* and it was awful in a way that should have been funny but wasn't.

Like you, daddio, he thought, his brain hot with anger and pressure.

Benji looked at the car's dashboard.

It had no modern LED display, just a series of dials. The speedometer's numbers glowed radium green. He focused on them, and breathed, and . . .

A silence cocooned his mind. The Feeling of Magic.

In his waking life Benji knew nothing about cars, but in this moment he loved this car, his Cadillac, like a miracle. Her red steel and her chrome so bright and loud that she resembled a four-wheeled jukebox, her front grille grinning like a mouth happily eating up the road toward the horizon. He loved her.

It's not "my Cadillac," though, Benji thought. *She's my machine.*

She's my Dream Machine.

The speedometer's markings glowed like emeralds. Or like strange eyes peering through the dark. . . .

"The monster's coming." This made Benji look over. Past Judy, thin night fog levitated over the ground, giving the forest an enchanted, fairy-tale quality.

"Hmm?" he said.

"That monster's coming now for sure," Judy repeated, and shivered as the movie's soundtrack grew shrieky with violins. Benji glanced at the screen. The movie's hero had just noticed the climbing full moon. Tufts of dark hair erupted from his waistband and the cuffs of his letterman jacket, like he was the victim of the world's worst and speediest case of puberty.

His date shivered again (a little theatrically). "I don't know that I want to watch this anymore," she told him softly.

Now it was Benji's turn to hide disappointment. "Say, that's all right. We can go home. Sure."

He shifted the Dream Machine into reverse, to take them out of their temporarily enchanted night.

The girl's hand appeared on top of his, stopping the gear change.

"I didn't mean I want to *leave*," she said, and smiled in a singularly brain-melting way.

(As if on absurd cue, the teenage monster wolf-called at the moon: *How-WOOOO!*)

The audience screamed, and Judy leaned in, the cinnamon of her breath meeting his lips—

The Dream Machine exploded.

Or at least it felt so: Judy's face was sailing in and *BOOM*, the car was smashed with a deafening human scream. She and Benji jumped and fell back in the seat. The scream wasn't the audience's; it didn't even sound like the movie's.

"What in the *hell!"* Benji shouted.

"—adio!"

"What!"

"That radio damn stupid *radio!"* she screamed. She snapped the volume dial hard to the left; the dial of his brand-new radio came off in her damn hand.

The primal, desperate-sounding scream filling the Cadillac didn't stop. If anything, it crescendoed. And Benji realized the doom voice wasn't just a shapeless howl.

It was *singing.* It was rock 'n' roll, American doo-wop, a young man belting the song like he hoped his passion could shatter the globe and reshape it into something unimaginably beautiful:

Ohhhhhh, I'm the one leaves a place, and never spies a familiar face,
And that's the way I like it, since you asked!
See, honey, I'm the Voyager—see, tramping the journey is my story, sir,
And I'll tell you why right now, since you asked!
The man who asks cannot understand, can't know the heart of the voyaging man.
I prefer the horizon to a past!

Judy opened her door, spilled out of the car, looked up into the sky, and shrieked.

Light flooded the Dream Machine. Green light, but nothing

like the radium dashboard. Brilliant green light from the sky, blinding him and turning the night fog into neon ghosts. And in the amphitheater of his own mind, even louder than the elemental rock 'n' roll, Benji heard a new voice:

MR. FAHRENHEIT, MY NAME IS MR. FAHRENHEIT, I AM MR. FAHRENHE—

Benji woke up falling down, yelped, and thudded onto his bedroom floor.

He groaned into the hardwood floor, then rolled onto his back. For a few moments he just lay there, rubbing his side, heart hammering his rib cage. The sky in the window above his bed was a pale blend of crayon blue and pink. *That girl*, he thought. *Who was she?* The dream had been so detailed, almost more like a memory, but he didn't think he knew her in real life. Still, there was something familiar . . .

She'd reminded him of Ellie. Maybe that was it.

He disentangled himself from his blanket as he stood, then reached over to slap off his clock radio. Right before he did, a voice spoke from the radio:

"See, honey, I'm the Voyager!"

The moment was vaguely surreal, the weirdly high-definition dream spilling into reality. He stared at the radio, his brow knitting.

"See, tramping the journey is my story, sir!"

With a sense of urgency that surprised him, he slapped the switch to silence the song.

Must've just heard the song in my sleep. That's why I dreamed about it—

"The man who asks cannot understand, can't know the heart of the voyaging man. I prefer the horizon to a past!"

Benji whirled toward the door, feet snarling in the blanket, catching himself on the bed. The song had come from some-where downstairs.

He opened his door. The hall and the steps to downstairs were dark, all the lights turned out.

"Papaw?" he called.

No answer.

He called out again and there was only silence, save his echo and the song, which seemed to be coming from the den. Benji felt a thin, hot lash of paranoia and hurried down the steps, remembering last night, the barricade, how exhausted Papaw had looked. Benji couldn't stop an image from coming into his head: his grandpa sprawled out on the den's rug, mouth crooked and slack, gaze empty, chest silent.

But Benji threw open the den door, and nobody was inside. The song from the hot-pink jukebox faded as the chorus repeated the singer's preference for the horizon to a past. Then just silence from the speakers. Benji didn't know the jukebox could pick up radio signals, which it must have been doing since it was playing the same song as his clock. How had the jukebox turned itself on? *Well, this thing isn't exactly in great shape.* He unplugged it from the wall.

The kitchen and living room were also empty. Ditto the driveway alongside the house.

I guess Papaw really did have to work all night.

Which was, in fact, what Benji had almost done. Once they'd installed The Saucer Thingy Thang (as Zeeko had christened it) in the tree house, Benji had felt wired with adrenaline and excitement, wanting to spend more time with the pod, to inspect it or whatever. The night so far had been a blur, all fire and velocity, which was memorable but not particularly condu-cive to examining the discovery of the century.

It was egglike in shape, which brought to mind "invasion of the pod people!" sci-fi clichés. But when Benji ran his gloved hands across the pod's quicksilver surface, it was flawlessly smooth, no cracks, compartments, seams, or doors. Whatever the pod was, it didn't seem to be meant to be opened.

He remembered the pleasant electricity he'd felt when he'd touched the pod with his bare hands at the quarry, and was filled with an urge to make direct contact again. He bent to put his ear against the pod, but CR grabbed him before he touched it. "New rule," said CR, looking both nervous and slightly annoyed. "Don't put your face against anything from outer space ever."

Benji nodded, still staring at the pod. "I don't even know where to start," he said.

"Start with what?"

"*This*, obviously," Benji said, laughing a little. The moonlight in the tree house was thin, but the pod glowed with it. "We should . . . test it or something."

CR sighed. "Test it. Hey, pod, who was the second president of the United States?"

"John Adams," Zeeko answered.

"Show-off," Ellie smirked.

"No," Benji said, "I mean we should try to figure out what it is, what it's made of." In Roswell, people had tested the strength of the "saucer shrapnel" using matches and hammers and knives. The metal had been impervious. So the witnesses said, anyway.

"Banjo, it's late. CR needs his beauty rest," CR said.

"You can go if you want."

"I want."

"I want also," said Zeeko, and yawned. It seemed insane to Benji that anyone could be tired right then.

"I'm calling it a night," CR said, "a crazy, cluster-fuggin' night. Come on, Banjo. New rule number two: Nobody hangs out with the Thingy Thang alone. Okay, man?" He said it with such genuine concern that Benji had just nodded in agreement.

But CR isn't home. He's got morning practice, said a voice inside Benji's head now. *And I've still got a few minutes before I have to leave.*

He felt a momentary indecision . . . but no, he didn't want to lie. And he didn't feel comfortable going against what CR said.

Benji went back upstairs, pulled on his hoodie, jeans, and sneakers. He had practice after school for Friday's homecoming assembly, parade, and game, so he tossed his folded tux into his backpack alongside his collapsed top hat.

When he grabbed his rumpled coat from the floor where he'd dropped it last night, the small piece of saucer debris he'd picked up at the quarry, the one that looked like a silver question mark, tumbled from his hoodie pocket.

The object landed with a *ping*. He stared at it, considering. Then he put it in his backpack, covering it with his tux.

Benji biked to school, the sun a lemony wedge in the sky, the clouds crisp sky-ships sailing easy. The morning felt bigger somehow, but also more personal, the way your birthday does when you're a kid.

He stopped off in the crowded, fluorescent cafeteria, the beckoning smell of breakfast burritos making his stomach rumble. By the time he got to the counter, first bell was ringing. He wrapped his greasy food-esque delicacy in several napkins, joined the crushing migration of students to class, and ate it in three bites on the move.

"Good morning, students," said Principal Branch's twangy voice over the intercom. "Remember that there will be no

breakfast served on Friday, due to preparations for the homecoming assembly."

"Howdy, Benjamin!"

Benji was passing the doors to the school's administrative
offices. He turned and saw something strange through the
doorway: Papaw, sitting on the edge of a secretary's desk with
his sheriff hat on his knee, waving to him.

"H-hi, sir," Benji said, surprised.

"I thought I'd come to school, see if I could learn somethin'
for once. So far I've learnt what it's like to fall in love, and I
mean *tumble*," Papaw said, pointing to the older-lady secretary
as Benji walked into the office. "But Brenda the Beauty won't
give me her phone number no matter how much I beg, can you
believe it?"

Brenda, whose looks were pretty modest, pointed to her thin
gold wedding ring.

Papaw shrugged innocently, then took the sheriff hat off his
knee and placed it on Brenda's head. "You make that look better
than I do," he said. "You keep that for a while."

Brenda laughed. For just that second, she *did* look a little
beautiful. It was this sort of moment that made everyone in this
tiny, futureless town love Papaw so much: He made them feel
special.

"Benjamin, help me ease my sorrows with a little conversation. Brenda, that fella's back in the conference room, is that
right?"

Papaw motioned for Benji to follow. They went into a small
hallway, cramped with filing cabinets and decorated with
pictures of old graduating classes, that led to offices in the
administration wing.

"There's somethin' important we need to talk about," Papaw
said. Now that he'd left "Sheriff Lightman" behind, his voice

was scratchy and tired. His eyes were red-ringed, underlined in blue. He really had been up all night.

And yet, for some reason, he didn't look as *old* as he had after his standoff last night with King Turd of Shit Mountain at the barricade.

"What 'fella' is back here, Papaw?" Benji said, trying not to sound nervous.

"A man who can help, I think. Benjamin, I've been tryin' lately—tryin' for a long time, truly—to tell you something, and time feels like it's runnin' out for me to tell you this particular thing. But I never know how to say it. The most important things are the hardest things to say—have you ever found that to be so?"

Papaw stopped a few steps short of the door to the conference room. He looked at Benji, and it took Benji a moment to realize that Papaw was waiting for him to answer—like, truly *waiting* and interested in Benji's response. In spite of his confusion, Benji felt a warm door open an inch in his chest.

"Yeah, absolutely, Papaw."

"Why is that? Mary and Joseph above, I sure don't know. But it turns out it's okay," Papaw said, his tired eyes brightening. "'Cause this morning I got a phone call, and it was like a message from heaven, ya know?"

"A call about what, sir?"

"A call from someone who wants to tell you the same thing I do: You've got one helluva future ahead of you. He asked for you by name." They walked to the door to the conference room; diffuse light filtered through the pane of fogged glass. Quietly, Papaw said, "I just *had* to come down and meet this fella in person. He and I had a good chat about you this mornin', and let me tell ya, son, he's eager to meet you."

Suddenly Benji realized why Papaw didn't look as old this morning. It was because he was excited.

Papaw said, "This fella's from the FBI. Now ain't that somethin'?"

Two times in his life, Benji had been sent to this conference room for meetings with the principal and guidance counselor (both times for talking to CR during class), and those had been two of the most existentially horrifying moments of his high school career. But as the doom-door swung wide now, Benji was too stunned to be frightened. What he saw inside didn't align with reality. The vicious lurch of his stomach wasn't from terror but from a kind of vertigo.

The world shifted under his feet, and Benji saw the dark man.

Past the conference room desk, the man from the FBI stood sharply silhouetted against the wall of glass on the far side of the office, gazing out on the white glare of the November daybreak.

Slowly, like a planet, the man rotated toward Benji. His suit jacket, his slacks, his necktie loosened at the knot: all of them were night black. His stark-white shirt was his only light item, and it shone as bright as a searchlight. *Black suit*, Benji thought wildly. *Man in black.*

And he became terribly aware of the question mark–shaped alien object in his backpack.

"*Mis*ter Lightman!" said the man, crossing the room, closing the distance between them. "How are you? I'm Agent Joshua McKedrick. But you can call me Agent Joshua McKedrick." He made a smile that never quite connected to his eyes.

Benji took the agent's offered hand, distantly hearing

Papaw's chuckle. Agent Joshua McKedrick's grip swallowed Benji's hand whole.

He was forty years old, tops, and stood only a couple of inches taller than Benji, but Benji still felt dwarfed. The agent was broad shouldered, perhaps that was part of it. His hair was pale gold, slicked back on a pale scalp; his eyes were hard gray like tombstones or steel. Stale cigarettes and stale coffee were on his breath when he spoke, which he did with a voice sharp with a big-city accent Benji only knew from movies. Boston? New York? (Benji'd always felt vaguely inferior whenever he met people from big cities.)

As the agent ended the handshake, Papaw said, "Well, Agent McKedrick, I'm real sorry to do this, but I should get back to the station. Paperwork calls, y'know?"

"Absolutely, Sheriff. I deeply appreciate you coming down."

"Truly my pleasure. I'll see you tonight, Benjamin. Agent, again, it was just so good to meet'cha."

As Papaw left with a wink Benji's way, Benji felt the low panic of an irrevocable mistake, like he was little and had just gotten home and realized he'd left his favorite toy back in the park, and now the night was gathering and he just knew in his heart he would never see that toy again. Maybe McKedrick really wasn't here for any reason connected to the saucer; probably he wasn't. But Benji was still scared, ill prepared, and one of Papaw's favorite phrases flitted through his mind:

If you want to dance, Benjamin, you've got to pay the fiddler.

"So," said the agent into the silence that spun out after the door clicked closed, "I hear you're a man with some amazing secrets."

What. The. Ass?

Benji began, "What do you mean—?"

"Hold on, I'm going to sit down, kid."

Homecoming decorations were stacked around the room, so at the moment, only two chairs were open. McKedrick sat in the leather chair the principal always used. Benji started to sit in the other, less-comfortable chair reserved for students, but when his butt was halfway down, McKedrick grabbed that chair, too, swinging it away, stationing it in front of himself as a footrest. His shoes were black, but shined to a glow. "I got a sore back like you wouldn't believe, sorry, kid."

"No problem, I don't mind standing."

"Do something for me: sit down. I'll get a sore neck, too, if I have to keep looking up at you." McKedrick winked. Which seemed friendly enough.

But there was something strange about it—maybe the way the rest of his face stayed slack—that made Benji uneasy.

The only other place to sit was on the room's heater, which was built into the wall beside them. It was so low that he had to look upward at McKedrick. It made Benji's butt uncomfortably hot. He scooted forward, balancing on a sharp corner. "So. You were saying—"

"*Right!*" McKedrick said. "You're a man of hidden talents. I've gotta say, Lightman, your results were mindblowers."

Benji blinked. "'Results'?"

McKedrick snagged a manila folder from the conference table. He opened it and riffled through some papers inside. "Your West-Test scores. Your analytical thinking, your math, your comprehension of abstract uses of language. I won't say the scores are off the charts, but they're close enough for government work. Ha."

It took Benji a few moments to even figure out what McKedrick was talking about. *Wait . . . those tests from last year?*

The West-Test was a standardized test everyone had to take at the end of junior year. It was supposed to help people choose a career path or whatever, but honestly, almost everyone thought of it as kind of a joke.

"Oh," Benji said. "I had no idea people actually, like, used that stuff."

"Usually we don't. Law enforcement agencies get your scores, though; the armed forces do, too. But honestly, most of us think of it as kind of a joke."

It was mostly just Benji's relief, but he couldn't help it: He laughed.

"Nonetheless, we make exceptions every once in a while if we find people like yourself."

"Like me?"

"Special people," McKedrick said casually. "Sometimes you come across an individual, and you simply know said individual is destined for greater things. Call it professional intuition, but if you spend enough time in my field, you learn to listen to that voice. The truth is, those people often aren't even aware of their own extraordinary quality. That's a tragedy for the United States of America. We conceal our secret aspects at our own peril, you know. That's another thing you learn in my field."

Benji nodded, powerfully flattered but still confused.

"Listen, I am loath to pry, but the sheriff mentioned that you hope to stay in the area for college."

Benji felt his shoulders twinge back microscopically. *Well, it's not really* me *who's hoping to do that.* But he nodded.

"Have you ever thought of government work?" When Benji made a politely noncommittal sound, McKedrick laughed good-naturedly. "Of course not, kid! What kind of dream would that be? It can be a decent enough gig, though, no lie. You might've heard we're creating a new criminal justice program at Indiana U? New forensics lab, a house for mock crime scenes. Real *CSI* stuff, minus all the people taking their sunglasses off *oh-so-dramatically* all the time. If you're interested—and with a head like yours, I say in all sincerity that I hope you will be—I'd like to see about setting you up with a full scholarship. It'd be an easy commute for you, and we can always use another good man."

Benji didn't quite know how to respond; it was all so sudden, so bizarre. More than anything, he simply felt good that this big-city guy thought so much of him.

Except . . . just then, something bothered Benji. McKedrick made all this sound awesome, but wasn't he really just offering to make Benji a cop? Maybe a different and shinier version, but ultimately another unit in the automated line of The Lightman Family Tradition.

Don't think that way. He likes you. Why can't you just enjoy it?

"Sounds pretty cool," Benji said.

"It is. Lot of mysteries out there, kid."

Benji waited for him to go on, but McKedrick only kept staring, the sentence clinging suspended in the air between them. *Lot of mysteries out there, kid.*

A sound shattered the silence: second bell, which signaled that classes would start in two minutes. Benji flinched, then laughed a little at himself, slightly embarrassed.

McKedrick didn't smile back.

McKedrick watched.

"So. Do you have a pamphlet I can check out?" Benji asked, shrugging his backpack on as the bell stopped screaming.

"Not with me," McKedrick said, "but absolutely I can get you one. The rest of my day's packed, but I can come by your house first thing tomorrow to drop off the literature."

Why can't you just bring it to school? "I have practices before school, unfortunately."

"Practices! Wow, I do not miss being young. How long do those practices last?"

"I think tomorrow's is from six until school starts at seven thirty."

"And they're not even paying you for it. The real world is a better place, kid. In any case, just so you are aware, we'll give you a standard background check before the process moves forward. Any history of drug use and underage drinking will rule you out."

"I cannot overstate how much that will *not* be a problem," Benji deadpanned.

McKedrick just peered up from the chair. The agent had a kind of relaxed confidence, a man utterly at home in his own flesh. But there was something in the clear gray eyes that gave the impression of a machine ticking stealthily in his skull.

"Just one last item before you go, chief," he said. "Something's been troubling me. That plane crash last night. A pilot with a perfect record is flying in good weather, and he just drops outta the sky like Wile E. Coyote? I'm not a NASA man, but something about that doesn't quite calculate."

A thread of adrenaline stitched inexplicably through Benji's veins. He nodded noncommittally.

"You wouldn't know anything about that," McKedrick said, "would you?"

"Why would I?"

"Weren't you out last night?"

The unease gathered in his gut. *Why is he asking this?* "No."

"You weren't? Because the sheriff said—"

"Oh. Yeah, no, we drove by. But we didn't see anything until it was over."

McKedrick's gaze grabbed Benji's and wouldn't let go. In another life, he could have made a killing as the world's greatest hypnotist.

"It's an unpleasant situation, don't you think? Not that it's my assignment, but I've heard how serious football rivalry pranks can get around here."

Benji again gave a vague nod. McKedrick's insinuation that anyone in Bedford Falls would have sabotaged an airplane was funny, even ridiculous. McKedrick seemed smart. Why would he believe that?

He doesn't, Benji thought, and it was then that his instinctive grasp of magic (call it professional intuition) offered him a conscious realization: McKedrick wasn't really interested in the plane crash. He was misdirecting Benji.

For what?

"I'm sure I can trust you," McKedrick said, "to tell me if you hear or think of anything strange, isn't that right?"

"Yes, sir."

"Sure I can. You're a smart kid."

"Thanks."

"You're a smart *kid.*" The emphasis made his point as sharp and unmistakable as a knife: You're Little League, sonny boy, and I'm the damn New York Yankees. All at once, Benji felt like a time traveler: not a senior in high school at all, but a little boy, heartsick and scared, about to be punished by a man in a uniform. He pictured McKedrick taking away the pod—

And he felt something strange.

Rather than feeling helpless, Benji suddenly thrummed with a kind of low electrical anger. It was an emotional electric field so powerful that it made his skin feel like it was vibrating.

It was alien to him.

And it was beautiful.

"We were just cruising." Benji shrugged. "I better get to class."

McKedrick's gaze trailed over Benji's shoulder. Benji realized: His skin actually *was* vibrating. The silver saucer shrapnel was buzzing in his backpack.

McKedrick saw Benji's utterly shocked expression before Benji could disguise it.

"What have you got in there, kid?" McKedrick said in response to Benji's strange reaction. McKedrick stood, and for one millisecond, something flashed in his eyes that shocked Benji: something like compassion, or pity. *I know you're in over your head, Lightman. Don't you lie to me.*

"I dunno," said Benji. "But it came from . . ."

. . . outer space . . .

". . . it came from *you*," Benji finished, and moved so smoothly that McKedrick did not notice Benji's hand retrieving a small silver object from his coat pocket. Benji reached up and pulled that object from McKedrick's ear, and showed it to the agent.

A joy buzzer.

McKedrick gave a single dry, confused chuckle.

And Benji, filled with a gorgeously reckless courage, said, "Out of this world, right?"

Benji strolled into the hallway and rejoined the stream of students, feeling an urge to shout to the population of the planet,

GUESS WHO IS A BADASS?! He settled on smiling, the fantastic metal of adrenaline filling his mouth. Even when the tardy bell rang and a group of stragglers jostled into him, he felt untouchable. Lighter. *So this is how CR always feels,* Benji thought. He stopped walking, just paused right there in the middle of the main hall, watching the last kids rushing into classrooms while the echo of the bell faded. And then the doors shut and the hallway filled with that almost-eerie almost-silence that you hear only and always when you're walking through school with no one else around. It was oddly exhilarating, that feeling—like you had this power or freedom that all the kids tethered to their desks didn't, even though really you were just going to the bathroom. *So this is how I'm always going to feel,* Benji thought.

He went to the bathroom.

Nobody at the urinals or sink; no feet in the stalls. He locked the last stall behind him, kneeled on the scuzzy floor, and tore open his backpack. The silvery cylinder lay at the bottom of it, smushed between his tuxedo and community college brochures. The curve in the metal looked a little like a kid's drawing of a smile.

No, Benji corrected himself. *Like a question mark.*

And now the Question was silent. Cautiously, he put his index finger on it. Buzz-less.

So he lifted it. The Question caught the bathroom fluorescents, bathing the interior of the backpack with a video game treasure-chest glow. He turned it in his hands. Fractals of light washed over the graffitied stall walls.

Here's a question: What the ass just happened in the office? Benji didn't know. All he knew was that rather than feeling powerless, he'd felt almost mighty. And the Question had seemed to somehow respond to that intense emotion.

Like magic.

Presto.

And for once, I kept my magic secret.

Change-o.

10

The rest of the morning felt a month long. When the lunch bell finally rang, Benji not-quite-jogged to the new wing of the school. The school's main building was really old, like days-of-disco old, but in the early 2000s it seemed like Bedford Falls's future was one big fat check from the natural gas companies, so the city cut down some forest land to build the new football stadium, and also added this new wing with computer labs and a huge auditorium. A plaque beside the auditorium double doors read: *To all fine arts, this theater is dedicated.* It was currently occupied by the football team, who were watching a video, projected on a portable movie screen, of rival Newporte High's latest game. Coach Nicewarner stood by the screen, illustrating Newporte's weaknesses with a laser pointer.

Benji spotted Ellie at the small audiovisual control booth in the middle-back of the auditorium. There were several boards covered in the buttons and sliding switches that controlled the auditorium, but Ellie was focused on her laptop.

Benji wove through the plushy blue-and-gold seats. "You've got your independent study period this afternoon, right?" he said when he reached her.

Ellie glanced up. "Howdy to you, too."

"Sorry, hi."

The glowing red eye of a laser pointer hovered on Benji's chest. "You got something real important to say to all of us, son? You got a message from the pope?" Coach grumbled.

Benji waved without apologizing, took the stool next to Ellie, and mostly whispered, "I need your help."

"Ellie," Coach called, "fast-forward to the end of the fourth quarter, would'ja, hon?"

Ellie offered Coach a plastic smile, punched a key on the control panel, and told Benji through her teeth, "When a man asks a question that ends with 'hon' or 'sweetie,' I always want to answer, 'Ew.'" She punched another key; on the movie screen Newporte resumed pummeling the other team at normal speed.

"I'll write that in my diary to make sure I remember, Tootsie-Wootsie," someone whispered to Benji's right. It was CR.

Ellie casually scratched her cheek with her middle finger— *not* smiling, Benji noticed.

"You need to watch the game, don't you?" Benji asked CR.

"Nah, I already did, like, three times. I had a double period of Phys Ed this morning." Ellie laughed under her breath. "What?" CR said.

"Two gym classes," Ellie said, "because you simply can't fit all there is to learn about the intricacies of indoor kickball into a single ninety-minute block?"

"Damn, Eleanor, moody much? I guess I'm not the only one having a double perio—"

"Nope!" Benji said warningly, raising his hand in front of CR's face like a stop sign.

CR stared at it for a moment, then at Benji, like he didn't understand what Benji was doing. Then, with a confused tentativeness, CR gave the hand a high five.

Ellie snapped her laptop shut, and just before she did, Benji saw that a Word document named "Short Film Narration" was open—a *blank* document. She slid the computer into her backpack. His chest tightened. It wasn't like he'd never been caught in the crossfire between CR and Ellie before. When they'd dated sophomore year, they'd bickered practically all the time. Benji had been the Switzerland of those conflicts: studiously neutral. During their rare post-breakup fights, Benji was always reminded of their prior relationship, which was unpleasant on a number of levels.

"Ellie, don't go," Benji said. "CR, apologize. Right now."

CR's mouth dropped open. "What?"

"Do it," Benji said. His voice was strong, free of the anxiety that usually tethered it. "I'm serious."

CR stared at Benji another moment, then cocked an incredulous (and condescending, frankly) half smile. "Oh, I'm *very* sorry, Eleanor."

CR, Benji thought angrily, *can you just not be yourself for a while?*

Ellie might have left anyway, but right then the door at the back of the auditorium opened. The silhouette of a skinny guy in dad clothes carrying two full-to-bursting duffel bags stepped through. Benji smiled. Zeeko made his way to them and dropped the bags to the floor, breathing and sweating pretty heavily.

He held his hand out in front of Benji. "That'll be a zillion dollars," he said.

"Did you get everything on the list?" Benji asked.

"You're welcome," Zeeko said.

"Sorry, thank you."

"I'd say 'Don't mention it,' but you already didn't." Zeeko sounded maybe a little hurt, actually, but he went on. "How's it going, kids? Ellie, dahling, you look upset, which is upsetting me."

Ellie smiled in spite of herself. "Yeah. It's Christopher Robin."

"Uh oh, a two-name offense! His social skills do leave something to be desired—specifically, social skills."

"Ha-ha," CR said. But he was grinning, and whatever tension lingered in the air had gone.

"I got most of your list, Neil deGrasse Tyson," Zeeko said to Benji. "If I took any more, the hospital would notice. And I need it back tonight." He pulled a crumpled piece of paper covered in Benji's handwriting from his pocket. "What's with leaving a note in my locker, though? Did your phone break?"

"Oh my *God*," Ellie whispered. She had opened one of the duffel bags and found some of the inventory. Benji had a moment to worry about how she would react, but when she lifted her face, it was lit with a kind of nervous delight. "Are we doing a science project, Benji Lightman? Are we going on a *field trip*?"

Benji nodded, feeling the happy zing of that "I have the ultimate hall pass" freedom.

"I left the note," he told Zeeko, "'cause we need a rule: no texting about anything even slightly related to Thingy Thang. If we *absolutely* need to talk about it, call. But no voice mails. Also, Ellie, before we go, make sure you turn off Find My iPhone. And Find My Friends. And Foursquare and Whisper. And Frequently Visited Places on Google Maps and location-based reminders, and, umm—"

"Why the paranoia?" Ellie said, looking concerned.

"Just being absurdly careful," Benji replied, quoting Ellie from last night, because he'd already concluded he shouldn't say anything about Agent McKedrick, at least not yet. And Benji really *wasn't* paranoid, at least not exactly. He just wanted answers, felt an extraordinary urge to go to the pod and try to make sense of everything. All his life he'd carried a vague anxiety that he was Missing Out on the Good Stuff. Now, for the first time he could remember, he thought he might know how to make that anxiety and longing vanish. If he could just understand the pod, just make sense of why the saucer had come . . .

Ellie nodded at his response, the sides of her mouth twitching adorably at the secret code.

CR, playing catch-up, asked, "When's this happening, Banjo?"

"Now."

"'Kay, I'll drive."

"Oh. Yeah, I mean, it's just, it might take a while, and I know you've got class."

"Just computer lab, and I was gonna skip anyway. Besides, I don't want you spending time with that thing without me." CR might just be acting protective. But he almost seemed more *defensive*, like he was trying to say *My hall pass is bigger than yours.*

Well . . . whatever. Benji was taking a day off from soothing CR's insecurities. To keep things light, he said, "Thanks."

Zeeko excused himself, saying he had to go help his dad in the community health truck, which that afternoon was hanging out in the Kroger parking lot.

Benji picked up the duffel bags filled with (among other things) stethoscopes, scalpels, bone saws, and radiation detectors. It was showtime.

Papaw's cruiser wasn't in the driveway, but Benji still told CR to wait in the truck. Ellie hopped out with Benji, and after they'd verified the house was empty, Benji helped CR back his truck up the driveway to the tree house in the backyard. The feelings of excitement grew stronger as he physically got closer to the tree house. Images of touching the pod again grew clear in his mind, like a video unpixelating on a better internet connection. He kept thinking of the years of carnival mornings with Papaw, and how although the world right now had none of that predawn visual mystique (it was just typical Indiana winter afternoon weather, low steely skies binding the brutally cold air), it *felt* like he'd always hoped those carnival mornings would.

As CR turned off the truck, wind gusted. The oak limbs around the tree house chattered. Wearing a fashionable-but-way-too-thin thrift store peacoat, Ellie shivered.

"Want to borrow my scarf?" Benji asked.

"What scarf would that be?" He wasn't wearing one.

He reached up his sleeve, pulled out a long, rainbow-colored "infinity scarf," and wrapped it gently around Ellie's neck. "You keep that for a while," he said. "You make that look better than I do."

Maybe it was just the cold, but roses appeared in Ellie's cheeks. "Benji Lightman," she said, laughing a little, "you can be so damn cheesy sometimes."

"I'm not sure if that's a compliment."

"It is."

For once, she was the one who broke eye contact.

As CR got out of the truck, his phone beeped.

"Stow it in the car, buddy," Benji said.

CR checked the screen. "Coach wants to know why I left. Also he's telling me for the billionth time not to do a revenge prank against Newporte this week. Which, I dunno, are you guys *sure* you don't want to do it?" CR frowned when Benji and Ellie nodded. "Well, thank you, World, for pooping my party. Just let me text him back."

Benji sighed inwardly and took out his own phone to turn

it off. But actually, it already was. When Ellie checked, hers was off, too. He remembered how so many metallic and electronic objects had gone bananas at the quarry when the saucer arrived. He realized he was closer to the tree house than CR—maybe fifteen feet from the ramp.

"Come over here first," Benji said to CR.

CR, texting, took a step forward and, *beep*, his phone went black. "The hell?"

Benji couldn't help but feel a small thrill. "It's the pod, I think. It's like a force field."

"What, seriously? Thanks for telling me! I don't have Apple-Care, bro!"

"No, the phone's fine. It just won't work while you're close to the pod." CR still looked annoyed or something, and Benji thought, *YOU CAN BUY A NEW PHONE. YOU CANNOT BUY A NEW POD.*

"Oh," CR said. "Well, I guess at least I don't have to worry about pictures getting online again."

Benji felt a reflexive disappointment that the pod was unphotographable—the phrase "pics or it didn't happen" flashed in his head like an obnoxious neon sign. But, after a moment, he really *liked* the idea. He wasn't sure whether he eventually wanted to tell the world about the pod, but until he decided, it was comforting, even exciting, to know it was unsharable (and un-Share-able).

It was almost, he thought, like the pod *wanted* to be kept hidden.

They donned the radiation protection Zeeko had given them: three thick lead-lined aprons used by X-ray technicians in hospitals. Benji pointed out the little green card under a plastic sheet on the chest of the aprons. On the off chance that the pod was radioactive, he explained, the green card would turn yellow. On the off-off chance that it was *dangerously* radioactive, it would turn red. "But don't freak out. The card changes colors before the radiation gets strong enough to hurt people."

Then, duffel bag in hand, he led the way to the tree house ramp, the upward spiral to their chamber of secrets.

The snow on the ramp was untouched, the lock on the door still in place, just as he'd left it last night. He didn't think McKedrick knew about the pod or anything, and certainly didn't expect McKedrick to come kicking in the door to the tree house shouting, "REACH FOR THE SKY, YOU POD-HARBORING SONS OF BITCHES!"

But seeing the smooth powder on that ramp was a relief, partly because Benji's own footprints from last night had been erased. Not that Papaw would have spotted the prints, rubbed his stubble, and instantly deduced, "Oh, dear God above, my grandson is concealing wreckage from an alien vessel in my very own backyard!" But Papaw *might* wonder why he was suddenly interested in his abandoned tree house.

Benji spun the combination into the lock, unhooked it, and opened the door. Ellie and CR followed him inside.

Light leaked through the boarded windows and gaps in the walls. When the door sealed shut behind them, the nostalgic smell of pine bloomed with such intensity that Benji had to momentarily close his eyes against the feeling: a joy that hurt.

He still couldn't see much when he opened his eyes. He pulled out the matchbook he'd grabbed from the kitchen and dragged a match across the strip. *Lumos!* some part of him whispered as it sparked. *Where did* that *come from?* he wondered, half smiling.

Then the pod glimmered into view, quicksilver in firelight, and as Ellie drew a sharp breath beside him, Benji's half smile went full. Snow had slipped into the tree house and spread a thin, bright carpet across the floor; the pod itself tossed the match light in a hundred directions, the firelight whirling over the walls like a carousel. It all gave the tree house the slightly otherworldly feel Benji'd always associated with holidays at night, and the pod was the Christmas tree.

"CR, could you pass me that lantern?" Benji asked. He was struck by an in-church feeling that he should be polite and reverent, and added, "Please?"

CR grabbed the scuffed red camping lantern off the trunk in the corner. Papaw had gotten it for Benji when he was maybe eleven. They always had two birthday parties for Benji: one for his friends (or, until CR moved in, *friend*) with a grocery store cake that came under a plastic bubble, and another "for the family" . . . which always comprised an awkward slice of cobbler split between Benji and Papaw at Dave's Dine-In out on the highway. Papaw would slide his gift, wrapped neatly in newspaper, across a tabletop that was checkered like a picnic blanket; Benji would open it and begin the time-honored childhood ritual of pretending to be happier with your gifts than you really are.

Sometimes Papaw would say a word or two about the gifts.

"That bat is a Louisville Slugger, just like what Babe Ruth used."

"That biography is about Benjamin Franklin—your namesake, Benjamin, a real self-made man if ever one walked these United States."

But mostly Papaw let his notes (written on Bedford Falls Police Department stationery) do the talking. *"To Benjamin— This lantern's a* Coleman! *Good American family company. Maybe we'll go camping & have a fine time. Happy birthday— Sheriff Robert Lightman."* They never did go camping, but the lantern remained Papaw's most memorable gift. Benji had seen the faint impression of ghost letters on that note, and later on, he gently rubbed the lead of a pencil sideways across the letters. The message materialized: *A lantern for you, because you're the light of my life.* How beautiful those words were. They pierced him like an arrow, and he thought for one fleeting instant that he understood the deeper chambers of his grandfather's heart.

But no. Of course no. The moral of that story wasn't what Papaw had written, but what he had erased.

Now Benji tipped some lighter fluid he'd gotten from the house into the lantern, then lit the wick with the match. A bright vertical flame blossomed, cutting through the gloom.

He lifted the lantern to the radiation-detector card on his apron. "How am I looking?"

Ellie gave him the A-OK sign.

"So, what's step one, pod-wise?" CR asked.

Benji glanced at Ellie. In the lamplight, she looked even prettier (and hotter, honestly) than usual, her face flushed with excitement, her green eyes sparking. "There is no instruction manual for the impossible," he said.

They shared a private grin.

Benji kneeled down a few inches in front of the pod, motioning for Ellie and CR to do the same. The highest point of the pod was even with their hearts.

He set the duffel bag on the floor. In addition to all the medical equipment Zeeko had supplied, Benji had added some of his own items from the house. Now he pulled out the first one: a square electronic box, roughly the size of a deck of cards. It was a stud finder, a carpenter's tool that you could run along the surface of walls to find "studs" (solid pieces of wood or metal, basically) hidden inside the walls.

He handed the stud finder to CR. "Go ahead," Benji said.

"Go ahead what?"

"Go ahead and make the joke I know you want to make."

CR's goofy-huge smile spread over his face. "Banjo, we're like a married couple in a nursing home. It's disgusting. I love it." He placed the stud finder against his chest and depressed the device's single button. The device beeped, and a small green light on the top lit up. "Found a stud!" CR said.

Maybe it was just the desire to ease the tension between them from the mini confrontation in the theater, but CR's joke still made Benji laugh.

"How did that work?" Ellie asked, confused.

"Extremely well," CR said.

She swatted the air like she was dismissing a gnat. "How come it could turn on? Doesn't the pod interfere with electronics?"

Benji had thought about this already, actually. At the quarry, when the saucer had made its first appearance, the engine and headlights of CR's truck had turned on by themselves. But Ellie's RustRocket station wagon, a much less modern vehicle, hadn't reacted at all.

"I think it only does it sometimes," Benji said, "and mostly with things that have digital parts, not just basic batteries."

"Why?"

"No clue."

Ellie frowned a little, not quite satisfied. "I never thought I'd say this, but I really wish I'd taken more science electives."

Benji took the stud finder back. Though he had an urge to use his bare hands, he knew CR would object, so he tugged on his gloves, then moved the stud finder toward the pod cautiously. A fun house–mirror version of Benji, reflected on the pod, did the same. He touched the stud finder against the silvery surface; the pod sang a thin, cheery musical note: *diiiing!*

He pushed the button. This time, the little light turned red.

He carefully traced the stud finder along the pod, first side to side and then top to bottom.

The indicator light on the stud finder stayed red the whole time.

"So the pod's empty?" Ellie asked.

"I suppose," Benji said, feeling weirdly disappointed.

"Then why's it kinda heavy?" CR said. There was a note of concern in his voice.

"We're dealing with interstellar technology here," Ellie said in a terse voice that made CR blush. "The pod could be made of a new element, for all we know."

"True," Benji said. *Although, admittedly, I took as little science as legally possible, too.*

He put the stud finder back in the duffel bag, and pulled out Item Number Two.

A stethoscope.

CR still looked a little stung by Ellie's reply, and as soon as he saw the stethoscope, he recovered by saying, "Okay, pod, now turn your head and cough." Benji gave a chuckle, and even Ellie had to smirk.

Benji plugged the eartips of the stethoscope into his ears. For a trial run, he ran a thumbnail across the listening pad of the stethoscope. The noise in his ears was like the rumble of distant thunder.

After placing the listening pad on the pod with the same gentle caution he'd used with the stud finder, Benji's heart gave a series of quick, hard beats: He thought he heard something shift within the pod, and then (his heart seemed to stop) swore he heard a voice within the pod *speak*. He held his breath, straining to hear.

The voice he'd heard became clear: *"Yoooouuuu're the next contestant on* The Price Is Right*!"* The stethoscope was just picking up the sound from ancient Mrs. Bainbridge's TV next door, which (to Papaw's annoyance) she blasted all day, every day.

So that was a little frustrating . . . but *only* a little. Mostly, as the "science project" continued, Benji felt nothing but a mixture of happiness and curiosity. All their radiation detectors stayed green as he used progressively more aggressive equipment from Zeeko's bag and Papaw's toolbox. First, he tapped a wood-carving chisel against the pod. The chisel was sharp steel, but it didn't leave so much as a scratch on the pod, even when CR stabbed it pretty hard.

Next up was Papaw's blowtorch. An inch-long blue flame emanated from its pistol-like tip. Benji held the fire against the surface of the pod, then inspected the spot it had touched. No burn mark, no discoloration at all.

The pod also stood up invincibly to efforts with both a manual bone saw and a handheld device with a spinning blade that Benji was pretty sure was used to cut skulls. The invincibility was amazing, but even better was the feeling Benji had through all the experiments: full *immersion*.

Part of it was that the itchy urge to check his phone (which he'd never really known he'd had) had vanished.

But the best part was the feeling of *mattering*, the certain knowledge that he was living a centrally special moment in his life. The only really important feeling in the world, he realized, was that the things you experience matter, that they *mean* something, like all the pain and inadequacies are only pixels in this beautiful bigger story you can't see yet. Most people refuse not just to see the story, but to acknowledge even the possibility that it might exist. Maybe that was why Spinney and Papaw tried so hard to claw back in time: They couldn't summon the kind of courageous faith required to face all the uncertainty and possibilities of the present, so they clung to the certainties of the past.

And Benji knew now that every last bit of his own pain and

embarrassment and fear had been worth enduring. It had meant something. If he didn't quite know whether he believed in God, he knew he believed in the future, and in fate. No obnoxious voice from stadium speakers or a drunk FIG or his grandfather's defeated sighs could convince him otherwise. He was strapped in the cockpit with stars in the glass. He was outsmarting the known universe.

Or at least that was how he felt until they decided to hit the pod with the magnetic hammer.

When Benji pulled out the hammer, the sound of Mrs. Bainbridge's TV told him they were going to have to leave soon to get back in time for their one-thirty classes: Drew Carey had just wrapped up the Showcase Showdown, and Wayne Brady was happily welcoming the live studio audience to *Let's Make a Deal.*

CR had been growing antsy as time went on, at one point actually pacing, hunchbacked, around the small tree house. Now he hopped gracefully out of his sitting position to his feet, lifted the corrugated tin cover from one of the windows, and peeked outside in the direction of Mrs. Bainbridge's living room picture window. "Yeah, Wayne Brady's on. It's one o'clock . . . holy shit!" CR breathed.

"What?" Benji said.

"Look at that dude break-dance. Look at him go! When I grow up, I wanna be Wayne Brady. Banjo, if I got in a fight with Wayne Brady, who would win?"

"I think we've got time to try one more thing," Benji said, trying to ignore him.

CR looked back at Benji. "Yeah, it was a trick question anyway. I would beat myself up, because I refuse to lay a finger on an American treasure like Mr. Wayne Brady." He spotted the small yellow hammer in Benji's hand. "Ah, Banjo. A damn spinning saw doesn't work, and you're breaking out the Playskool tool set."

"CR, you can leave," Benji said. "If you want to stay, cool. If you're bored and want to go, also okay." He wasn't mad, just stating it as a fact.

He couldn't quite see CR's reaction; the sunlight through the window silhouetted him. CR's shoulders maybe seemed to tense, but when he spoke, he was friendly enough.

"I'm just saying, if Bob the Builder finds out you stole his hammer, he's gonna be pissed." CR let go of the sheet of tin; it swung down and covered the window again.

Benji tightened his grip on the roofing hammer's black rubber handle. CR was right: The hammer did look small. But its tip was magnetic, and that detail seemed to matter; the saucer had apparently come alive last night when the magnetic winch touched it, after all.

Benji lifted the hammer, preparing to give the pod a firm tap. Outside, Wayne Brady was telling a contestant to choose between Door #1, #2, or #3.

Benji hesitated with the hammer in midair. An image popped insistently into his head, of Ellie using the hammer instead.

"Ellie, do you want to do this one?"

She scooted over to his side of the pod, then said, "How about we do it together?"

Benji agreed. He had been wearing gloves this whole time, and now CR suggested that Ellie do the same. (For a moment Benji felt an inexplicable, strange anger, then shook his head to clear it.)

With a voice suggesting the fate of the world would pivot on her decision, the contestant informed Wayne Brady she wanted to go with Door #2.

Benji tried to put his hand lower than Ellie's on the rubber grip, but there wasn't quite room. "Oh, c'mon," she said, laughing a little, and placed his hand on top of hers, all their fingers intertwining.

She whispered, "One, two, you-know-what-to-do."

There was already an electric quality in the air, and that sensation—as if all the atoms inside Benji had begun to crackle—only surged as the hammer arced down toward the pod.

Right around the time Door #2 opened, Benji saw the first thin blue thread of electricity leap between the pod and the hammer. The lucky contestant gave a hysterical shriek. The single thread forked in two: a lightning bolt in miniature.

All this happened in milliseconds, quickly enough that Benji didn't have time to find out if the contestant had been shrieking from joy or something else, and quickly enough that they couldn't stop the hammer from striking the pod. An inch away, the hammer jerked out of their hands, the powerful magnet taking hold. As the hammer made contact, the delicate electricity flared brilliantly, multiplied, and spread, enveloping the entire pod in a complex web made of a hundred threads of dazzling light.

There was an electrical *zap* sound, like a great circuit breaker in Dr. Frankenstein's lab sizzling to life. Benji felt a *WHOMPF*, an invisible wave of power rushing outward from the pod. It was like wind but also nothing like wind: The wave traveled *through* him, making his fillings zing. He fell onto his back. As the shock wave left the tree house, the walls shuddered.

For a moment, Benji was totally still, propped up on his elbows and staring at the pod as the web of light crackled out of existence. He looked at Ellie, who had crashed onto her back, too. She stared at him with eyes wide with shock and something like exaltation.

He scrambled up and lifted the cover off a window just in time to watch the effects of the invisible shock wave ripple across his neighborhood. One by one, the streetlamps lit themselves in broad daylight. Lights in the houses switched on and burned bright. Mrs. Bainbridge's TV blared a deafening commercial about reverse mortgages. Car alarms whooped. Radios sang discordant joy.

And then, all at once, it was over. The streetlamps went dark, and the alarms went silent, and Mrs. Bainbridge's TV resumed its normal volume. It was just another afternoon in the neighborhood in Bedford Falls, Indiana.

Except it wasn't.

"Kiss my ass," CR whispered shakily. He'd fallen against the wall on the other side of the tree house. His face pinched into an expression rarely seen from CR: absolute and honest fear. "What was that?"

Benji looked down at the plastic radiation-detector card on his chest. His card and everyone else's was the safe color, green. The magnetized hammer, which had been stuck to the pod, clanged to the ground. When Benji would test the hammer later on, he'd find that the magnet no longer worked. Next door, Mrs. Bainbridge's TV now gently explained that wearing adult diapers was nothing to be embarrassed about.

"Wh-what do you think this is? Banjo?" CR asked. "Not, like, what do you think it's made of. What do you think the pod is, period?"

Benji couldn't find his voice. He'd asked himself what the pod was a hundred times since last night, of course. Before his close encounter with Agent McKedrick, Benji's best (if disheartening) guess was that the pod was nothing more than the final random fragment of the miracle of the century.

But then the Question had come momentarily alive . . . then

this pod had unleashed a wave of enigmatic energy. . . .

We own this magic, Benji thought. *These . . . these machines. They're our secrets, but holy shit, they're not just little freaking toys we play with, tricks that only seem amazing when we use our imagination. They touched the rest of the world. They have that power.*

We *have that power.*

And the same booming voice he'd heard in the dream about the drive-in filled his head, speaking a name just alien enough to suggest something extraordinary: *I AM MR. FAHRENHEIT.*

Finally, Benji answered CR: "Whatever it is, it's important. And we're going to figure it out. We're *meant* to." His voice was completely steady.

"You sound pretty damn sure about that," CR replied, surprised.

Benji smiled. "Yeah. I am."

"Me too, Benji Lightman," Ellie said. "Hot damn, *me too.*"

You grow up being told you'll change the world. Maybe for most people becoming an adult means giving up on that belief, and letting the world change *you.* But Benji—Benji and Ellie— wouldn't let that happen. They were on the eve of gathering fate. It was all happening, and she was in it with him completely. And it was then, for the first time, that Benji began to understand that Ellie might be falling in love with him, too.

11

Benji, CR, and Ellie made it back to school just in time for their last classes. After the experience in the tree house, the rest of the day seemed torturously boring. Evening had fallen by the time Benji's after-school practices ended. When he got home, Papaw was in the living room polishing his work shoes.

"Benjamin!" Papaw said, looking exhausted and excited, like he had when introducing Benji to McKedrick. "How'd the meetin' go?"

Before Benji could answer, their landline phone, the one used only for police business, rang. Papaw grimaced, picked it up, and said, "Sheriff Lightman. This better be good."

Benji was about to go to his room when Papaw hung up. "That plane crash has opened an unbelievable can of worms," Papaw said, frowning. "We were inspectin' the crash site and came across a cannabis field on Deegan's property. The whole property's roped off. I get the pleasure of giving the DEA a tour at five thirty in the a.m. tomorrow."

"I'm sorry."

"You and me both. So, that meetin', how was it? I bet it was interestin'."

Benji answered honestly. "You have no idea, sir."

Papaw smiled.

Benji woke up the next morning just before dawn. He'd managed to sleep only a little, his dreams filled with images of the drive-in and the Dream Machine Cadillac, but he didn't feel tired at all.

After Papaw had left around five thirty to show the DEA Deegan's field, Benji called the school's band director to let her know he wouldn't be able to make it to today's six a.m. parade practice. It had been a long time since he'd faked a stomachache to skip out on something; he thought he did pretty well, especially considering that his legs were bouncing with excitement the whole time.

He thought about calling Ellie, Zeeko, or CR to come over, but even if they were awake, they'd be too busy: Ellie was constantly in the media lab finishing the nostalgia-a-thon video for the assembly, Zeeko in the community health truck with his dad, CR at morning practice. Still, despite being alone (perhaps *because* he was alone), Benji smiled. He could spend time alone with the pod, and the thought filled him with relief and anticipation as strong as any he'd ever felt.

Benji grabbed his old laptop, which took a couple of minutes to boot up. As he waited, he looked out his window at the tree house. It all still seemed so unreal. Not just the pod and the Question, but that expression on Ellie's face yesterday, the way roses had appeared in her cheeks when he gave her the scarf.

But it is real. Actually, it's the realest thing that ever happened to me. He felt like he *existed* in a way he never really had before.

When Windows finally loaded, he opened the browser and

put it into Private Mode. (Despite the shock wave from the pod, his phone still worked fine, but he felt more comfortable using the laptop because he wasn't sure if his search history showed up on their cell phone bill.) As he had last night, he checked the local TV station's website. After scrolling past several headlines about Friday's homecoming game, he clicked on a headline reading *Bedford Falls Power & Light Co. Outage Reported.*

The story still just said that the power had gone off very briefly due to a surge, which the power company was investigating. There was nothing to indicate anyone suspected anything extraordinary had occurred.

Satisfied, Benji jogged downstairs. He went out the front door, making sure Papaw hadn't unexpectedly returned while Benji had been online.

As soon as Benji stepped onto his porch, he heard a squeal of brakes.

At the end of the street, a black SUV, which had been turning onto his road, bucked to a stop. In contrast to the older cars in the neighborhood, the brand-new SUV practically glittered. Benji stared. There were government plates on the front of the car. Although he couldn't quite make out the face, he could tell the driver was wearing a black suit.

Is that McKedrick? Maybe he's dropping off the pamphlets.

Except, no. Benji had told him he had practice this morning. Why would McKedrick come now, in spite of thinking Benji wouldn't be home?

The SUV reversed quickly, did a U-turn, and sped away.

What if, Benji's mind whispered, *he was coming because he thought I wouldn't be home? What if he wanted to have a little look around?* Paranoia stiched into Benji, his mouth suddenly spitless.

I can't keep the pod here anymore.

12

"You want to do the thing? SERIOUSLY?!" CR shouted.

"ASAP."

"You want to do the thing ASAP?! (Hut-hut-hike.)"

The center snapped the ball into CR's hands. The offensive and defensive lines collided, the sound like firecracker pops in the wintry air of the after-school practice. CR faded back several yards, checking for a receiver. Seeing none, he momentarily looked back to Benji on the sidelines.

"I LOVE this, Banjo! What changed your mind?"

"You're being blitzed."

"I'm BEING BLITZ—*oh, shitty shit.*"

Two defenders surged through holes in the offensive line. They were zero trouble: CR tucked the ball into his elbow, deked left before dashing to the right, and the poor JV defenders, who had dived to tackle him, got nothing for their efforts except mouthfuls of snow and laughs from the hundreds of people watching the practice from the stadium's bleachers.

With the effortless grace of his mighty and Einsteinian arm, CR let the football fly toward an open receiver on the very far end of the field. The throw was a spiraling leather missile slicing through the flurries, and the crowd gasped in a kind of exalted amazement.

CR didn't seem all that interested. He was bending over to help the defenders up even as the receiver downfield pulled the pass into his chest and sprinted into the end zone. Men in the stands shouted, "Hell yes!" and "Go, Magic, go!" and (this one made Benji laugh out loud) "God bless America!"

Coach Nicewarner blew his whistle, clapping. "Don't think we can end better than that! That's practice, gentlemen!"

CR took off his helmet, his hair matted and sweat soaked, and jogged toward the sidelines. In the cold, his head steamed a little. There was a murmur of excitement from fans in the stands, but CR didn't go for them. He stopped in front of Benji, looking him straight in the face.

Benji worked to appear calm, which was tough after the most uncalm day he could remember. After seeing the SUV, he had waited at the house until Papaw got back from work mid-morning; he didn't feel safe leaving the pod at the house, and he didn't think McKedrick would come back if Papaw was home. Benji had told Papaw he'd forgotten his history book, then biked to school, spending the rest of the day trying to figure out what to do. He didn't know if McKedrick had been in the SUV, let alone if he knew anything about the saucer. In fact, as the day went on, Benji felt increasingly confident that things would work out the way they were meant to: perfectly. But he refused to take the chance.

"I can't believe you want to do the prank, Banjo," CR now said quietly, beaming. "What changed your mind?"

"I was just thinking that it's something I know you wanted to do for a long time," Benji said.

"What a sweetie pie my friend is." Then CR giggled, pulled

Benji in, and gave him a noogie. It was too affectionate, too loving, for Benji to get mad. After CR was finished, he kissed the
top of Benji's head with a cartoon sound: *mwah!*

"So we should figure out what we're gonna do, right?" Benji
said.

"Oh, baby, I know what we're gonna do. I've only been planning this for a million years. Step one is, we need to grab Zeeko
and tell him to get some of his dad's supply of Icy Hot. And you
know those things the cheerleaders use to shoot shirts at the
games?"

"The T-shirt cannons."

"Right, we're gonna go grab those bad boys, too."

So they grabbed those two bad boys from the field house
equipment closet. They found Zeeko outside the stadium gates
with his dad in the community health truck (which looked like
a silver-plated UPS truck) and got him to come with them. After
they bought a couple of additional supplies from Walmart,
Benji called Ellie. She sounded excited when she picked up,
and after Benji explained the plan and asked her to meet them
at his house, she said, "I want you to know, Benji Lightman, that
I'm doing this only because I am a better getaway driver than
Christopher Robin, and I do not want you to get in trouble. See
you in ten minutes."

"Why do we need to go to your house?" CR asked Benji after
they'd hung up.

"I just have to grab a couple things."

But it was just one thing, really.

Adrenaline had helped Benji move the heavy pod into his
magic steamer trunk by himself earlier. But the adrenaline had
faded. Papaw was in his bedroom, trying to catch up on sleep. As
Benji struggled to quietly pull the trunk from the closet where
he'd hidden it, CR jogged over and said, "Allow me, buddy."

Before Benji could object, CR picked up the trunk. He grunted. "What you got in this thing, a dead body?"

"Some new props for the assembly tomorrow. I was thinking we could drop them off in the theater at school after the prank. Ellie's got a key, and I wanted to get there early tomorrow to practice anyway."

CR looked at him a moment, and Benji could not read his expression. Then CR just said, "Sweet!"

They decided to take the RustRocket because the guys from Newporte High School in Indianapolis might recognize CR's truck. After they loaded the magic trunk into the back of the station wagon, Benji took the front seat, and he smiled. Ellie was wearing his scarf.

After you passed through some woods outside of Bedford Falls, the journey to Indianapolis was mostly farmland, just a panorama of cornfields bisected by the highway. Every once in a while a gap appeared in the rows of corn, and there would be lines of natural gas mining machinery, motionless and rusting in the snow. Even on cloudy nights like tonight, you could see Indianapolis miles before you actually reached it, the skyscrapers and lights of downtown flying high above the plains. During every minute of the fifteen-minute trip to the city, with a giddiness Benji couldn't help but love, CR bounced in his seat and seemed to talk in one continuous, breathless sentence.

"Holy crap, y'all, this is so exciting. Like, I can feel my butt tingling right now. Do your butts tingle when you get excited? Well, I can't be the only one. I just want to click my heels right now, just click my heels like a damn leprechaun! Zeeko, pass me those paintballs. Thank you, Dad Clothes, you are my bae. These Newporte d-bags deserve it, am I right? These big-city guys are all the same. Their big-ass companies stomp on little towns and then they go back to their mansions and wipe their big asses with hundred-dollar bills."

"I think you're confusing the Newporte football team with Scrooge McDuck." Benji laughed.

CR giggled. "'Hey, Newporte, shut the duck up!' I'm gonna say that! They'll be all like, 'Whaaaat?'"

"You don't want them to recognize your voice," Benji said.

"You're right, not my best idea. But people mess with my Banjo at their own peril. Banjo, you are my bae. Zeek, you're sure Icy Hot can't kill someone, even if they get it on their balls? Sweet, sweet. Guys, I can't believe this is happening. Can you believe we're seniors and we're doing this? This is exactly like I imagined being old would be. *I love everything so much right now!*"

Everyone cracked up.

From what Benji could tell, the north part of Indianapolis was the fancy-pantsiest part of town, with lots of McMansions and upscale restaurants and a pair of Apple Stores. They turned off the main road and drove past the huge main Newporte High School building, which looked so spotless that it almost gleamed in the night air. After making their way through the manicured campus, CR told Ellie to park the RustRocket on the far edge of their football stadium's enormous parking lot, just past the reach of the field lights.

Everyone followed CR's lead and got out of the car, hearing the distant football practice sounds: shoulder pads colliding, whistles chirping. With a ten-thousand-seat capacity, Bedford Falls's stadium was pretty big, but Newporte's dwarfed it. It looked like it could seat fifteen thousand, and from the parking lot Benji could see their Jumbotron, which must have been twice as big as the one in Bedford Falls. The players' cars, parked by the gates, were different than you'd find in Bedford

Falls, too: brand-new SUVs, as well as some low-riding sports cars that seemed hilariously optimistic for an Indiana winter.

CR grabbed a duffel bag from the trunk of the car, checked the time on his phone, and said, "Okay, here's what's up. It's six fifty-two right now and their practice ends at seven, so we better hurry.

"Step One: Eleanor, you're gonna be the distraction. I got this idea from a book we had to read for class. It was about this guy at a boarding school and he was obsessed with dead people and this girl who was smart but moody but *hot*, so okay. Pretty good book! Sad, though. *Shit*, was it sad! Anyway, Eleanor, drive the Rocket over to the other parking lot, the one way on the other side of the field. At exactly six fifty-eight, cell phone time, light these babies up." He dropped his duffel bag to the ground. As the canvas flap fell open, its cargo tumbled out: two dozen long, red, cylindrical sticks, topped with black fuses. He had tied all their fuses together, so that one spark could light the whole thing. "They're bottle rockets. I got 'em on sale last year right after the Fourth of July. Told you I'd been planning this forever, Banjo!

"Okay, Step Two: While everyone's distracted by the fireworks, me and Zeek go in the locker room and rub Icy Hot in all the seniors' underwear."

"Let it be noted," Zeeko said, "I'm only participating because I feel it is my Christian duty to make sure CR doesn't sterilize anyone."

"Good man," CR said. "So once their balls are on icy fire, some of the guys will probably freak and come outside, which is when Banjo launches the paintballs out of the T-shirt cannons. Banjo, here's a tip: Be sure you don't aim where people are. If you want to hit them, aim *just* ahead. Aim where they're going to be.

"Eleanor, you have to be back here by the time the paintballs fly, 'cause we're gonna have to haul ass out of here. Cool? Okay, now the disguises!"

He grabbed the Walmart bag and handed them four ski masks. They were hot pink, with little poofy balls on top. They had obviously been designed for tween girls, and CR had obviously thought this was hilarious. He tugged his mask on. "So how hot do I look right now?" he asked, then headbanged as he played heavy metal on an air guitar, the poofy ball jigging.

"It's six fifty-six," Ellie said impatiently.

CR threw his air guitar over his shoulder. "All right, buddies, let's go make history!" He and Zeeko jogged toward the field through the shadowy parking lot.

"See ya real soon, Benji Lightman," Ellie said as she drove off.

Benji opened the plastic tub of assorted-color paintballs they'd gotten from Walmart. He divided them equally into the large barrels of the two T-shirt cannons, then checked that the CO_2 tanks, which launched objects from the guns, were screwed in tightly. He adjusted some nozzles so the guns would shoot with the maximum amount of power.

And then he waited. He put on his mask, which was too tight. Still, as the seconds ticked, he was surprised to feel a delighted, nervous thrill. This was actually pretty fun.

Or at least it was, until 6:58 came and went without Ellie igniting the bottle rockets. The practice was ending, all the players heading back to the locker room. Benji's phone buzzed with a group text from Ellie.

Fireworks r duds! Won't light! Get out of the locker room!

"Oh, shit," Benji said. Right then, from all the way across the parking lot, he heard several shouts of surprise from the Newporte field house.

Doors burst open and CR and Zeeko dashed out. Inexplicably, CR kneeled between a couple of the Newporte players' cars, like he was praying. As some of the Newporte guys followed them out, CR looked back and shouted in a high falsetto voice, "We just fed you a revenge sandwich with a side of justice!" He and Zeeko sprinted across the parking lot toward Benji, sprinted like men possessed, arms churning, poofy ski mask balls bopping happily back and forth.

"Shoot!" CR screamed in that high voice. Benji realized he was trying to disguise his voice. "Shoot the d-bags *now!*"

Benji picked up both T-shirt cannons and fired simultaneously. They kicked against his shoulders, two jets of gas ejected from the barrels, and there the paintballs went, a multicolored swarm rainbowing through the night.

The amazing Technicolor onslaught peppered a few of the Newporte guys who had been chasing CR and Zeeko, but it wasn't a direct hit; he'd forgotten CR's advice about aiming for the future. Still, the shock of the assault made the players momentarily retreat behind their cars, which had just received rather psychedelic new paint jobs.

The Rocket peeled to a stop a few feet away. CR scrambled into the passenger seat, Benji and Zeeko in the back, CR shouting and half laughing, "Go go go go!"

"CR, I can't believe you did that!" Zeeko said, ripping off his mask. "That was too far!" He was as angry as Benji had ever seen him.

"What did you do?" Ellie said, speeding from the parking lot.

"I slit a bunch of their car tires," CR said.

"Wait, wait, isn't that an actual crime?" Ellie said.

"I had to do it or else they'd be able to chase us!"

And it seemed hard to argue with that logic, but unfortunately, as they turned onto the highway out of the city, they realized that the Newporte guys *were* chasing them. A pair of new SUVs trailed them, gaining as they entered the panoramic cornfields.

"Lose 'em, Eleanor! Take a shortcut!"

"Point the way," Ellie said sarcastically. It was all cornfields for miles, with just a single lane heading in either direction. "If we make it back to Bedford Falls, maybe they'll stop chasing us. Buckle your asses up, boys."

She floored it. The Rocket might have been pretty much a piece of crap, but it was *Ellie's* piece of crap, and she knew exactly how to take it to its outer limits. They accelerated, miraculously putting distance between themselves and their pursuers. By the time they reached the foggy, winding forest roads just outside of Bedford Falls, they were at least a mile ahead of the SUVs.

Right then, there was a cry from the Rocket's engine.

They'd been racing at a good seventy miles per hour. Suddenly, the Rocket *lurched*, bucking so violently that Benji flew into the headrest in front of him. The engine emitted a sound like a pack of rabbits being tortured.

"Ellie," CR said, "tell me that's not what I think it is."

"Don't you do this," Ellie said to the car. "Don't you dare." The Rocket answered by lurching again. It was dropping speed at a prodigious rate. You could have counted the pine needles on the roadside trees.

"Go!" CR slammed his fist into the dashboard; the glove compartment sprang open like a jack-in-the-box, ejecting gum wrappers and DMV documents. "Come on, you piece of shit from hell, *MOVE!*"

But the Rocket wasn't in the listening mood. It staggered forward up a small rise in the road with all the power of a dying tortoise, finally just stopping dead, motionless and dead in the middle of the road.

CR spoke with a small voice. "Are they still coming, Banjo?"

Benji didn't have to look back to know the answer. But he did. "Y-yeah."

CR opened his door. He stepped out, staring at the road behind the Rocket, his eyes wildly wide. The headlights of the casually opulent vehicles of the Pride of Newporte High approached through the fog like illuminative doom. Benji stepped onto the road, watching his friend growing white in the gathering light. CR looked nothing like an athlete with otherworldly talents and an infinite future. He looked like a little kid, and it was so sad, and somehow frightening, that Benji had to turn away.

"Oh my God!" Benji exclaimed.

CR looked at him.

"There's a road! We can hide the car over there!"

Benji pointed at the miracle he'd just spotted: an opening in the dense forest, a hundred feet ahead of the Rocket on the other side of the small hill where the Rocket had died. It looked like an old access road, overgrown with weeds, the entry partially blocked by a small log. If you weren't looking for it—say, if you were in pursuit of people who had icy-burnt your balls and launched a horde of paintballs at you—it would have been invisible. Where it went, who knew? But it was a *chance*.

"Ohhh, thank *God*," CR said.

"I'll push!" Benji said. "Ellie, put the car in neutral and steer toward that road!"

"Wait, I'm way stronger, shouldn't I push?" CR said.

"No, go move the log off— Zeeko, get out and help me— We just need to push the car over the hill, then we can coast down to the road—GO, CR!"

CR didn't carry on the argument: A half mile back in the fog, the SUVs finally turned onto the straightaway, the yellow headlights now glaring directly at them like the lambent eyes of a dragon. CR sprinted to the road.

Zeeko scrambled out and joined Benji behind the car. Together, they pushed against the RustRocket's bumper with every bit of the slim measure of strength they possessed.

"*Neutral*, Ellie!" Benji shouted.

"It is in neutral!"

Oh, Benji thought.

The Rocket inched, inched . . . Finally it crested the small rise and, as the road sloped down, the car began to move without Benji and Zeeko's efforts. They jogged to catch up and jumped into the backseat; with the log removed from the road, CR sprinted to the Rocket and leaped into the passenger seat.

"Faster, Ellie, c'mon!" CR said. Benji looked back and could see the SUVs' headlights gaining, just a few hundred feet back on the other side of the hill.

"I can't make it *go* any faster!" Ellie said.

And Benji suddenly understood there would be no grand escape, no last-minute heroics. *We're going to get caught*, he thought, closing his eyes. *We're going to get caught, and they're going to take my pod away.*

"Help us," he breathed, to God or nothing or everything. *"Please help me."*

Benji's eyelids glowed.

He opened his eyes. The trunk area was washed in subtle light. He looked in the direction of the SUVs, expecting to see them exploding through the final barrier of the fog.

But no.

This light wasn't coming from the headlights. It originated from the bag wedged beside the steamer trunk. Benji's backpack.

The Question is in my backpack.

The gaps between the pack's metallic zipper glowed like the smile of a jack-o'-lantern that contained a neon-green flame.

Open the bag, a voice deep inside him whispered. A high-definition image of him reaching into the bag filled his brain.

CR and Zeeko opened their doors, trying to speed up the Rocket by pushing against the ground with one leg. Mesmerized, Benji crawled over the backseat and into the cramped trunk area, sitting between the trunk door and the steamer chest, staring at the backpack.

The glow became brighter, painting the whole floor of the Rocket's trunk with radiance.

"Benji," Zeeko said, peering over the backseat, "what are you doing?"

Open the backpack, Benji.

The backpack, untouched, slammed down on the floor of the Rocket's trunk.

The zipper screamed open.

The Question launched out, slamming into Benji's palm as if magically summoned. The tip of its straight end was green: terribly gorgeously atomically green.

"What in the name of God . . ." whispered Zeeko.

The Rocket's trunk popped open of its own accord, exposing Benji to the open air.

"Yes, Benji, push!" CR screamed. *"Push, push, they're almost here!"*

The headlights were just on the other side of the hill and final rim of fog.

The Question vibrated in his grip, the green light on its tip blooming. Just beneath his index finger, a small curved piece of metal sprang out of the body of the Question.

A trigger. It looks like a trigger on a gun.

"Banjo, please, push!"

But Benji aimed the Question out the back of Rocket, and *pulled* the trigger instead.

Like an arrow ignited, like a missile of almighty light: That was how the power burst forth from the tip of the Question.

The force of the blast blew Benji backward several inches, slamming him against the magic trunk, pinning him there.

For the first time in history, the Rocket lived up to its name: Propelled by the continuous blast of the Question, which was acting as a handheld afterburner, the Rocket hyper-zoomed forward, quaking like it might burst into a thousand particles.

"WHAT THE AAASSSS?!" Benji screamed.

Everyone in the car shared roughly the same sentiment.

"Ellie, look out, the trees!" CR screamed.

Ellie heaved the wheel, aiming the Rocket toward the access road. The tires squalled and smoked, sending the Rocket into a wild fishtail. The Question's blaze swiped across the trunks of trees on the opposite side of the road. Benji saw that the Question wasn't emitting a steady stream of energy at all: It was firing a rapid sequence of compact green ovals, which flew like the tracer bullets of an atomic machine gun. The moment the ovals struck the tree trunks, the trunks vanished, vaporized from existence. The ruined trees roared and crashed to the road like cyclopses slain.

Oh my God oh my God, Benji thought, *this thing is a ray gu—*

"Benji," Zeeko cried from the backseat, "whatever you're doing, stop doing it!"

"I don't know how!" Benji said, but then he remembered his finger was on the trigger, and finally let go.

The Question stopped blazing instantaneously.

Still, momentum hurtled them forward on the unpaved downhill road. Ellie wove, working the brakes but skidding on frozen earth, navigating the RustRocket on a daredevil course of trees and turns, tossing Benji back and forth in the trunk. He grabbed the headrest on the backseat and white-knuckled it.

An eternity later, the Rocket escaped the woods, shooting into some kind of open expanse. Ellie slammed the brakes; Benji pitched forward and felt something hard strike his leg. The Rocket skied over the snow for another fifteen feet. Then it came to a stop, its energy expelled, its passengers silent, its Prank Night escape complete, its tires smoking softly in the hissing snow.

Benji's whole body was electric with his heartbeat. He let go of the headrest. Swallowed several invisible cotton balls. Remembered that breathing was a thing.

He gaped at the question mark–shaped object still in his hand. The trigger had receded back into the body of the Question. It looked like unextraordinary metal. There wasn't so much as an afterglow on its tip.

Benji dropped the Question, like something deadly, onto the floor.

It's not "the Question," he thought, stumbling out of the trunk. *Oh my God, that's not what it is* at all.

The Rocket's doors opened.

Ellie stepped out first, shaking and pale, one hand on the Rocket to steady herself. Zeeko spilled out his own door beside her. For a moment Zeeko peered up at the sky full of stars, like a philosopher in contemplation. Then, bending at the waist like an English butler, he puked between his boots.

Still in the passenger seat, CR slammed his shoulder again and again against his door. Benji saw the paneling had been dented during their impromptu rendition of Mr. Toad's Wild Ride. Finally, the door wrenched open with a rusty *reeeeek.*

"Banjo, are you okay?" CR said as soon as he stepped out. He looked even more frightened than he had when the caravan of Newporte SUVs had been about to shatter his singular hope. He was staring at Benji's forehead. Benji felt it and found a thin line of blood.

"O-oh. I'm good. Fine," Benji said woodenly.

With a look of intense relief, CR hugged Benji. After a moment, he said, "What happened? Did the gas explode?"

"What?"

CR stared at the rear of the Rocket, dumbfounded. "I thought the back of the car, like . . ." He mimed an explosion with his hands. The motion made him grimace in pain; he began rubbing his right shoulder.

He has no idea what just happened, Benji realized. He suddenly felt afraid to tell CR. He couldn't have predicted anything like this would happen. But he'd still lied about what was in his magic trunk.

CR, still kneading his arm, took a sharp breath. "You okay?" Benji asked.

"Just yanked something in my shoulder when I was moving that log. Hey, where'd your trunk go?"

"My friends call me a liar . . ." somebody said softly.

They turned toward Zeeko. Benji saw that they were in a kind of valley, ringed by woods on all sides. The valley, weirdly, was studded here and there with random, waist-high metal poles.

"Benji," said Zeeko, standing upright and wiping his wrist across his mouth, "what did you do? What was that thing?"

"What're you talking about?" CR asked, confused.

"But my heart keeps racin' higher . . ." that same soft voice said. But Zeeko hadn't spoken.

Neither had Ellie. In fact, Ellie looked like she couldn't have spoken if she'd tried. Eyes huge and afraid, she moved past Zeeko, staring at something in the dark valley behind Benji. He turned to follow her gaze, and he realized several things at once.

His magic trunk lay twenty yards behind him, thrown free during the RustRocket's last moments of mayhem. The trunk's lid was open crookedly, like a broken mouth, one of the hinges busted. And beside the trunk, brighter than the steam rising around it, was the pod.

"No. No, Benji, you did not bring that," CR said, but he was cut off by another voice, a singing rock 'n' roll voice, 1950s superstar "Bronkin'" Buck Strong, one of Papaw's very favorites, rushing toward them from every direction like a tide of amplified teenage joy:

"My friends call me a liar! But my heart is racin' higher! Baby, when you love me, OOOO, I just catch on fire!"

Benji was not just in a valley: He was standing in the middle of an abandoned drive-in theater.

A vast movie screen rose white and frayed at the far end of the field. A ripe crescent moon hung beyond it, veiled in clouds but visible through an ancient hole in the screen. Facing the screen and broadcasting the music were the drive-in's speakers (they looked like old radio microphones), mounted on all those endless metal poles. As Bronkin' Buck's voice floated in the air, weak blue sparks zapped from several of the speakers, like circuitry receiving a charge after an age of corrosion.

"I dreamed this place," he whispered to himself, goose bumps rippling across his body. "Didn't I?" No, he told himself, he couldn't have. He'd just wound up here by accident, because of—

"Yes, when I least expect it," sang the night, *"I just catch on FIRE!"*

Benji felt his heart halt. He looked back at the pod. "Are *you* doing this?"

A new voice sang the answer in a style that was, unmistakably, 1950s doo-wop:

Ohhhh, my dear, don't you know
That it's true?
When I speak, I speak
My words only for youuuuu.

A mystical astonishment filled Benji. "It's talking to us," he said . . . and began to smile.

On Prank Night, in a long-lost movie wonderland just outside of Bedford Falls, Indiana, the pod from another world had spoken across the airwaves with pure teenage sound, and Benji Lightman thought: *First contact.*

"*What,* exactly, is talking?" CR said softly behind Benji.

Benji started to tell him it was the pod. But that wasn't really right, was it? Until this moment, he'd thought of "the pod" as only interstellar debris, incredible and miraculous in theory, but ultimately nothing more than mindless shrapnel. Yet if it was broadcasting its answers to him, then the pod wasn't random detritus. The night of the shootdown, Benji had been witness to a spaceshipwreck, and inside that seamless cylinder was its sole survivor.

"I think it's the pilot of the saucer," Benji replied.

The speakers responded in a voice taken from another doo-wop recording: *"Heyyyyyy, B-I-N-G-O!"*

Benji couldn't help it: He *giggled.* So did Ellie, who was standing beside him now. He looked over, and she did something that surprised him: In the moment of shared wonder, she took his hand, and squeezed it, once, warmly.

A billion questions for the pod streaked through Benji's mind all at once. *Where are you from? How old are you? Why did you come* here—*not just Earth, but Bedford Falls?* He couldn't quite locate his voice, though. For all he knew, this moment, this moment right here, was the most pivotal exchange since the first prehistoric man had spoken with the first understandable language, had given his ancestors the power of knowledge that would outlive himself. Benji felt dwarfed, thunderstruck by a sense of history.

Finally, he said, "How are you speaking to us?"

The musical night, sung in the style of a sock hop slow-dancer: *"I think this is magic, my dear."*

Ellie (whispering): "My God, Benji . . ."

Benji: "Can you speak in your own voice?"

CR (whispering): "Banjo, stop. . . ."

The musical night: *"Don't you know, I'm spee-eee-eeechless?"*

Zeeko: "I know that song. It's really old. My mom used to listen to it on YouTube when she was learning English."

Benji: "Can . . . can we help you out of the pod?"

The gorgeously manic voice of Ricky Richman: *"Talk all you want, but ya ain't comin' in!"*

Benji laughed. "How come?"

The speakers were silent. For a long moment, the only sounds Benji knew of were his and Ellie's breathing, hissing in the frozen air of the Midwest winter dark. Then the clouds that had dimmed the moon broke apart, and a single brilliant moonbeam soared through the hole in the great movie screen. It looked like the dream-beam of a film projector, as if the movie screen, which had held so many fantasies, was offering one in return. The beam landed on the pod, making it gleam like a holy relic. Benji and Ellie gasped together.

So, at first, he didn't pay much attention to what happened

next. The snow around the pod began to stir in a soft wind; then the fine powder swirled a couple of feet high, forming a funnel that made him think wildly of the tornado that had delivered Dorothy to Oz. The funnel revolved as the wind grew stronger . . . except, he realized after a moment, there *was* no wind.

"Ho. Lee. Shit," Ellie said.

In midair the snow took on new and impossible shapes: It rearranged itself into a flying saucer, roughly the size of a football. A smile twitched at the edges of Benji's mouth until, without warning, the front of the saucer "exploded." The violent burst of snow hit Benji like cold mist, and the rest of the snow-saucer crashed to the ground.

The speakers finally answered his question: *"Darlin', don't desert me. Youuuu've already hurt me."*

Benji winced. "We hurt you when we blew u—" He paused. *I don't want to say "When we blew you up."* Feeling faintly ridiculous, he said, "When the incident involving a gaseous blast occurred?"

"B-I-N-G-O."

Benji cleared his throat, feeling the need to offer a diplomatic apology. How did diplomats talk? "Well, umm, on behalf of my people, I offer my apologies to you from us. We here—my friends and myself—simply thought you may have been doing something that could have conceivably been a plan—or scheme, if you will—to bring bad harm to us—"

Ellie nudged him. "Why are you talking like Sarah Palin?"

Benji blushed, then continued, "On Earth, we've got a term called 'big miscommunication.'"

Silence from the pod.

"Can you maybe come out when you're feeling better?"

Silence from the pod.

"Are you alone?"

Silence.

Ellie (whispering): "Well, *this* is certainly awkward."

Benji tried to change the subject. "So. Where do you come from?"

The silence spun out. How long did it actually last? Benji didn't know. But it felt portentous in a way no other silence of his life ever had.

Ohhhhhh, I'm the one leaves a place, and never spies a familiar face,
And that's the way I like it, since you asked!
See, honey, I'm the Voyager—see, tramping the journey is my story, sir,
And I'll tell you why right now, since you asked!
The man who asks cannot understand, can't know the heart of the voyaging man.
I prefer the horizon to a past!

That's the song from my dream, Benji thought, feeling an electric surge through his body. *And I'm in a drive-in, like in the dream.*

He mentally replayed the dream. The radio had malfunctioned. The sky had blazed green. And a voice filled with almighty power had thundered through the amphitheater of his skull. *What if the pod was. . . was talking to me in that dream? What if it was trying to tell me something?*

"Your name," he said, "is it Mr. Fahrenheit?"

"Come closer and I'll tell you, my dear."

A hand grabbed Benji's shoulder. He jolted. CR had stopped him. "Benji," he whispered, "keep a good distance from that thing." His narrowed gaze was locked on the pod. Benji recognized his expression: It was the same calculating, subzero glare

CR used against an enemy defender at the line of scrimmage. "What if it wants to get back at us for hurting it?"

"That's not what it wants."

"How do you even know?"

"I . . . it's weird, but I can feel it," Benji said. He was thinking back to how he'd felt since retrieving the pod from the saucer. He'd experienced foreign feelings of power; he'd had strange mental images that were so clear, they seemed to come via a high-def broadcast. . . .

"I think maybe the pod has been, like, *connecting* to me. My brain, I mean."

CR wore an expression that said, *Maybe I've heard of crazier things. I just can't think of any right now.*

"Don't you guys feel it?" Benji said. "Or see pictures in your head? Here, maybe if you get closer to the pod."

Now Zeeko and Ellie's faces echoed CR's. Nobody moved closer.

Holy crap, I'm the only one it's happening to. He didn't understand why the alien (*the Voyager*, he thought with a trill of happiness) did not mentally and emotionally communicate with anyone except him. But there was something vaguely thrilling about it.

"It wants to understand us, I think," Benji said. "To ask us things. It came here for a reason, you know? And of all the people in the world, *we're* the ones it wants to talk to."

"Banjo, seriously, did you hit your head or something?" CR whispered, then said aloud to the pod, "We shot you out of the sky. Scale of one to ten, where are you, anger-wise?"

The pod stayed silent.

"Why isn't it answering me?"

The pod, via the Southern twang of "Rebel" Roddy Dee: *"You'll never be my buddy, cause you're a fuddy-duddy."*

Benji laughed. "What?" CR asked.

"I don't think it likes you, man," Benji said.

"That's what we call a bull's-eye, smart guy."

Now Ellie and Zeeko laughed, too. CR's jaw dropped; he looked at the pod, goggle-eyed. "What a *dick!*" he breathed.

"Listen, I know the whole *psychic-alien* deal sounds insane," Benji said. "But even if I'm wrong about that, there's another reason I know it's not mad: It helped us get away from the Newporte guys. Here, look at this." He jogged to the RustRocket, got the ray gun, and showed it to CR. "This is what made us go so fast."

"What the hell is 'this'?"

Benji smiled, almost goofy with happiness. "Right, so admittedly this makes me sound like a villain on *Dr. Who,* but, *say hello to Mr. Ray Gun.* I got it at the quarry after the saucer explo—after the gaseous blast."

"And it didn't seem important to you to tell us you had a laser pistol? Just like you didn't happen to mention the alien pod was in your trunk?"

Benji's cheeks prickled. "You're making it sound worse than it is. I didn't even know the gun was anything but shrapnel until it acted weird yesterday at school."

"What?" CR spluttered. "You took that thing to *school*? You took *a gun from outer space* to school? Jesus, we get suspended for having *tobacco* in school!"

"But I'm saying I didn't know there was anything weird about it until I was talking to this guy. . . ." Benji trailed off.

"What guy?" said Ellie.

"Well, first let me just say there is no need to freak out."

Not exactly a reassuring speech, there, Benji.

He took a breath. "It was a guy from the FBI."

CR made a sound like a growl, like a scream he was keeping

locked in his throat, and pivoted on his heels, away from Benji. Zeeko's brow knit in confusion; he raised his palms and mouthed, *FBI?*

But it was Ellie's reaction, more than anyone else's, that punctured the joy and brought home the gravity of what he'd said. It wasn't just that she looked furious and frightened and even a little sick. It was that she looked so . . . *disappointed* in him. And betrayed.

"This FBI guy," CR said, voice clipped, crouching down on his heels, still not looking at Benji, "does he know anything about the dick-pod over there?"

"No, he was asking about stupid stuff, random stuff. It was boring, honestly. He mentioned the plane crash, and asked me to talk to him if I heard anything weird about it. But I don't think he knows anything."

"You don't think so."

"N—" Benji began, but CR didn't let him finish: With all the grace and speed of a great and terrible tornado, CR burst up from his crouch and whirled toward Benji. He had something in his hand. A snowball. CR roared. This wasn't playtime.

Benji ducked, raising his arms. The hard-packed snowball smacked the ray gun, which spun from his grasp, rang cheerily like a tuning fork, and vanished into the snow a few feet away.

"Do you know what could happen to all of us?!" CR screamed.

"Calm down!" Benji staggered backward as CR stomped toward him. "We're not going to get in trouble!"

"'Get in trouble'? Hiding an alien, keeping a weapon like that, lying to a government super agent: You don't get in trouble for that stuff, Lightman. You get *disappeared* for it!"

"CR, stop!" Zeeko said.

"Seriously? You're on his side?"

"Who said anything about sides?"

CR only glared at the pod. "We have to get rid of this thing," he said. "Right now, before anyone finds out we have it. I said so ever since we shot it down. You're not talking me out of it this time, Lightman." CR's gaze landed on something in the snow to Benji's right. And he dived toward it.

Benji felt what seemed to be the Voyager's anger, but he was motivated by his own.

"NO, PLEASE, CR, DON'T!" Benji shouted, lunging for the ray gun, and then, hardly aware of it and not really understanding why, he added: *"YOU COWARD!"*

CR scooped the ray gun from the snow and aimed it at the pod.

If he had used the weapon before, had known that you had to hold the ray gun for a moment before its trigger would present itself, he really might have destroyed the pod, and "Mr. Fahrenheit," too. But that was Benji's secret, and he sacked CR, tackling him from behind, the gun arcing out of CR's hand.

They spilled to the ground. CR cried out in pain and grabbed his injured shoulder. He kicked Benji off him, and as Benji was launched backward into the air, he saw, out of the corner of his eye, Zeeko sprinting toward them.

Benji's head hit Zeeko dead-smack on the chin. With the combined factors of the strike, Zeeko's sprint, and the slick snow, the result was almost cartoonish: Zeeko's feet flew out from under him, banana peel–style. He crash-landed on his back in the snow.

For a second, CR and Benji just looked at each other, gawping. Benji's head hurt a little, but Zeeko had plainly taken the worst of it.

"I didn't mean to do that, Zeek!"

"Dude, dude, hey, are you all right?!"

They helped him to his feet. He blinked, shell-shocked.

Ellie hurried over. "Oh, Zeek, this will help," she said, and gently placed a handful of snow against Zeeko's already-swelling chin.

Zeeko replied: "MMMAAAAAAAAHHHHHHHHHHHHH!" He plopped back down, cross-legged in the snow.

The injury (and Ellie's reprimanding stare) mollified Benji and CR a bit. But CR's voice was still hot with anger when he said, "Why do you need this, Benji? Why are you so obsessed with this thing? Why can't you just be happy? It could ruin everything for us."

"For you."

"What?"

"It could ruin everything for *you*. That's what you really mean, isn't it? You're a coward, Noland. Your life was just so perfect, and now you're pissed because it's the moment when someone other than you gets to do amazing things, too."

"'Amazing things'?" CR scoffed. "You're not *doing anything* amazing. If anything's 'amazing,' it's that thing, not you. You're playing dress-up with aprons Zeeko stole from the hospital, and pretending you're Steven Spielberg in a shitty tree house, and feeling like a badass for lying to the only friends you ever had. Yep, really amazing there, buddy! You know what? I think you're *dangerous*, Lightman. I think we made that plane crash. I think the tractor beam ripped that plane right out of the sky."

The idea hit Benji with the force of a roundhouse slap. He didn't know what to say.

"You can't just throw something like that in our faces," Ellie said. Benji felt a flood of gratitude. "You were there, too. And you don't even know if it's true."

"You don't even know it's not."

"Please," Zeeko said from the ground. "Please, stop. . . ."

Everyone looked down. Zeeko sounded like he was going to cry.

"You're friends, you three jackasses. Okay? There are so many things in this whole situation we can't understand. Maybe we're not meant to. But for the love of all that is good on this dumb planet, will you just remember how much you've been through together? That's the only way we'll make it through this in one piece. So please, *please*, can we just talk about what's actually important here?"

"What's that?" Ellie asked softly after a moment.

Zeeko peered up. "My face, Ellie," he said. "My beautiful Goddamn face."

Coming from Zeeko, the profanity was the equivalent of a *nuclear* f-bomb. Benji guffawed. CR went, *"Whaaaat!"* Ellie's hand popped up to cover her wide-open mouth. Zeeko's gesture was as sweet as it was vulgar: In spite of having been bashed in the face, he was trying to lighten the mood and heal the rift between his friends. Maybe all the king's horses and all the king's men couldn't put it back together again, but Zeeko would still try. His religiosity was annoying sometimes, but how many people tried so hard to act decent?

"Do you think anything's broken?" CR asked.

*"Every*thing, actually. Nah, but truly, I think I'm okay. I'll have Dad check me out in the morning."

CR nodded, awkwardly patted Zeeko on the shoulder, then turned to Benji. "We still need a game plan," he said, sounding more civil, if still rather tense.

"Fine. But we're not going to even talk about destroying it. That is not going to happen," Benji said.

CR obviously wanted to debate this, but instead replied, "So, we turn it in, then?"

Benji swore he heard an infinitesimal squeal of feedback,

like an angry protestation, from the drive-in speakers. Nobody else reacted, though. Was it only in his head?

"We'd be admitting we were hiding it," Ellie said. "Remember how you think it would get us in trouble? For the record, I'm convinced not at all that it would get us sent to a CIA Black Site. But . . ." She glanced at Benji, a brief but cutting look of hurt and something approaching disgust. "But it's a maybe," she finished.

Benji's stomach knotted.

"Also," he added quietly after a moment, "I . . . I don't want them to do, like, an autopsy on it."

"But this FBI guy, if he even works for the FBI," CR said, "if he finds the pod and wants to keep things quiet, what stops him from doing an autopsy on *us*?"

Will you just stop thinking like that? Can we just slow down? Can we just start over?

"We need leverage, right?" Ellie said. "Something we could threaten to do, or expose, if anything happened to us."

"Like what?"

"A video of the pod?" Benji said.

"Nope. It zaps everything digital, remember?"

"You recorded something on the ice the other night, didn't you?"

"Yes, and a staggering five seconds of film it was, too," Ellie said curtly. "Come on, Benji."

"A picture . . ." Zeeko said.

"Well, but even if we used an old camera, Zeek, it might screw up the film."

"No, you guys, I know exactly what to do!" Zeeko said breathlessly, springing to his feet. "We need to X-ray it!"

They looked at him uncertainly. "You want to sneak the pod into a hospital?" Ellie said.

"Won't need to. We've got the community health truck. A lot of really rural hospitals around here can't afford much medical equipment. It's awful, almost third world, my dad says, and he should know, since he is literally from the third world. A lot of the coal miners downstate, near Kentucky, they die from black lung disease just because they never get X-rayed in time. Which enrages me, but here's the good news: The community health truck has an X-ray machine in it. I think it'll work for us. Sincerely! The machine takes X-rays and sends them to this computer, which is in an operator's booth. Everything in that truck is lead-lined, so it blocks radiation." He beamed. "Guys, the truck is basically an X-ray mobile, and I've got a copy of the key."

Ellie raised her eyebrows, impressed.

"The computer's even got Wi-Fi. Dad emails the X-rays to patients or other docs sometimes," Zeeko went on, more excited every moment. "He and I have to use it pretty much all the time for the next couple days, but we'll be finished on Friday after school. That's when we can take the X-ray."

"I've got to watch game film then," CR said. "And the parade's going on right before the game, too."

"So Ellie and Benji and me can do it. We'll still have a couple hours between school and the parade. Then we can set up a bunch of, like, automatic posts that would go up online— Facebook and Reddit and stuff—if we didn't 'check in' with them after a while. And Benji, this way, you'll get to see what's inside the pod, too. You wanted to know more about it, so even if this FBI guy isn't looking for the pod, you'll still have what you wanted. Right?"

"I don't know. I guess." But not really. It wasn't enough. There was so much more he wanted, *needed*, to know.

"You know what, Zeek?" CR said, smiling. "I'm a wee bit gay for you right now."

"Thanks! I've always thought we had a 'will they or won't they?' vibe." Zeeko smirked. "One thing, though. We can keep the pod hidden until Friday, but what if something happens to us before that? Ellie, I know there's not a lot of footage from the lake, but can you put the memory card someplace safe, where nobody can find it?"

She shook her head. "I feel like people not finding it would defeat the purpose, Zeek. But . . . I could stash it someplace where nobody would find it until after the game, and then they would *definitely* find it. That way, if nothing happens and we *do* get to do the X-ray, we can just go get the memory card back."

"Where would you put it?"

"I have to go to the carnival tomorrow to film a couple things for the homecoming video for the assembly; they're going to have all the rides operational for whatever shots I want to get. And the carnival doesn't open until the day after the game, right, so I could just wrap the card in a bag, write a message on it, and hide it in the top Ferris wheel car or something."

"What d'you think, Banjo?" CR said. "It's a pretty solid plan, right?"

It was. Benji did not really want to admit it, but it was. He nodded, but his insides churned with a panicky sadness.

For the last few days, the pod had been a miracle, an actual wish reeled from the sky. Ten minutes ago, it had been speaking to him, the promise of an answer to every question ever asked about the universe.

Now, it was an insurance policy for their survival.

Jesus, Benji thought. *How did this get so screwed up so fast?*

Through all this, the pod had not spoken aloud, but Benji could sense a desperation radiating from it. What was it thinking? Did it think less of him?

"I'm really sorry," Benji said. Zeeko and CR and Ellie looked genuinely touched.

But he hadn't been talking to them.

They spotted a cinder-block projection booth across the valley from the tattered movie screen. CR kicked the door open, and when he flicked his lighter, a pair of raccoons, which had been dining on cockroaches, skittered away from the light. The smell was a nightmare, the worst parts of a cellar mixed with the worst parts of a sewer. And it was here, *here*, that they were going to hide Benji's pod.

Framed posters hung on the walls, ghostly with age, advertising long-forgotten monster and "hot-rod" movies. They reminded Benji of his dream. He still had so many questions for the pod, for Mr. Fahrenheit. Leaving the pod behind without speaking with it more felt like the ultimate betrayal. Not just a betrayal of Mr. Fahrenheit, but a betrayal of the version of the world and of himself that Benji wanted to create. He'd gotten his "moment," and he was letting it slip right through his fingers.

Now they all trekked back toward the Rocket. CR found the ray gun and put it in the magic trunk, insisting on leaving it here with the pod. Benji nodded, and together they lifted the pod into the trunk.

When CR turned away for a moment, Benji quickly tried to pull the magnet-on-a-string magic trick he had hidden in his sleeve, to make the ray gun secretly zip up into his jacket.

CR clapped him on the shoulder.

The gun slipped silently from Benji's fingers, back into the trunk.

"Ready to go?" CR said, and if he knew what Benji had been doing, he didn't show it. He just snapped the trunk closed, barely allowing Benji time to pull out his hands. The two of them carried it to the projection booth, leaving both pod and ray gun in the farthest corner of that rotting place.

As they went back to the RustRocket and fixed the car's loose fan belt, Benji was overcome with a sense that a clock was ticking. His plans hadn't worked, his friends hadn't helped, and he was lost, confused, frightened. He looked back at the booth as Ellie drove them away, and for one moment he felt a cold resolve, as if things would be okay because nothing was going to stand in his way. Then they left the drive-in, and it was gone.

PART THREE
THE DAY BEDFORD FALLS STOOD STILL

Hey hey, fellas, are we cookin' with grease?
Uh-huh, we're goin' nuclear (to say the least).
—The Atomic Bobs

The magic of today, however, is not like the magic
of yesterday. The art of deception, like other arts,
advances with every swing of the pendulum.
—Thomas Nelson Downs

13

The note on the kitchen table read:

Out back, pal. Come & talk, OK?

"Pal"? Benji thought. It was early Friday morning. In the two days since they'd left the Voyager at the drive-in, nothing out of the ordinary had happened. He hadn't even seen McKedrick in town. The world just felt depressingly normal, all school and homework and FIGs, as if the amazing events with the pod had never happened. The only real difference was how utterly disconnected Benji felt from everyone: He hadn't spoken to CR in two days (the first time this had ever happened), and Zeeko was too busy helping his dad with the community health truck. Worst of all, Ellie, the one person who might have made him feel better, was occupied by her duties for the homecoming assembly. He couldn't even feel anything from the creature in the pod, as if its psychic signal were out of range. In the few hours Benji managed to sleep, he was dreamless.

He walked across the kitchen and looked out the window.

What he saw gave him pause. Papaw was outside, all right, in the detached garage in the backyard. Benji rarely saw the garage open: At one time, Papaw had intended to make it into a man cave, but it was so disorganized and cluttered with boxes that the project had petered out. And that had been years ago.

What the heck's he doing?

Papaw's police cruiser was also in the backyard and mostly blocked the view. Plain curiosity took Benji outside without a jacket.

As he approached, he half laughed under his breath, a little astonished at what Papaw was wearing. Blue jeans. Green T-shirt. It wasn't just weird because of the cold, but because a button-up shirt and crisply ironed slacks were Papaw's idea of "really letting my hair down" attire. Humming tunelessly under a caged lightbulb, he bent over the open hood of a car (not the cruiser) in the garage, working elbows-deep in the engine. A protective blue tarp, bungee-corded over the roof and grille, covered the rest of the vehicle. He sometimes worked on the town's cop cars, but Benji couldn't remember him ever bringing one home. Benji didn't ponder this too much, though, because another thought occurred to him that made him laugh: With Papaw's remaining hair slicked back and his T-shirt tucked into his snug jeans, he looked like the world's oldest "greaser."

"Good morning," Benji said, a few steps from the garage.

Papaw's head snapped up, smacking the hood. He dropped a wrench, which clattered into the engine. "Aw, hell, you old fool," he muttered. His voice was scratchy and spent, wrecking any illusion of youth. As he reached into the engine, the loose white flesh of his throat fell over the T-shirt's collar; his arms were thin, and pale like fish. Benji felt that fear again, like he'd felt at the police barricade, that awful knowledge of Papaw's old age. . . .

"What's the word, pal?" Papaw said, retrieving the wrench.

"*Pal*"? Benji thought again. "Nothing, sir. Working on a cruiser?"

A faintly sad smile crossed Papaw's face. "I guess by God you could call it that." He paused, thoughtfully thumping the wrench against an open palm. He muttered something about having the wrong tool, then turned to inspect the shelves and wooden workbench behind him. They were populated by a half-dozen old galvanized cans filled with tools.

Benji took the opportunity to glance around. The garage was smaller than he would've thought, although that may have just been a consequence of the covered cruiser. A tiny space heater hummed on the floor, the glowing coils splashing red light across the concrete floor and cinder-block walls. A few cardboard boxes sat stacked in the corner, looking like abandoned things, their surfaces bruised and bulging with damp. The top box was the only one not sealed by age-brittled tape, and Benji lifted the flap. A melancholy smell that could only be described as "forgotten" rose up. The box held paper, mostly. A roadmap of California; several yellowed paperback novels, all with covers depicting pistol-packin' cowboys and prodigious-busted women. Benji glanced at some curled loose-leaf paper, inked with some doodles of guitars in the margins and cursive handwriting he didn't recognize. . . .

He spotted a name on the top corner: *ROBERT LIGHTMAN, HISTORY, 4TH PERIOD, 5/30/59.*

Holy crap, Benji thought, smiling a little. The idea of Papaw in school was sort of astounding. *I mean, I know he went to school. But, like, he* really *went to school.*

Papaw was still occupied. Benji quietly dug deeper.

Through a gap in the notebook papers, he saw some kind of large black-and-white picture. He pushed aside a few interesting items (including a 1958 Bedford Falls High School yearbook that he noted to check out later), then carefully pulled the photo out.

The photo was actually part of a poster. Text was laid out on the poster in such a wild (and, uh, grammatically unique) way that it took a moment for Benji to understand.

HEY, TEENS! READY? . . . FOR SOME ROCK AND ROLL!
ONE NIGHT ONLY!
BEDFORD FALLS' OWN MUSIC SENSATION!!!
(WILL THEY CONQUER THE NATION??)
FIND OUT! . . .
. . . AT THE HOMECOMING CARNIVAL!!!

The photo showed three teenage guys in matching '50s-style suits: black jackets, skinny ties. The drummer was seated behind the snare-and-bass kit, and the other two musicians stood in front, leaning into a shared microphone. It should have all felt staged and super cheesy, and in a way, it did: The singers were trying both to mime singing *and* grin directly into the camera. But there was something about the picture that made it really charming. Maybe it was everyone's smiles, which gleamed as crazy-big and shiny as the singers' guitars. Or maybe it was the perfect-for-the-era name of the band, hand-painted on the bass drum: *THE ATOMIC BOBS!*

Where have I heard that name before? Benji thought.

All at once, several ideas collided in his brain.

The Atomic Bobs had been a local band. He'd heard them playing on the jukebox when he found Papaw passed out in the den. (*"Put us three young men together, hey, and what are our jobs?"* sang a guy's voice in his head. *"To move your soul with rock 'n' roll! We're the Atomic Bobs!"*)

And the singer on the left side of the microphone, while

infinitely younger, was Robert "Bob" Lightman. Papaw.

"Whoa," Benji breathed. He glanced over at Papaw, who was still absorbed in his search for a tool. Benji felt his heart pumping in a hard and unpleasant way.

He looked back and forth between the past and present Papaws. It was just so hard to reconcile them. It wasn't like he'd thought Papaw had come out of the womb already seventy years old, wearing a hat and gun and saying, *Mother, your hard work today is much appreciated. Now please point me toward the nearest police station.* But Benji had never actually seen his grandpa so young. *Or so happy*, he thought.

"You know what I was thinking 'bout today, pal?" Papaw said softly, returning to work on the engine. "I was thinking of that fire. Thinking of coming out of the woods and seein' you layin' out in front of that house. That was the worst moment of my life, Benjamin."

Benji blinked. "It was?"

"I never told you that. Never told anyone, because . . . because I didn't *want* to, *that's* why." Papaw's voice bore a dull anger— *anger at himself?*—that caught Benji off guard. "Well, who would want to speak about it? I wish I could forget. Sometimes I think I'd sleep a lot better if I could. You don't remember me taking you down that hill from the house, do you, Benjamin?"

He didn't. He remembered opening the House's cellar door, and the smoke-induced hallucination of a figure in the cellar right before he passed out, and then CR pulling him and Ellie to safety. After that, all he remembered was waking up in the hospital.

"No, sir, I don't remember that at all."

"Well, there's a blessing, at least," Papaw said without conviction. "You looked dead. Just dead, a little-boy corpse in the grass. Mary and Joseph above. You started coughing but still couldn't breathe, really. I picked you right up and carried you off that mountain. I kept thinking, *I'll die for this child. Dear God, if You are truly God, take me instead of him.* The world doesn't work like that, though. Never did and never will. Which makes you question many good things you once took on faith."

Benji stepped toward Papaw slowly, mesmerized by what he was saying.

"I started talkin' to you while I was runnin'. 'Don't leave me, honey. Not you. Not *you.* Don't you dare go away, boy.' The paramedics met me halfway up the hill. I screamed when they tried to take you outta my arms. I hadn't hardly noticed them at all."

Benji stopped on the opposite side of the hood from Papaw, the engine silent and complex between them. The sharp ghost scents of machinery, oil, and rust drifted upward: a darkly romantic smell. It was the smell of something visible but utterly unknowable, a territory on a map marked "Uncharted." It reminded Benji of being a little kid and seeing his grandfather through a doorframe, looking into a bright mirror while he shaved, a figure as large as a mountain and every bit as unshakable.

Papaw didn't look unshakable now. As he raised his gaze to meet Benji's, Papaw's eyes shone with tears.

"Benjamin, I know the pain you've been in. This is not an easy world to grow up in. I can be a hard man. But I am trying, I am trying so much to make you understand: *You can make something wonderful here.* You can do anything, whatever you want, here in Bedford Falls. Because wherever *you* are, *you'll* be there. And you are the wonderful thing, Benjamin. That's exactly what you are."

For the first time in Benji's life, emotion lay unhidden on Papaw's face. The sight of it was overwhelming, even frightening, but it pierced something inside Benji. He felt that sense of the world tilting, the looking glass refocusing, just as he'd felt at the drive-in as he spoke with Mr. Fahrenheit.

Maybe that's enough, Benji thought. *Maybe staying in Bedford Falls can be enough for me.* Maybe part of the reason he'd wanted to leave was that he hadn't really thought Papaw cared about him. Maybe Benji didn't have to be a voyager to be happy.

"Thank you, Papaw," he finally said.

Relief washed over Papaw's face, like he'd given up on opening a lock and just now, completely unexpectedly, gotten the combination. "Oh dear Lord, boy, did your grandpa just accidentally make sense?"

"I think maybe." Benji smiled. Papaw guffawed, then there was a moment of quiet, when they both tried to think of something to say.

Papaw's gaze drifted to the poster in Benji's hand, which Benji had forgotten he was holding.

"Where in *the* hell did you find *that*?" Papaw said, eyes big, walking to Benji's side of the car.

"The box over there. This is you, right?"

"Me or the *other* ugliest man on Earth."

"Hey! People always say I look like you!" Benji laughed.

"Well, you got the good parts of me." Papaw winked, then whistled admiringly at the picture. "Haven't gave this a thought in I don't know how many years. Look at that hair, Benjamin! A man could walk into that hair and never find his way out!"

Benji laughed again, a feeling of utter contentment sweeping through him. "So did you, like, sing?"

"Oh, hell no. That's just a bit of 'Hollywood' for the picture."

"I don't think I know the other guys. Their names are 'Bob,' right?"

"Like I said, you got the good parts of me."

"Huh?"

"Your detective work, there. You're a natural."

Benji's smile faltered a little.

"But no," Papaw said, "you wouldn't know those old boys. The one behind the drums, that's Bobby Volpe. Couldn't carry a tune in a lunch-bucket, but could he play that kit! Could he ever!"

"Are you guys still friends?" Benji regretted it as soon as he said it. Papaw didn't really *have* friends.

"No, Volpe, he graduated a year ahead of us," Papaw said, frowning a little. "He stuck around town for a few months. He said it was because of the band, but really it was his sweetheart; she was still in school. Well, she truly broke his heart, and he beat feet outta town in a hurry after that. Maybe he wanted to leave anyway. I heard tell at the time that she only broke up with him because he'd tried to get fresh with her best friend. I think sometimes we make things go bad just so it's easier to say good-bye. Anyhow, he became an army man. Never heard a word from him again. Not a once."

Benji nodded, trying to think of something to say that might lighten things.

"The other fella on guitar is Robby King," Papaw went on. "He sounded okay, but I tell you what, he *looked* a helluva lot better. Girls would scream when he sang, and mind, this was before those British bands came over. It felt so good, being on that stage. Lord, it truly did. Like I wasn't even myself."

"You guys sounded pretty great on that record."

Papaw looked up. "What record is that?"

"It was playing on the jukebox the other night. You were asleep in your chair."

"Oh," Papaw said, but he still looked confused. "I didn't even know that record was still in there."

"So, wait, you guys made an album? Did you have a record deal?"

"No, that would have just been a recording of the carnival show. It was live on the radio around here. Felt like a real big deal at the time. I doubt we were as good as we thought we were, though. As the man said, 'The older I get, the better I was.'"

"No, you were good, Papaw," Benji offered. "We should listen to it."

Papaw sighed, and said, simply, "No, Benjamin, we should not." He looked back at the poster. "Maybe we would've made a fancy, big career for ourselves, but that ain't what life had planned. Robby died that night. Drunk driver. Senseless as hell. I sold my guitar after his funeral." He paused. "But you know what, I don't regret selling it. I wouldn't have met your grandmother otherwise. And what's a good life, anyway? It's workin' and makin' a better life for your blood. That's all. Go to Timbuktu and it's true. That's all there is to life: struggle and people you care about. Ay-uh, that's exactly the size of it."

But the confident rhythm Benji knew so well wasn't in Papaw's voice, then. Papaw didn't sound like even *he* believed what he was saying. Actually, it seemed as if he were trying to convince himself, as much as Benji.

"Let's put that away now, Benjamin. No, you know what, let's just clear these boxes out; the garbage is going today."

Papaw took the poster from Benji's hand. Benji felt his heart twist. Papaw was obviously upset, and Benji felt it was somehow his fault, for showing him the poster in the first place.

Yet Benji also felt a little angry as he watched Papaw stuff the poster into the box. Anger at what, he wasn't quite sure. . . .

A question formed in his head.

"Why were you thinking about the fire, sir?"

"I was just thinking of Shaun Spinney, I guess. Remember I said Shaun Spinney's parents would show up in my office to sue me? I was not wrong. But I just started thinkin' about how it's my own fault. What I did to that boy the other night at the barricade was mean and it was low. The worst thing you can do to a person is not tellin' them what they are. It's telling them what they never will be."

Papaw shivered, though Benji noticed no wind.

"So you just thought of the fire because Spinney was there?" Benji said, weirdly uneasy.

"Well, partly. Like we were saying, Benjamin, maybe a lot of your trouble is that you've been trying to become somethin' you aren't. I'm old enough to know that you don't need that kind of trouble. Your father went off looking for a big adventure, too, signed up after 9/11, thinking he had some patriotic duty. And your government thanked him kindly by giving him a vehicle as fragile as a Campbell's Soup can."

Benji felt his cheeks burn. "I've never said I've been trying to become something I'm not."

"Well, you pretty much did."

"No. I didn't." *You just never listen to me.*

Benji realized something: As wonderful as Papaw's kindness felt, Benji couldn't open his heart to that kindness without letting Papaw's stubbornness come in, too. Papaw said that traditions are gravity, things that kept you from floating off, and there was something beautiful in that idea. But even it cast a shadow.

Gravity doesn't let you go, Benji thought. *Never. It just sucks you down on the earth.*

"You know what I don't get, Papaw? I don't get why you and every other adult in this town tell kids, 'Shoot for the stars, follow your dreams!' But then, the second we get to high school, you say, 'Well, time to be realistic.' What does that even *mean*? You say that's just the way life is, but it's only that way because you're too afraid to change it."

Papaw actually flinched. But Benji couldn't stop; he'd kept all this fear and anger pent up inside him too long.

"I don't get why adults say young people should know about politics and current events, but when we try to talk about them, we get told to shut up. You say, 'Believe in yourselves! *But don't be proud.*' 'Dress nicely, feel good about how you look! *But don't be vain.*' 'Be a self-made American! Never let the past define you! *But don't forget where you came from.*' Don't you people know what you're doing to us? If you want us to believe in everything, we can't believe in anything."

"Now listen, pal—"

"Don't call me that. You don't get to just be my friend when you're feeling bad and want someone to talk to."

Anger flared in Papaw's eyes, but it was fleeting. He put down the box and raised his palms, like, *let's slow down here.*

"Benjamin, I think I'm not saying things right. I haven't slept more than a few hours this week—nightmares, I don't know why—but I'm tryin' to tell you I'm proud of you. For God's sake, that agent fella came by again last night, wanting to talk about you."

Benji's anger congealed to cold fear. "W-what? He's still in town?"

"He is. That's what I mean, honey."

"What did he say?"

"Well, I don't know. Not much, I guess. He wanted to talk to you, give you a few pamphlets you asked for."

"Did he leave them?"

"No, he said he'd give 'em to you hisself. Benjamin, what's wrong?"

"Nothing," Benji said, and turned and walked out of the garage as Papaw called his name. Benji stopped halfway across the yard and looked back. The first edge of dawn had seeped into the sky, and it and the space heater conspired to color the snow dark red. He didn't know why McKedrick had come, but Benji was afraid, afraid of a lot of things just then. He wanted to say something to Papaw, but he could think of no way to warn him without telling him everything.

Finally, he said, "Be careful today." Papaw only looked confused. Papaw was from innocent times. His dreams were small-town dreams. And in that case, Benji realized, it's hard to imagine larger and more malevolent nightmares.

As Benji threw on his tuxedo in his room, he thought of how the United States government had only acknowledged flying saucer sightings because of a death.

It happened in 1948, when an air force test pilot named Thomas Mantell radioed his control tower that he'd spotted something flying a few miles ahead, in the air over Fort Knox Air Force Base. *Negative, Captain,* the tower replied, *we've got nothing on radar.*

Mantell said, *I see it right here.*

Negative, Captain.

Dammit, guys, I've got eyes on it. Disc-shaped, appears silver. . . . Requesting permission to pursue, Control.

Negati—

The velocity, it's unbelievable! I'm increasing my speed to four hundred fifty miles per hour.

Captain, permission denied!

Five hundred— Five fifty—it's climbing now. I'm following, guys. I'm sorry. I'm telling you, I can catch this.

But he didn't catch it. Mantell pushed his jet to an altitude it wasn't meant for. His engine stalled out, and when the jet began to lose velocity and tumble, the friction of the atmosphere shredded the aircraft into a thousand pieces. The air force stated that Mantell most likely had seen ice crystals vaporizing in the ionosphere, or maybe a reflection of Venus. Smoke and mirrors, in other words.

When Benji read about that two nights ago, he'd tried not to think about it, because it seemed to him to be a depressing real-life Icarus warning about a man who died flying too high in pursuit of something amazing. But now, his heart thundering as he sped to school on his bike, Benji realized that was not true.

Mantell's mistake was not that he'd flown too high. His mistake was that he had not gone fast enough.

I can't let everything good slip away. I just can't bear that.

Because of all the FIGs and parents coming to school for the homecoming assembly, even the sidewalks were a traffic jam near the school, and Benji didn't make it there until just a couple of minutes before the assembly was set to begin. He worked his way through the backstage part of the theater, passing the football team, who were in their uniforms and would come onstage after he had done his Magic Mascot introduction. He didn't look for CR.

Benji reached the big silver door that opened onto the stage. A freshman, dressed in all black and carrying a clipboard and looking approximately eight years old, told Benji that his cue to go onstage was coming in less than a minute.

Benji zoned out, trying urgently to figure out questions about the pod. Why had the pod only played old music? The pod—the Voyager, Mr. Fahrenheit—had broadcast songs at the drive-in theater from the era where saucer sightings and films were at their peak. Movies, music, sightings: All had filled the earth and sky during the same weirdly innocent time. Was that just a coincidence? If not, why? If so, *why*?

The reason the Voyager was here was so literally out of this world that it was unimaginable. There *had* to be a connection, some purpose behind it all, but it was like sensing shapes in a dark room and not being able to find the light switch.

No, that's not what it's like. It was more like trying to retrieve a memory, or being on the very edge of understanding a déjà vu.

That doesn't make sense, though. Why would it be a memory?

"They're just about ready," the freshman said to Benji.

And so Benji opened the door, and saw memory.

He froze. He'd expected to walk onstage and be looking straight out on the auditorium, packed for the assembly. But he'd forgotten about the homecoming video Ellie had edited. A retractable movie screen hung from the rafters above the stage, and on it, right in front of him, brighter and larger than life, stood the eleven-year-old boy Benji had once been.

Benji-in-the-video was walking between parallel rows of kids who sat in a high school auditorium—the very auditorium that Benji-in-the-present was in as well. The boy wore a tuxedo jacket, cargo shorts, and flip-flops (?!). Heartstring-tugging violin music swelled on the soundtrack. Benji-in-the-video's hands were shaking, which you could see because the high-definition camera itself was so steady.

"You'll go on after the video ends," whispered the freshman.

Benji nodded absently, still gazing at the screen. "God, I remember that day. Wow," he whispered, a faint smile coming across his face. "Fifth-grade countywide talent show."

The freshman looked more confused than interested, but that didn't matter: Benji was mostly talking to himself. "This was the first time I ever did magic for an audience." *And this was when it all began for me and Ellie.* "It was awesome, I mean, like, perfect. Watch, this part's great!"

Benji-from-the-past faced the elementary school audience to debut his act.

Benji-in-the-present watched it in his memory before it even played onscreen. He'd pulled a neon "infinity scarf" from his tuxedo, shown the audience he had nothing else in his hands, then tossed the scarf into the air like an indoor arcing rainbow, a millisecond of misdirection so he could produce an iPod Nano (preloaded with his magic-act music) from inside his sleeve. Not to brag or anything, but it really had been a flawless performance. Now here it came, on the screen—

Benji's forehead knit.

The movie didn't match his memory.

The differences were small, almost dismissible at first. For one thing, a few feet behind Benji-in-the-past, the school principal who doubled as the emcee was standing glumly, arms folded, looking like he was in actual and literal danger of falling asleep. Next, Benji-in-the-past did a good enough job of producing and tossing the scarf . . . but he completely mistimed the next move, so the falling scarf didn't disguise his iPod grab at all. The only way it could have been more obvious that he was pulling the iPod from his sleeve was if he'd said "Lay-dees and jee-entle-men, I am now pulling an iPod from my sleeve!"

The kids in the audience are laughing at me, Benji thought, stunned. *What the hell? This has to be the wrong tape. . . .*

There was a time-cut in the video. Now it showed the boy operating like a maniac in mid-show, his hands twin blurs of activity: cards from vapor, cards *to* vapor, a magic wand appearing from nothing and then gone again in a flash. Behind the boy, the principal applauded, nodding for the audience to do the same.

Slow DOWN! Benji thought, cringing. The boy was doing everything way too fast, like he was afraid of being caught, or like he feared there would never be enough time to show you all the things he wanted to share, never enough time in the world. But his speed smeared it all together, so the tricks never had a moment to settle and *exist*.

The boy was trying to do everything at once, and so he wound up doing nothing at all.

He looked so terribly happy, so oblivious.

The soundtrack swelling, the video paused on a freeze-frame of the boy brandishing a wand straight at the camera.

"Now, please welcome your Bedford Falls mascot: Benji Blazes!" a deep voice boomed through the auditorium.

Just before the screen began to ascend to the rafters, the video faded to a new image: Benji-now, looking upward. It took him a second to realize that this was a live broadcast, filmed by a camera somewhere backstage.

". . . cue cue cue c'mon cue!" whispered the freshman frantically.

Dry ice billowed forward dramatically as the screen rose and revealed Benji to the audience, who let loose thunderous applause. A brilliant spotlight flew through the dark and speared him. He took an uneasy step forward, blinded and still dumbstruck by the tape.

Speakers in the theater blared to life, the soaring violins that opened "A Mighty Magic" suffusing the world in stereo. Benji flinched, though he'd rehearsed this entrance dozens of times. He felt oddly motion sick, as if tumbling out of control and gravityless. He took a clunky step toward the footlights.

"A mighty magic is the greatest joy," sang Ben McQueen through the speakers, a 1950s voice drenching the auditorium in romance, *"a mighty magic between a girl and boy."*

The audience clarified into individual shapes. It was a full house; people even stood at the back of the auditorium.

Middle-aged men wearing faded letterman jackets. Moms in cheerleading outfits that no longer quite fit. It hurt. Oh, it hurt so much to see them. And it occurred to Benji that he was once again in a haunted place, that in these days of homecoming, Bedford Falls became a harbor for people chasing phantoms of their better pasts. They sat in the auditorium, enchanted by this elevated moment, but the spell would wear off soon.

"A mighty magic, why don't you give it a chance?" sang the speakers. *"Tell me your secrets at the Homecoming Dance."*

That was Benji's cue to let two decks of Bicycle cards eject from his sleeves. His pulse knocked behind his eyes. When he tried to speak, his throat clicked drily.

I went into the House, and that changed nothing, he thought. *I got the pod, and it changed nothing. I've spent so long waiting. I keep thinking there's more time in the future for amazing things.*

But so did everyone in here.

He could see the A.V. control table, halfway up the center aisle. . . .

"Do you feel it? I know that you do," the song continued, and in front of a thousand people, Benji closed his eyes, trying to open his heart and nerves to the melody. *"Oh darling, let's make each other's dreams come true. . . ."*

He thought he felt something in his chest opening like a rose after rain. He was almost sure this was his moment. In this same room, so many years ago, he had screwed up the first time he and Ellie met. He felt an overpowering, panicked need to redeem his mistakes. And yes, this would be a dramatic gesture, but why was that bad? This had to be the moment.

What if it isn't?

He couldn't bear to think about that.

It *had* to be.

"*Give us the chance and you'll see, a mighty magic is our destiny. . . .*"

The announcer tried to push on: "Uhh, ladies and gentlemen, once again, welcome your Bedford Falls Ma—"

Benji opened his eyes.

"Ellie Holmes," he said, "I love you."

14

His voice echoed.

Someone a world away gasped.

"I'm *in* love with you," Benji said.

A girl said, "Awww." Not Ellie.

A silence spun out forever. He stopped just short of the footlights, at the edge of the stage.

"Ellie?" Pause. "Are you here?"

Soft reply, from the center aisle: "I'm here."

The footlights and the spotlight created a starfield; he couldn't see her. Aware of a few people whispering, he hopped off the stage. Finally, he could almost-but-not-quite see her: Ellie, walking down the aisle, walking through a silence so profound that her footsteps echoed up up up to the high rafters of an auditorium where a little boy had met a girl with a smile that could remake the world, a boy who had melted down in his seat and understood, deep in his heart, why it was called *falling* in love.

Ellie stopped a few steps from him, and she looked . . . scared? He felt a moment's fear, too. This was something he'd dreamed of for years. *Keep going,* he told himself.

Between Benji and Ellie there was only the silence and blinding light. The world didn't shift under his feet, like he'd dreamed it would.

"Ellie, please say something," he said.

But she didn't, and the spotlight shifted and she was obscured by the beam, and Benji could not stand the silence. So he did the only thing he could think to do:

He stepped forward, took her face into his hands, and kissed her.

Kissed her.

Applause: a deafening Big Bang of applause.

Kissing her, he thought, and all his nerve endings were amplified and alive and terrified and gorgeous. He closed his eyes. Her lips were warm, cinnamon-sweet on his, and he could feel her pulse quick beneath his fingers at the soft curve of her jaw.

She pulled back.

"Benji, no," she whispered.

He blinked. The applause stopped.

She stepped away. "I just— I can't. You— Can we please leave?"

Benji stared. Couldn't move.

And then, suddenly, Ellie was grabbing him by the wrist, pulling him up the aisle with her as the infinitely awkward silence gave way to a few tentative laughs. She led him through the door, and they were in the hall, the antiseptically, cruelly fluorescent hall.

As the door shut behind them, the tentative laughter in the auditorium gave way to a full tsunami of it. Ellie leaned toward him, and there was a moment when he thought she was going to kiss him back. Instead, she grabbed the microphone from his lapel. "Screw you, asshats," she said into the mic. Her voice resounded over the speaker system, followed by a sound like a cannon as she threw the mic to the ground.

She just stood there staring at it, eyes down. Her hands went to her hair.

Talk to her. Just say the things you always wanted to say.

"I'm in love with you, Ellie," he said. "I think maybe you already knew that, because I've loved you since the first time I saw you. Anyone who really sees you would."

"Benji . . ."

He waited for her to go on. She didn't.

"But—but maybe you don't know *why* I love you. I love you because you change me. You make me feel excited to exist. There's this voice in my head, always telling me I missed out on something important a long time ago, something about being happy that everyone knows but me. I spend so much time trying to get that voice to stop. But the only time it ever stops is when I'm with you. I walked into the House for you, Ellie. You're real magic, you're the sky at night, you give me the future, and I love you."

"I've known you forever. I care about you so much," she said softly. "But I honestly have just no idea who the hell you are sometimes. Why do you always do this?"

"Always do what?" When she didn't respond, he went on, fighting to keep his voice calm. "I feel like I'm saying everything wrong? I—I know right now I don't deserve you—"

"THAT!" she said, looking up. He was struck again by how very sad she looked. "'Deserve me'? Benji, I am going to tell you something I've wanted to tell you for a long time: *I am just a person.* I am not going to fix you, or make your life more special, or make you 'better,' whatever *that* means."

He recoiled. His face burned. A hole ached in the deep center of his stomach.

"Ellie, stop."

"No. Why do you have to make everything A Very Special Moment? Why do you feel like everything has to be perfect and wonderful and pure? Nobody can live up to that, and it makes me feel like shit for not living up to it, and then I'm pissed at you for *wanting* me to. Do you think you're going to win me by being brave and believing in yourself?"

"Shut up!" he shouted. "Why are you making fun of me? Do you *want* to hurt me?"

Her face softened a bit. It just made him feel pathetic. "No. God, no. Never. I'm trying to understand why you're hurting yourself. Listen. You said I'm 'the night sky.' I'm what you want, I give you the future. Except I'm not, and I don't. Don't you know the night sky isn't the future? The sky is a time machine that only goes in reverse. Everything you see up there, all the light from every last goddamn star, it's all the past."

The black hole in his stomach was an expanding, relentless ache.

"And I think that's what you're really after, Benji. You're trying to go back and fix all these imperfect moments from when we were kids. Well, I can't do that for you."

"Okay," he said weakly, because it was the only word he could get out. He turned away from her, his vision swimming.

Ellie was wrong when she said he was trying to alter his inalterable childhood. He did not want to change the past . . . but it had changed anyway. Her reaction, coupled with everything else falling apart, hadn't just shattered his every hope and idea of his future: It had also destroyed how he'd imagined the pain of the past, as merely the darker prologue of a sunlit future. For the real terror is not that the past cannot be altered. The real terror is this: The past is so very fragile, and when it shatters, you do, too.

He walked into the cold air of outside and toward the bike rack. Somebody grabbed his sleeve. He threw the grasp off and spun. It was CR.

"Banjo, holy shit. I mean ho-lee *shit*, buddy. How you doing? Stupid question," CR said, and before Benji could react, CR pulled him into a hug. And not a bro hug, either, but his first-ever full-on "it's going to be okay" hug. Benji's arms stayed locked at his sides, but he didn't move away. Partly from shock, mostly from gratitude.

"I'll tell you one thing, Banjo: This town might be dying, but if they ever want to get tourists to come, they can just put up a sign on the highway: 'Welcome to Bedford Falls, Home of the World's Hugest Set of Testicles.' You're bulletproof, man." CR finally let him go.

Benji looked away, setting his jaw as the horizon blurred. He wanted to get on his bike and pedal, just pound until his muscles shrieked and his mind went numb and he tipped over the rim of the world to someplace better and new. *See, honey, I'm the Voyager.*

"I made a mistake," Benji said. "Understatement. I can't breathe, man, I can't breathe."

"You are."

"I can't believe I did that. God! I'm an idiot, I looked like an idiot—"

"Banjo, *stop!*" CR said, suddenly stern and loud.

Benji looked at him. "Don't use your damn quarterback voice with me. I really can't take you trying to boss me into feeling better."

"What? That's not what I'm doing, man. I'm just trying to help you calm down."

"This is not a situation where you calm down, CR. You 'calm

down' when things look bad but are going to be okay. This is *never* going to be okay, do you understand that? Can you imagine what it's like to not know things are going to work out for you? Can you please, for once, for one second, think about that for me? Because I don't think you can."

CR glared at him. *"Stop. Calling. Me. Stupid."*

"What?!"

"I swear to Christ," CR said, seething, "I can break a lot more than your heart."

For a moment, the two of them stood staring at each other, reality-as-it-had-once-been ripping away between them. Then Benji said, "Why don't you go back to your party?"

He unlocked his bike from the rack.

CR grabbed the bike and threw it to the ground.

"What the hell!"

"What happened back there changes nothing, Lightman. Nothing," CR said, inches from Benji's face. "I don't care how bad or lost or whatever you feel. You are not keeping the pod."

"I wasn't even thinking about that."

Except, he realized, he had been.

He needed it. Now, more than ever.

"I think you were, Lightman."

"It's safe. The alien isn't dangerous. I know. I can feel it, I can almost understand why it's here."

"What makes you so special, Pod-Whisperer?"

Benji had thought about it a lot, and he wished there was some mystical reason. But he didn't think so anymore. "I don't know. Maybe because I touched it without gloves when we first found it. Nobody else had direct contact."

CR smirked. "So I guess it's not because you were 'the chosen one,' then, Benji Blazes?" he said mockingly. "Yeah, I didn't think so. You know what you are? You're a moon, Lightman.

You'll always follow people around and never shine on your own. It's pathetic. Maybe I should be used to it by now. Ellie sure seems to be."

Benji's fist rocketed upward. CR caught the punch inches away from his cheek, his hand swallowing Benji's whole.

"If I let go, are you going to play nice?" CR said.

"I don't want you to let go," Benji said coldly.

CR's eyes narrowed in confusion and in something approaching fear.

"Christopher Robin?"

"Yeah?"

"You're peaking early, asshole."

Benji snapped his fingers.

The FireFingers flashed; the handheld fireball ignited. CR screamed, reeled backward, stumbling on his own feet and landing on his tailbone on the sidewalk. He gaped at his wounded hand with almost comically wide eyes, then plunged it into the snow beside him. "No no no no," he was saying, "no no no no." And he didn't even look angry.

He looked like a terrified little kid.

15

When the adrenaline faded, Benji almost passed out. He'd biked Bedford Falls taking random roads with furied speed, sprinting standing up on the pedals, only vaguely aware of his surroundings: men on ladders hanging parade decorations on Main Street, cars he nearly sideswiped when he zoomed through stop signs.

And then it hit him, a direct shot dead-center in his gut, on a forest walking trail behind the town park. He squeezed his brakes, almost flipped over his handlebars, and stumbled off the bike. He put his hands on a tree to steady himself. Air whistled from his mouth but he couldn't get his breath. He closed his eyes. *Why did that happen?*

He felt guilty; he felt innocent.

I shouldn't have done that, one part of him said.

CR shouldn't have, either, another part said.

What if I ruined his life?

Benji made himself suck several deep breaths. He could hear wind in the trees, and the sounds of the river gentle behind him, and little kids laughing in the park. He tried to focus on those things. They were good things.

He opened his eyes.

There was a used condom between his feet.

And all at once, rage burst in Benji bitter and bright and he seized his bike and sprinted to the trash-strewn riverside and hurled the bike with all his strength like a shot-putter. The bike arced over the water, wheels revolving, spokes clicking and catching the sun, and for one moment it seemed to hover, enchanted, at the top of its arc. Then it crashed into the mud-brown water.

"I don't understand," he said. "I just don't understand any of this."

What is there to understand, Benji? hissed a voice in his head. *You keep acting like all of this—the saucer, Ellie, even the freaking House—has to* mean *something. But what if it doesn't? What if you're just trying to believe those things because they're beautiful? What if it's smoke and mirrors?*

What if you're just some asshole who won't. Grow. Up?

A feeling of freezing enveloped Benji. Above him, black branches sliced at the cruel white sky. He felt so small, but not like a kid: He was unimportant, stranded and abandoned, a dot marooned on an uncaring map. He felt a dark door opening deep inside himself, a creaking door that he'd tried to deny existed—and then had locked down—and then had nailed shut because something terrible had knocked on the other side of that door for his entire, pathetic life.

The monster was the world, the real world, and it wanted to swallow him whole, it wanted to take everything good and hopeful and pure inside of him away.

No! Benji thought, and it was like he was throwing his weight against the door. *Mr. Fahrenheit is real, too, dammit! Life doesn't have to be so much shit! I don't care if nobody else believes me. I still believe the pod is good. I* have *to believe something can be amazing.*

Then look in the pod, said a voice in his head.

He waited in the woods for a long time, and as afternoon faded to evening just before five p.m., he walked through the cold toward home.

Every time Benji turned a corner, he expected to be grabbed by a mob of Bedford Falls football fans and torched at the nearest stake for hijacking the homecoming rally and burning CR's hand. He took backstreets, hearing the crowd lined up along Main Street, imagining them ten-deep on the sidewalks, some of them waiting in lawn chairs for the parade to begin at five thirty, in twenty minutes or so.

Finally, he reached his street, and was once again surprised by what he saw: Zeeko was sitting on Benji's front steps.

"Benji!" Zeeko cried, springing up as soon as he saw him. "Good God, boy, where you *been*?" Dressed in dad jeans and the letterman jacket he'd gotten for being the football trainer, he jogged to meet Benji on the sidewalk.

"H-huh?"

"My brain's been going nuts here!" Zeeko looked a bit angry, but mostly relieved. "I thought maybe something was wrong. Where were you?"

"In the park," Benji said, still confused.

"The park? While I've been worried sick about you?! Okay, I sound like a mom, deep breath, Zeeko," Zeeko said. "But when you didn't show after school to get the pod, and Ellie wouldn't answer my texts . . ."

"Sorry, Zeek. I just assumed you wouldn't want to go with me, after what happened at the assembly."

"The assembly? I wasn't in school today. Excused absence since I had to help Dad." Zeeko motioned across the road. Parked in front of his house was the community health truck, a huge silver vehicle plastered with *BIOHAZARD* and *RADIA-TION* signs. Its back doors were open and Benji could see the inside, which resembled an ambulance. "What happened at the assembly?" Zeeko asked.

"You really don't know?" Zeeko shook his head. "You haven't talked with anyone today?"

"I talked to CR for about two seconds when I was waiting for you. He came over to see my dad."

"Is CR okay?" Benji asked quickly.

"He was a little grumpy. Well, God's honest truth, he was actually a b-hole to me when I asked if he knew where you were. He said he had more important things to think about."

"But physically he was okay?"

"He burned his wrist in home ec and Dad bandaged it. Why?"

Benji didn't answer. Too many emotions were warring in his head. So CR was fine and hadn't told anyone the truth about what Benji had done to him. Benji felt relieved, and if anything, now even guiltier about what had happened.

"Benji? Hello?"

"Sorry. Did you say something?"

"*Yes*, I said we have to hurry. We're going to miss the parade, but I don't want to miss the game, too."

"Hurry to do what?"

"X-ray the pod! I went and got it after school. It's in the med truck."

"Wait, you brought it *here*?"

"Yes, Benji, I did. We promised each other we'd do this

important thing together. That's serious, whether you take it seriously or not," Zeeko said with uncharacteristic sternness. Then he looked closer at Benji and softened. "Whoa, hey, are you okay? Skipping out isn't like you, dude."

"No, I'm not," Benji said, too emotionally exhausted to lie. "Everything is falling apart. Nothing is how it's supposed to be."

"How is it supposed to be?"

"I don't know. I'm just— All of this is going to be over soon, you know? And best-case scenario, it will have been the most and only amazing thing that ever happened to me. I'll be stuck in this town forever, and my life is going to suck—"

"Oh, hush yourself, please." Zeeko laughed.

"What?"

"Listen to me. You, my dear buddy, have a tendency to be a *touch* overdramatic and a wee bit panicky if you don't know exactly what's going to happen. Things are effed up now, that's a fact, fair enough. Maybe you're not going to get everything you want. Maybe you can still get that apprenticeship at the Magic Lantern, or maybe that won't happen, either. But sometimes things turn out *better* than your plan. I think it's because of God's plan, but either way, I am absolutely sure you'll get through this. Your life is not going to suck. And you need to trust me on that, because I am so much smarter than you that it ain't even funny."

Despite himself, Benji laughed. "Thanks, Zeeko."

"Now let's get to work, huh, buddy? Let's find out what's behind Door Number Pod."

"I'm gonna change out of my tux first, cool?"

"Sure. I'll get the machine warmed up."

"You want to X-ray it here?"

Zeeko gestured at the empty street. "There is literally nobody else around."

"It's Papaw's day off, though," Benji said, his gaze flicking to the house.

"He's not home. When I was looking for you, I knocked for about twenty minutes straight."

As Zeeko headed to the X-ray mobile, Benji felt a thread of disquiet stitch through him.

He went to his house, unlocked the front door, and opened it.

And everything changed.

He understood something was wrong the moment he crossed the threshold: When he took his first step into the house, it *splashed*.

Benji looked down, and lifted his foot. The ancient hardwood floor was splotched with a thin layer of red liquid. His gaze followed the erratic trail of water up the length of the dark hall. The liquid was leaking from beneath the door of Papaw's den.

No.

And then he was running down the hall, throwing open the door to the den. Papaw's orderly world had been thrown into chaos, his recliner flipped, his lamp shattered.

But Benji didn't see anyone.

"Papaw?"

Someone whispered, *"See . . ."*

Benji whirled, heels shrieking in the water. Papaw's jukebox lay facedown on the floor in a ring of broken glass. The piping that normally conveyed the bubbling water upward had been shattered. Its neon lights flickered and zapped, painting the room sporadically red.

"See, honey, I'm the Voyager—see, tramping the journey is my story, sir," the jukebox sang at the volume of a whisper. *"I prefer the horizon to a past. . . ."*

And in the time it took for that lyric to finish, Benji looked around the room again. There was no reason to feel relieved. The wallpaper was shredded from the walls, there was a revolver lying in the corner of the room, and *oh God oh God*, what had happened to Papaw?

Something stirred outside the den.

Benji stepped into the hall and heard the sound again, like the breath of someone in pain, from the kitchen.

"Papaw?"

No reply.

Some part of Benji understood that it could be dangerous to go into the kitchen, that he might well find McKedrick waiting there, but Benji could not *not* go. What if Papaw was in there, hurt or something worse?

Like the den, the kitchen was empty except for the wreckage. Chairs were reduced to shards of wood, the faces of cabinets torn off the hinges. Benji tried to turn on the lights; even the bulbs had been smashed. The windows had been, too, and when a breeze slipped in through one of the missing panes, he heard the sigh again, but understood it wasn't a sigh. It was only something softly fluttering behind him on the kitchen table.

"Mary and Joseph above," he whispered.

The note lay on the table, held down by a block of kitchen knives. In the chaos of the kitchen, the neat square of Bedford Falls Sheriff's Desk Stationery looked surreal, like a smile in a nightmare of murder.

Benji picked up the note. The message on it was a violent scrawl, the paper ripped where the wild pen scratched through.

In the long history of notes from his grandfather, Benji had never received one as short as this. Just three letters. Just a single syllable. But the message screamed off the page like a siren so deafening that his sense of reality splintered, finally and irretrievably, like a looking glass tumbling from the imagined stars and shattering against the uncaring earth.

RUN

16

Run.

But paralysis seemed to have fused him to the spot.

Run.

But what had happened here? Where was Papaw?

Run; but what if he's dead?

The cold breeze haunted the kitchen again.

Benji turned slowly. Through the ruined window, he could see Papaw's cruiser. The door of the garage was open. The covered car Papaw had been working on this morning was gone. *Then . . . maybe he got away*, Benji thought, his brain seeming roughly a million miles away from his skull.

Away from what?

Away from here.

!!RUN!!

And finally, Benji did.

His footfalls splashing, he stumbled, tried to catch himself as he hit the floor, and accidentally activated one of the cardshooters hidden in his trick-loaded tuxedo sleeves. A blizzard of Bicycle cards fluttered out before he picked himself up and dashed down the hallway.

He reached the porch and opened his mouth to scream for Zeeko to run. He stopped himself, his gaze snapping left, right, his nerve endings ignited with paranoid terror. *Is McKedrick here?* Benji didn't see anyone, not even Zeeko; the rear silver door to the X-ray mobile was shut.

He heard a gunshot.

Except, no, not a gunshot: Perhaps a mile to the east, a yellow firework bloomed, a billion frantic dandelion sparks descending like a swarm. It was five thirty p.m. in Bedford Falls, and the homecoming parade had begun.

Benji walked toward the street, not quite daring to run, feeling vulnerable in the wide space. He reached the X-ray mobile, found the rear door locked, knocked on it. "Zeeko!" he said softly, but new fireworks boomed, drowning out his voice. *"Zeeko!"* he said louder, and pounded.

Zeeko's grinning face appeared in the small porthole-shaped window in the door. "What's the magic worrrrd?" he said.

"Open the door!"

"Incorrect."

"Zeeko, OPEN IT!"

"One more time from the top, dahling."

"Zeeko, OPEN THE FREAKING DOOR—PLEASE!"

Zeeko congratulated Benji and began a brief lecture on the virtues of patience as he finally cracked the door. Benji threw the door wide and launched himself into the vehicle and slammed the door behind him.

"What the eff's wrong with you?" Zeeko said.

"Something happened to my Papaw," Benji said, peering out the porthole window onto the street. His panting breath fogged it.

"What?"

"The house is wrecked up. Some kind of fight." Benji tried to wipe the fog from the window but only succeeded in smearing it. He looked back at Zeeko. "The agent knows now, somehow he found out, and he came looking for me."

Zeeko gaped at him, thunderstruck. "Why isn't he here? If he knows, why isn't he here waiting for you?"

"I don't know! We have to do the X-ray *now*, Zeeko. If they took Papaw, that's the only leverage we've got to get him back. Where's the pod?" Not waiting for an answer, Benji moved past Zeeko. He'd mentally compared the interior of the X-ray mobile to an ambulance before, but that was wrong. The vehicle was more like an armored car, mixed with a mad scientist's lab. It was divided into two sections: X-ray chamber and general med center in back, and driver's section in front, separated by a silver wall.

Benji walked past something that looked like a phone booth. He glanced inside for the pod, but saw only a computer and monitor. It was the radiation-proof station for the X-ray operator.

"The agent?" Zeeko said, still stunned.

"Yes, the agen—*ow!*" He'd hit his head on some kind of machine that hung from above, situated on a circular track in the ceiling. It looked like a bone-white mechanical arm pointing toward the chamber floor. At the end of the arm was an orb, like a great blinkless eye. This was what generated the X-rays, Benji realized. He finally spotted his magic trunk sitting in shadows in a back corner.

"The agent!" Zeeko repeated. His tone, now not stunned but frightened, made Benji look back.

Zeeko was staring out the porthole window in the door . . . and suddenly, brilliant white light, far brighter than any firework, blazed through the porthole, dazzling all the surfaces in the chamber.

A black SUV had come around the corner at the end of the street. The vehicle was identical to those of the Newporte crew, but of course it wasn't them. It was McKedrick, the man in black, and now, at long last, Benji really was going to be vanished.

The SUV barreled toward the X-ray mobile, its high beams ignited like the eyes of a fairy-tale monster.

Benji threw the lid of his magic trunk open. The pod glimmered inside. He reached under it, searching. "Where's the gun?"

"What?"

"The ray gun, Zeeko!"

"Y-you have it, don't you?"

No.

The SUV peeled to a stop fifteen feet away.

Agent McKedrick, black jacket whipping in the wind, stepped out into the night. He had the fire-eyed look of a man in focused pursuit of his prey.

"Kid!"

"Holy shit," Zeeko breathed.

"Lightman, I'm going to need you to exit your vehicle right now," McKedrick said with terrible calmness barely disguising fury. "I'm going to need you to do it with your hands up."

Almost without Benji realizing, McKedrick was within one step of the X-ray mobile. The agent reached for the door.

Benji grabbed the inside door handle in the same moment McKedrick grabbed the one outside. McKedrick was strong, almost impossibly strong, and the door came open an inch, two, three. Benji hauled back, arching his back and throwing all his weight into the effort. He managed to shut it again. *"Zeeko, lock it!"* he cried, and Zeeko did.

Through the window, Benji's and McKedrick's eyes met, inches apart, separated only by the pane.

"No more games, kid!" McKedrick shouted. "I've been to the quarry! I know something happened there, and I've got a pretty damn strong intuition you and your friends had something to do with it!"

"Where's my grandpa?"

McKedrick didn't seem to hear, or maybe care. "There are men in my business who will do terrible things to you. You and everyone you love. They can be here within the hour. You are in over your head, kid. You are not playing with fire; you're screwing with an atomic bomb. Now, come out. Be a man and come out and let me see what you're hiding. You have no idea what can happen to you if you don't."

"Bullshit! You already hurt Papaw!"

McKedrick again refused to acknowledge what Benji had said. He only stared at Benji with that awful but eroding calm. He glanced around the streets, as if scanning to confirm they were truly alone. Then he looked back at Benji.

"Your call, kid."

McKedrick stepped back, reached into his jacket, and pulled out a handgun fitted with a long silencer.

Screaming, Benji and Zeeko fell backward onto the floor. A bullet slammed into the outside of the door, punching a dimple into the heavy, radiation-proof metal, which had barely stopped the bullet.

The silenced pistol chirped again, and the door handle was blown out of the door. Malformed by the bullet, the twisted metal flew toward them.

Zeeko screamed and grabbed his bicep. Blood spurted between his fingers.

"Are you okay?!" Benji said.

"I'm SHOT! I am sort of SHOT!"

"You want to live, kid?" the agent said. He tried to open the door; a piece of the shattered handle was stuck in the jamb, and the door wouldn't budge. "Get out!"

"Can—can you still work the X-ray, Zeeko?"

Zeeko went, *"Whaaaat?"*

A bullet flew through the porthole window. The glass crashed inward as the bullet embedded itself in the ceiling, missing the precious X-ray generator by inches. McKedrick's arm reached through the window, searching for the inner doorknob.

Benji shoved Zeeko into the X-ray's operating booth and ran frantically for the door that separated the driver's seat from the X-ray chamber.

"What are you doing?" Zeeko cried from the booth.

Benji threw open the door. The keys were in the ignition. "Hold on to something, Zeeko!"

He turned the keys, gunning the vehicle to life. If they X-rayed the pod and put the picture online, they would have leverage. If they didn't, McKedrick could vanish them without worry.

Papaw, Benji thought. He threw the X-ray mobile into drive and rocketed away.

Correction: *tried* to rocket away.

The vehicle lurched forward maybe two whole feet. Benji pushed the pedal all the way to the floor. The steering wheel rattled, the engine whinnied, and the vehicle began moving at the pace of an impressive riding lawnmower. Panicked, Benji looked in the side-view mirror. He saw a stunned McKedrick fall off the back of the X-ray mobile and begin to chase on foot.

Zeeko appeared behind Benji. "The parking brake!" he said. He looked like he was wearing a sleeve of blood. With his uninjured arm, he yanked the emergency brake lever beside the wheel.

The vehicle's speed immediately doubled, sending Zeeko spilling and screaming into the X-ray chamber.

Benji heaved the wheel hard left like a mad sea captain; the vehicle tilted as it fishtailed, doing a one-eighty so that it was now aimed toward the exit of Benji's dead-end street.

The X-ray mobile zoomed past McKedrick's SUV just as the agent gave up the foot chase and ran back to his own car.

"Zeeko!"

"What!"

"Turn on the machine and X-ray the pod!"

"I'M SHO—"

"I know you're shot—*hold on!*"

Their vehicle reached the end of the road. Benji had to make a choice of which way to go, and he did so at random, swerving right, once again making the vehicle tilt dangerously close to tipping.

"I KNOW YOU'RE SHOT," Benji continued, "BUT IF YOU DON'T TAKE THAT PICTURE AND PUT IT ONLINE, WE WILL BE *DEAD!*"

"OKAY, OKAY, GOOD POINT, I'M DOING IT!"

Benji took another left, another right. The streets were empty except for the snow, a ghost town haunted only by the man in black. Benji could hear Zeeko struggling to get the trunk and pod positioned beneath the X-ray device. Benji took a narrow one-way street, hoping against hope he had somehow thrown McKedrick's tail.

But no. After perhaps a minute of the chase, he saw the SUV turn a corner only a few seconds behind them.

"Benji, the X-ray isn't working!"

Benji's stomach plummeted. "Did it get shot?"

"No, but the trunk is sliding all over the place! We have to stop the car somewhere!"

How? How was he supposed to do that? *We stop, we're dead.*

"What do I do?" Benji said. He looked back, staring at the magic trunk that pinballed back and forth with every movement. "What am I supposed to do?" he said to the pod. "You have to help me, what am I supposed to *do?*"

The pod didn't answer.

But the heavens did.

The night sky to the east boomed with a sudden great light. Blue sparks descended like a constellation caught and cascading on the same wind that likewise carried the brassy-sassy sounds of the Bedford Falls High School Marching Band.

Maybe half a mile away, Benji could see the fire department parking lot, where all the parade floats waited until it was their turn to join the parade.

A plan flashed in his mind.

We can stop the car if we do it in front of other people. That's the only way it will be safe.

Benji made a hairpin turn, directing the X-ray vehicle toward the fireworks. So it turned out they weren't going to miss the parade, after all.

17

The Bedford Falls Fire Department was an enormous, bright-red building, one of the last beneficiaries of the town's brief economic boom. The road Benji sped down fed directly into the building's parking lot, which was full of performers waiting to join the parade. Benji tapped his horn, driving very slowly through the lot, avoiding a convertible carrying last year's Homecoming Queen, a gymnastics troupe of little kids, and a dozen old men who wore fezzes and drove tiny go-karts (they honked indignantly back at Benji, their horns going "ah-*roooo*-gah!").

Zeeko appeared over his shoulder, wrapping his bleeding bicep with gauze. "God Almighty, buddy, tell me this is part of a plan."

Benji tilted his hand one way and then the other: *Kind of.*

In front of him was a queue of cars waiting to turn onto Main Street. The crowd on the sidewalks wasn't as big as it might have been, which made sense. This was the end of the parade, and the football team had already passed.

"Get ready," Benji told Zeeko, steering around the queue and cutting in front of a woman in an ice-cream truck. The X-ray mobile was nearly into the street.

Benji slammed the brakes when someone in black stepped in front of the vehicle, waving their arms over their head. "Whoa whoa whoa," said the same freshman who had directed him onto the stage at the assembly.

Benji cranked down his window. "Hi! Move!"

"Benji? What the—what are you doing?"

"I'm driving the community health truck."

"*Okay*?"

"It's in the parade."

"How *come*?"

"Because healthy living is magical! C'mon, move, we're next up, man!"

The confused freshman consulted his clipboard. "The truck isn't on the list. It says you were supposed to be on the football float?"

No more than fifty feet back, Benji could hear McKedrick's SUV scream to a stop. There was another chorus of *ah-rooo-gahs*.

Benji said quickly, "Right, they didn't want me to be on the team's float because I was stupid at the assembly today."

And this, at last, convinced the freshman, who gave a thumbs-up and waved Benji through.

He steered onto Main Street. The crowd cheered and waved hand-painted signs featuring the names and numbers of players. Ahead of the X-ray mobile, the mayor (who Benji recognized only because he was wearing a sash that read *MAYOR*) rode in a slow-moving blue convertible. The crowd applauded the mayor raucously—not because they were huge mayoral fans, but because he was throwing candy.

Benji noticed some people in the crowd gawping at his own vehicle. Feeling absurd, he grinned and waved.

There was a commotion behind him.

He leaned out the window, looked back, and what he saw made his stomach fall. He had hoped that McKedrick would stop the pursuit, at least for the length of the parade. Instead, the agent had abandoned his car and was weaving through the people on the sidewalk fifty feet back, barking into a cell phone, his eyes on the X-ray mobile.

"What do I do?" Benji said once more, although he held no real hope that Mr. Fahrenheit would speak. No answer.

"Zeeko, are you ready?"

"When you are."

"How long does it take to do the X-ray?"

"About a minute, give or take a few seconds."

Benji put the vehicle into park. At once, the X-ray machine hummed to life. McKedrick burst through the crowd now, no more than thirty steps back. Benji didn't think McKedrick would hurt him or even arrest him in front of so many witnesses. But Benji had to hold him off until the X-ray was done.

McKedrick has a gun, probably even some other weapons. And I've got nothing.

Except . . . he realized that wasn't true.

He had his tuxedo. He carried magic in his pockets in the same way a gunslinger hauls his iron firepower.

Magic's comprised of the same material that falls out of a bull's ass, said a voice in his head.

Maybe it is, Benji said back. *But maybe it will be enough.*

He grabbed his FireFinger gloves from his pockets, put them on. He reached up his sleeve and grasped the small but powerful magnet pinned to the fabric in there. He tugged the magnet, which was attached to a retractable string that ran up the sleeve to his armpit, and brought it out of his sleeve so he could hold it in his palm. With his free hand, he pulled from his inside pocket a three-inch silver cylinder: his collapsible magic staff.

His arsenal wasn't exactly a ray gun. But what other option did he have?

Benji opened the door.

The crowd greeted him with muted applause. He looked ragged, his top hat gone, his pant legs still wet from the jukebox water.

His mind was rocketing, searching the catalog of every performance he'd ever done, trying to find something useful. But this was not a freaking talent show.

This was a surreal standoff. Even McKedrick's *fashion sense* looked out of place. His expensive suit. His slicked-back hair. This impeccable big-city monster strode down a potholed road past country and small-town people in old winter coats. . . .

And inspiration struck Benji like a bolt.

"Hello there, 'Mr. Fancypants Newporte Indianapolis'!" Benji shouted in his most theatrical voice. "How generous of you to visit our humble little hometown! Do you know what we're going to do to your team tonight?"

McKedrick paused, two steps away: *What the hell you talking about, kid?*

Blinking to protect his vision, Benji snapped his fingers: light blast. McKedrick flinched, momentarily blinded; the crowd laughed and cheered this strange but apparently planned "fight" between their team mascot and the avatar of the big-city population that had always looked down on them.

Benji hurled a fistful of smoke pellets to the concrete, raising a thick cocoon that enveloped both him and the agent and obscured them from the crowd. Sightless though McKedrick was, his reflexes were terrifyingly attuned: As Benji lunged forward to clear the final distance between them, the agent was already reaching into his own jacket, reaching for the pistol in a holster beneath his armpit.

By a millisecond, Benji was quicker. He grabbed McKedrick's pistol with his magnet-bearing hand, felt the magnet take hold of the gun. The magnet and the gun zipped up his sleeve, cracking against his elbow but at least disarming the agent.

Now wind whipped the last of the smoke away, revealing them again to the crowd. McKedrick blinked twice, opened his eyes fully, and heedless of the crowd, he grabbed Benji by his tuxedo, pulling him closer, his hot, tobacco-rich breath like an invasion.

"Where is my Papaw?" Benji said, soft but furious.

"I don't care," McKedrick spat. "Damn you, listen to me—"

Benji opened his magic-staff-bearing hand in front of McKedrick's stomach. The silver collapsible staff expanded, hitting McKedrick in the gut, knocking the wind out of him and sending him to his knees. "*That's* what we're gonna do!" Benji announced to the crowd.

"Benji?" said a familiar voice.

He whipped around. Across the street was a raised wooden platform with television cameras broadcasting the parade on local TV. Ellie stood up behind one of the control panels, looking shocked by what she had seen.

Benji froze, unsure for so many reasons what he should say. McKedrick groaned, trying to stand.

"*It's done!*" Zeeko shouted from the X-ray mobile.

Benji dashed back into the vehicle. He spotted an alleyway between two buildings on the right side of the parade route. Luckily, police sawhorses were set up on the sidewalk there, so the entrance was clear. With a thousand confused stares trailing his vehicle, he steered toward the alley.

Once inside, he sped up as much as he could, taking turns through a series of alleys, trying to put distance between himself and McKedrick. Zeeko opened the lead door between the

X-ray compartment and the driver's seat. "We did it, my friend," he said. "Thank God."

"What does it . . . what does Mr. Fahrenheit look like?"

"The X-ray's still processing."

"Are you okay?" Benji said, nodding to Zeeko's arm.

"Define 'okay,'" Zeeko said, but laughed weakly. "The bleeding stopped. I love you and CR, but y'all need to stop beating me up." There was an electronic *beep* behind them. "Popcorn's done."

As Zeeko returned to the rear compartment, Benji turned into an alley a couple hundred feet long. By now, all the sounds of the parade were muted by distance. He steered around a Dumpster, almost to the end of the alley. . . .

"Benji," Zeeko said, "something's wrong." In the rearview mirror, Benji could see Zeeko standing beside the magic trunk, staring at the pod with an expression of confusion and unaccountable fear. Zeeko looked up and said, "The pod is e— *Benji, look out!*"

Benji's gaze whipped forward just in time to see a car screaming to a stop at the end of the alley a few feet ahead, cutting off the only exit. He slammed the brakes and instinctively heaved the wheel to avoid collision; the X-ray mobile slammed into the alley wall with a shriek of metal and sparks. Benji pitched forward, seatbelt-less, the steering wheel punching him over his heart, and for a moment his vision grayed out. And so that was why he didn't put up a fight when a shadowed figure opened his door, grabbed him by the jacket, and pulled him into the night.

18

Benji felt himself being slammed against the cold metal side of the X-ray mobile. He blinked, trying to clear his vision. All he could see was a vague shape, but the shape looked like himself, as if he was looking in a blurry mirror. A red light was flashing somewhere. He forced himself to take a deep breath.

"Benjamin," the blurry shape whispered, "are you hurt?"

Shock and relief surged through Benji. *"Papaw?"*

"Are you hurt, boy?"

"I—no. Zeeko is."

Benji's vision cleared a bit. Papaw didn't look surprised by the news that Zeeko was injured. "How bad is it?" Papaw said.

"He's okay."

"Who else is here with you?"

"Nobody. Papaw, what happened to you? What happened at the house?"

"Quiet, son!" Papaw said urgently.

In the red, whirling light thrown by the police flasher atop Papaw's car, Benji began to notice things: Papaw was wearing his sheriff's hat and uniform, and to Benji, those were normally the symbols and talismans of his grandfather's strength. Now a thin line of blood leaked out from the brim of Papaw's hat; the cloth of his collar was gashed.

But the worst thing of all was the look in Papaw's eyes.

Sheriff Robert Lightman's gaze was normally a bright hard gray, carrying the color and character of steel. But the gray had undergone a metamorphosis, changing into the shade of a sky tortured by an approaching storm.

For the first time in Benji's life, Papaw looked *afraid*, and somehow that was more frightening by far than anything that had happened tonight.

Hearing a squeal of brakes, Papaw and Benji looked down to the end of the alley that was not blocked by Papaw's car. There was not much light, only the pulse of the flasher, but there was enough to see. McKedrick had retrieved his SUV, and now he parked it about a hundred feet away, across the other end of the alleyway, sealing them inside.

McKedrick stepped out. Benji had felt victorious when he'd stolen the agent's pistol and "disarmed" him, but he realized now how stupid that had been: McKedrick was carrying a compact shotgun, something Benji had never seen anyone in law enforcement do.

"Lightman—both of you—it's over! Get down on the ground NOW!"

"Benjamin," Papaw whispered, "don't you say one thing or move one muscle."

And before Benji could reply, Papaw strode away to meet the man in black, who snicked off the safety of his shotgun and aimed it squarely at Papaw's chest.

Benji had, of course, zero intention of following Papaw's instructions. He began to chase Papaw but had only gone a few feet when he felt hands seize his arm.

"Benji, no!" hissed Zeeko, who'd gotten out of the X-ray mobile.

"Let me go, Zeeko!"

"Evenin', sir," Papaw said, greeting the agent as they neared each other, "and how the heck are *you*?" He sounded happy to see McKedrick, eager to charm his fellow lawman. As if Papaw hadn't noticed the rage on his face, or the death stick in his hands.

"Sheriff Lightman," McKedrick said coldly, "I believe you know Standard Operating Procedure. Put your hands on the back of your head and lace your fingers."

Benji thrashed in Zeeko's grip; his friend held tighter, bear-hugging him despite his injury. "For the love of Christ, listen to me," Zeeko whispered in his ear. "The pod—"

"What, now?" Papaw answered McKedrick, cupping a hand behind one ear. "Couldn't quite make out that last part, sorry."

"I tried to play nice. But you and your grandson are now property of the United States government."

"Papaw, he's after something we found! McKedrick, he doesn't know anything! Just take the pod and leave him alone!"

But it was like a nightmare: No matter how loud Benji yelled, Papaw didn't react, didn't even seem to hear him. . . .

"I think you hear me fine, Sheriff." McKedrick sneered. "Stop right there and put your face on the goddamn pavement."

Papaw replied, just a few steps from the agent, "Now listen, I know I look not a day over forty, but my hearin' aid is bein' fritzy. One more time, if you'd be so very kind. I wanna know what's got you *riled*."

And then fireworks detonated overhead, rendering the dark alleyway suddenly shadowless and vivid. Papaw looked over McKedrick's shoulder, toward the SUV, and he shouted, in a voice filled with the same fear Benji had seen on his face, *"Get the hell outta here, honey!"*

Panicked, McKedrick whirled, firing the shotgun in time with the delayed *boom* of the fireworks. Someone screamed, and everything in Benji went cold: It was Ellie. She'd followed them to the alley and had been trying to silently crawl over the hood of the SUV.

A hundred holes eviscerated the side of the SUV; the driver's window imploded. Ellie fell from the hood and landed on the ground on the near side of the vehicle.

Benji screamed, his fury at last freeing him from Zeeko's grasp. He sprinted toward Papaw and McKedrick, but most of all toward Ellie, not knowing if she had been hit.

The finale fireworks of the parade bellowed brightly, a billion points of apocalypse light illuminating the alley.

McKedrick pumped his shotgun, the weapon expending a smoking shell as he pivoted back toward Papaw.

Papaw tilted backward, violently backward, like a gunslinger falling to an inglorious death in a dusty street.

But he wasn't falling: He was preparing. He was cocking his fist back.

Papaw launched a haymaker punch at Agent McKedrick with the speed and grace of a teenage heavyweight champion. McKedrick took the cataclysmic crash across his jaw. His head snapped backward, a thin line of blood arcing from his chin like the flourish of a signature. He crumpled to the ground like dead weight, his shotgun skittering across the concrete.

Benji skidded to a stop, dumbfounded. Papaw rubbed his fist into his other palm, shoulders heaving as his punch echoed in the gray canyon of the alley.

"Sheriff! Hot *damn!*" Ellie cried shakily. Benji saw with blinding relief that she was standing up beside the SUV, brushing shattered glass from her pants.

The last light and sound of the fireworks died. Staring at the fallen McKedrick, Papaw said, "Ellie, honey, I want you to get in that fancy car and follow me out of here. Benjamin and Zeeko, I need to ask for your help carrying this man to the Caddie."

Benji flinched as a hand grabbed his shoulder. He turned back. The swiping fire of Papaw's police flasher swept over Zeeko's face. His eyes were wide as saucers.

"Benji," he said, "the pod is *empty*."

Empty.

Benji felt the word hit him like a depth charge, like a detonation heard but not yet felt.

"There's nothing inside," said Zeeko.

"You mean no 'Thing' inside," Papaw said. He finally looked at Benji. "The pod's empty because the beast got out, Benjamin. It came to our house. And It's in one hell of a bad mood."

There was the depth-charge shockwave: *BOOM.*

"What?" Benji said. "You *know*, Papaw?!"

But suddenly the whirling dome atop Papaw's car shattered, a miniature nova of sparks and glass. The frozen air seemed to plummet by ten degrees. All at once, Benji inexplicably felt like he was standing on railroad tracks that had just begun to vibrate beneath him. Something was coming.

Next moment, a sound like a siren amplified beyond imagining flooded the alley. He clapped his hands over his ears; Papaw, Ellie, and Zeeko did the same. The earsplitting sound awoke McKedrick, who attempted to prop himself up on his elbows.

"It's coming!" Papaw bellowed.

"Papaw, what's happening?"

"Mary and Joseph, I thought I might've killed It back at the

house today but It's still alive. We have to go, Benjamin, It's coming for y—"

The pitch of the siren changed, and Benji realized it was not a siren at all: It was a blaring musical note, a chord from a guitar, and now it was replaced by a young man's melodious voice:

"We got Captain Celsius, back there on the snares and bass! Yes sir, that's right, he's a rock 'n' roll ace!"

A manhole cover lay in the concrete floor of the alleyway between Benji and Papaw. The manhole cover began to quiver, then to dance. Sickly green light radiated from the sewer below.

"I'm Kid Nuclear, want to know my job?" the song went on. *"I'm the singer of the Atomic Bobs!"*

Spears of green light flew through the manhole cover holes like arrows of war fired at the heavens.

The cover erupted, spiraling into the air, higher and higher and eclipsing the moon, and just before the music died with abrupt finality, the phantom singer roared one last lyric:

"And hey, who's that on guitar tonight? Well, that's Bob Lightman, MR. FA—!"

And the Voyager rose.

Perhaps it was fitting, after all, that the moment should feel unreal: The arrival of the magically impossible had been rehearsed ten thousand times in Benji's dreams. It had been the shape of his hope, the great secret of his heart that he wanted to share with no one and the whole world.

Unreal, yes. But not like this.

Ever since he'd shot it from the sky, the creature had made Benji feel like a kid. But until this moment, as the creature emerged from the sewer, he had forgotten that childhood carried its own terrors. And the hole in the ground before him seemed to Benji to be a dark closet. It was the closet door you hear creaking beside you when everyone else at the sleepover is asleep but you are still awake. It was the door that you swear is shut but whose hinges softly cry as the clock downstairs is striking three and invoking the witching hour, when graveyards are reputed to yawn. It was every dark bedroom closet from all of kidhood's nightmares, and witch and werewolf and demon and vampire and dead kid are waiting in there, and if you try to move, the door will roar open like a dark eternal mouth, and it will be *their* black eyes you see flashing at you, *their* ice fingers that enwrap your naked ankles, and in the morning, all that will be left of you will be a streak of blood and the desperate, doomed tracks your fingers carved into the carpet.

The Voyager arose in a manner vaguely magnificent, like a fallen angel reascending. The terrible light that bound it was the color from outer space: ray-gun green. The creature was shaped almost like a human but then . . . but then not quite. Its skull was a misshapen bulb perched atop a neck as long and thin as a needle. Strange strings of flesh danced on Its face like the hair of Medusa. Its two arms stretched forever, ending with three-clawed hands. Between Its legs was a long tail similarly tipped by a kind of dagger. As the Voyager floated up, Benji saw It stood seven feet tall at the very least—how It fit in the pod was a mystery—and there were ridges of bones across the creature's whole body, as if God had made a mistake and put the skeleton on the outside.

Though Benji could not see Its eyes, he felt as though the creature were not just staring at him but *through* him. He stood mesmerized and terrified, unable to move.

A roar and a flash of light split the night. A chunk of brick wall beside Benji exploded. The Voyager spun in midair with somehow terrible grace, facing the source of the sound: McKedrick, staggering to his feet, his smoking shotgun in hand. The agent's shot had gone wild, but already he was pumping a fresh shell into the breach, zeroing in on the Voyager.

The creature lunged through the air before McKedrick could react. The agent screamed, bicycling his legs as the creature raised him off the earth with one clawed hand. The shotgun dropped to the ground, discharging uselessly. The Voyager raised Its free claw, but rather than strike the agent, It did something Benji did not understand: It placed Its palm to McKedrick's forehead.

The agent was like a marionette whose strings have been severed. His arms collapsed to his sides, his mouth went slack and silent, his eyes glazed to glassy orbs. . . .

Moments later, the creature lifted Its clawed hand from McKedrick's forehead. McKedrick snapped back to his senses. He thrashed in the Voyager's grip and began to scream. In pain. The Voyager was plunging a long silvery object into the agent's chest like a dagger.

The Voyager fired the ray gun.

The blast sliced straight through McKedrick. A rainbow arc of green light and red blood jetted from the back of his perfect black suit. Ellie and Zeeko screamed. McKedrick's body hit the pavement bonelessly.

Papaw, shoot It, Benji thought—and as if sensing the intention, the creature spun to face Benji. *"Shoot It now!"* he called aloud.

Past the creature, Papaw reached for his holster, but his arthritic hands betrayed him. He fumbled the gun, which clattered to the pavement. Benji reached into his tuxedo, remembering that the pistol he'd stolen from McKedrick was inside his sleeve.

"Benji, look out!" Ellie screamed.

The Voyager reached him. It placed Its death-cold palm on Benji's brow.

And his mind turned to flame.

He was hurled like a human bullet into a corridor of endless darkness.

He opened his mouth to scream, but he had no mouth. Nothing existed, nothing at all except for the black, cold velocity. He was searching for something: There was something in these corridors he needed, some kind of clue, something to guide his future—but what was it? Why had he come here looking for it?

Without warning, the corridor exploded around him and was no longer a corridor at all: It became a vast emptiness, gulfs of gravityless dark through which he soared alone. There were pinpricks of light in the ether. Stars, unimaginable light-years away. Benji looked back, and he saw a nearer star, furious and red, swallowing an entire world. . . .

Anger surged through him. This wasn't what he was looking for!

The vision of space vanished, and now Benji was—he didn't understand it—he was at CR's father's quarry in the daytime, holding some kind of electronic handheld device against the ground. The device began to beep, and Benji pulled out his phone. "This is McKedrick," he said in McKedrick's voice.

What is this? Why am I McKedrick?

"I may have something here in Indiana, ma'am," Benji/McKedrick said. "Nothing like we've seen before. The local police and DEA finally cleared out of the area, and there are definite traces of possible activity. There's a kid involved, more than one, perhaps. Ma'am, I'd like to see if I can talk some sense into him before Omega moves in. He seems like a decent young man, if naive, and I believe I can put the fear of God in him. It's possible the kid doesn't yet know enough to be dangerous. It's even possible I'm on a wild-goose chase, perhaps. Yes, ma'am, I understand the risk to the division. I assume full responsibility.

I won't let you down. And ma'am, if you don't hear from me by eighteen hundred hours, please feel free to send in the whole damn cavalry. . . ."

The corridor, again.

A light was growing ahead. He sped toward it. It wasn't an exit, but something like a mirror maze that had been flooded with smoke. The mirrors around him bore images of the night of the saucer shootdown. Seeing the images filled him with excitement. He was closer. Where were the ones he needed?

Now Benji felt a pain so overwhelming that it was as if the Voyager were dragging Its claws across his brain, flicking through gray matter, digging deep. He crashed through mirror after mirror, searching desperately. He saw the saucer shootdown again, then went further back in time to when he'd spoken to Ellie on the frozen lake during the quarry party. That conversation had reminded him of the House, and now Benji was thinking about the hallucination of the monster that had come out of the House's cellar. Inexplicably, the hallucination filled him, for the first time, with relief. . . .

"Get the hell away from my child!" Papaw roared a billion miles away.

A blast of light. Benji fell, hitting the ground hard. He looked around, dazed, seeing the pebbled plain of the alley's concrete floor. He was still where he had been before the creature touched him. In fact, it was as if almost no time had passed: A few feet away, Papaw was striding toward the creature with his pistol raised. The creature turned toward Papaw, raising its own, far deadlier weapon.

"Papaw, get down! It will kill you!"

The weapon Papaw brandished began to glow.

What? When did Papaw get the ray gun?

Three green ovals jetted out from the ray gun in Papaw's

hand, painting the world atomically. The Voyager reacted too late: It spun, sparing itself a direct hit but taking the shot midway up Its left arm. The impact sent the creature corkscrewing through the air; Benji ducked and saw Zeeko, who was behind him, do the same.

The creature slammed into a brick wall beside the X-ray mobile, sending fissures through the bricks.

The creature recovered quickly, moving across the wall with the speed of a spider. Still in motion, It raised one claw toward Papaw. It was holding the ray gun. Benji did not understand, because hadn't Papaw just had the Voyager's gun?

It didn't matter. Benji reached into his tux. His fingers found the pistol, tried to draw it out.

The alien and Papaw fired simultaneously. Impossibly and inexplicably, *they both fired ray guns simultaneously.*

Because both leaped to evade the other's blast, neither hit their target. Their bolts struck empty space, peppering the battle zone with brick and concrete.

Benji covered his head, then finally yanked the pistol free of the magnet. He drew the weapon, whirling on his heels, his gaze sweeping around the alley. He had no idea where the creature was.

Zeeko, who had dived to the ground when Papaw's shot sent the creature spiraling, stood unsteadily, searching the area around him, too. Benji tasted fine metallic fear at the back of his mouth.

He slowly looked in the other direction, where Papaw and Ellie stood. Holding fiercely on to the lip of a Dumpster, Papaw was struggling to his feet, still recovering from the shootout. His hat had fallen to the ground. Ellie walked to him, her footsteps the only sound disturbing the eerie quiet. She wrapped an arm around Papaw, helping him up the final few inches. Benji felt a painful clutch of gratitude.

"Sheriff, not for nothing," Ellie said, "but what in the blue hell is happening here?"

"Is It dead?" Papaw whispered.

"God, I hope so," Zeeko said.

I don't think he hit It, Benji thought, his mind still racing with adrenaline and a billion questions about how Papaw knew about any of this.

"Honey, fetch me my gun," Papaw said to Ellie. "I dropped it under the Dumpst—"

Zeeko screamed. The arms of the creature, glistening like wasps, had erupted from the shadows beneath the X-ray mobile.

The claws wrapped around Zeeko's ankles. Zeeko fell, hitting the ground face-first. "No!" he cried, clawing the ground as he was reeled toward the shadows. "Help me! Oh God, please help me!"

One claw reached out and seized Zeeko's forehead. Instantly, Zeeko went limp.

Benji fired his pistol at the shape in the dark. The shot was off by yards, way too high. Somebody pushed him to the side. The shotgun appeared over his shoulder, and fired.

The buckshot hit just below the driver's door of the X-ray mobile.

The front tire exploded with an airburst.

The shotgun pumped, then shot out one of the rear tires.

The X-ray mobile plummeted violently on the flattened rubber. In his mind, Benji felt a cold inarticulate rage and pain from the Voyager. The creature released Zeeko, Its arms vanishing back under the car.

Zeeko scrambled to his feet, tears of fear and relief in his eyes. "Oh holy Jesus, thank you," he wheezed. "Also, Ellie, thank you."

Benji turned and saw with a small shock that Ellie was holding the shotgun. "This is one of those moments," she whispered shakily, "when I am very grateful that my dad refused to pay for ballet lessons."

Papaw patted Ellie on the shoulder. Once again, Benji was bursting with questions, and this time, Papaw seemed to acknowledge it: He looked at Benji and, after a moment, nodded sympathetically. Still, he spoke only to Ellie. "That was smart thinking, Annie Oakley. But I need to see the body."

With the inexplicable ray gun in his hand, Papaw approached the X-ray mobile. He bent cautiously, peering under the vehicle a few feet away. He unfastened an LED flashlight from his belt.

"You guys," Zeeko said to Ellie and Benji, "something happened to me. When It touched me, I saw—"

Papaw clicked his flashlight's button several times. The flashlight wouldn't ignite.

"Here, Papaw," Benji whispered.

"Stay back, Benjamin."

Benji snapped his fingers, demonstrating the fire, and Papaw relented. They kneeled together. Benji put the pistol in his outer jacket pocket, snapped again. The phosphorescent flash was brief, the FireFingers nearly exhausted, and the light didn't quite penetrate the hiding place beneath the vehicle.

"Maybe we crushed It," Papaw said.

"Papaw, can you tell me what—"

"Snap again, boy."

This time his light breached the dark, barely.

"Again . . ." Papaw instructed. They moved a few inches closer. Benji snapped again, his heart a fist pounding at the base of his throat.

The fleeting light washed across almost everything beneath

the vehicle. At the farthest rim of his light's reach, something large shimmered in the dark.

Benji snapped, one final time.

The shimmering object was a manhole cover, standing almost on end.

Everything inside Benji froze.

He breathed: *"Trapdoor."*

"What?"

"Trapdoor—to the sewer!—" Benji stammered. He spun back toward the manhole the Voyager had first emerged from, knowing even as he did that he was too late, that he had been bested by the oldest trick in the book.

Ellie Holmes didn't see it coming. An instant ago, the creature had vanished down one manhole, into the dark network of pipes, and now, with a speed no conjuror had ever dreamed, It rematerialized from the hole behind Ellie. Hideous claws flew from the dark, seizing her by the waist. The shotgun flew from her hands and hit the pavement, discharging into the air. She cried out. Benji ran for her with every measure of strength his unathletic frame possessed, and when she began to fall into the dark pit, he dove, flying, arms outstretched, and there was one infinite moment when their fingertips grazed one another. . . .

Then she was gone, vanished, poof and good-bye, the sound of her scream fading into the catacombs below Bedford Falls.

He stared into the pipe, shock surging through him. Her voice grew softer, farther away, the wail of a little girl lost. A wild thought echoed in Benji's mind: *Ladies and gentlemen, for my next trick, I will make the love of my life disappear! And then someone—some Thing—will saw her in two!!*

Benji's torso was already into the pipe when hands grabbed

him and pulled him up. He threw them off—they were mean-ingless, nothing mattered except getting down there—but Papaw wouldn't let go.

"Son, stop!"

"Papaw, It's got her!"

"I know it, but you goin' down there won't do a thing to help."

"*I don't care!* This is my fault, let me go—"

"*Benjamin, listen to your grandfather, dammit!*"

Benji looked up at him.

"If there's a chance on this earth to save that girl, we'll do it. I swear to you. But I don't think the beast will hurt her yet."

"How do you know that?"

Papaw turned to Zeeko, who was sitting on the ground shak-ing and gazing a light-year away. "Zeeko, can you drive a stick? *Zeeko!*"

Zeeko snapped from his stupor. "Yes, sir. I can."

"Then get into that SUV and follow me. We may need two cars later. Benjamin's riding with me."

Gritting his teeth, Papaw pulled Benji to his feet, and as he led him toward the cruiser he'd stopped in front of the X-ray mobile, he finally spoke to Benji again.

"There are things you need to know, Benjamin. It's time to tell you all of them. It's well past that time, actually."

"Papaw, none of this makes sense."

"This is my fault, Benjamin. *My* sin."

"W-what?"

"I met this Beast before. A lifetime ago. I was . . . I was your age, driving this car like it was the only thing that ever mattered."

Confused, Benji followed his grandfather's gaze.

The car Papaw had driven here had a removable domed police light attached to its roof, but it was not a police cruiser.

It was a 1959 Cadillac. It had been pelted with debris, but even in the aftermath of the confrontation, it glowed like a moonlit dream.

Dream Machine, Benji thought. *That's the car from . . .*

"This is happening," Papaw said, the words catching in his throat, "because of something I did when I was younger. . . ."

Benji barely heard. He was staring at the side paneling of the Cadillac, which was covered by hand-painted words that time had faded but not erased . . . .

"OFFICIAL" CAR OF THE "ATOMIC BOBS"! BOBBY "CAPTAIN CELSIUS" VOLPE! ROBBY "KID NUCLEAR" KING! BOB "MR. FAHRENHEIT" LIGHTMAN!

PART FOUR
THE SKY IS A TIME MACHINE

Fire always has been, and seemingly will always
remain, the most terrible of the elements.
—Harry Houdini

Thank you, Bedford Falls! You've made this a real
unforgettable night! Drive careful out there!
—Robert Lightman of the Atomic Bobs
(Homecoming Carnival, 1959)

19

"When I was young," Papaw said, "my father told me the best thing about being a teenager is that it won't last long. He never bothered to tell me that it's also the worst part. Benjamin, remember that. As I'm telling you this story, please remember that and try to forgive me."

Benji nodded, speechless, numb, as Papaw drove the Cadillac out of the alley. Papaw switched on the mobile scanner on the dashboard. The dispatcher reported some fender benders and fights around the football stadium, and said a snowstorm was moving in from the east. Satisfied that there were no reports about the battle in the alley, Papaw turned the scanner off.

They steered onto the highway, Papaw's face pale in the thin, lonesome lights that baptized it.

"In the alley," he said, "that wasn't the first time I seen the Beast. It came lookin' for you at our house this afternoon. I fought It off, barely. But that wasn't the first time, neither. It's been to Bedford Falls before."

Benji was silent for a long time, still unable to process any of what was happening. "When . . . when did you see It?"

"A lifetime ago."

"You saw the alien a lifetime ago." Voice flat.

"Yes, son."

"Then, why . . . You said . . . You've never acted like you believed in anything like this, Papaw." He felt like he was trying to grasp an ungraspable thing.

"I *didn't* believe in it. I know it doesn't make sense, Benjamin. You'll understand everything soon.

"I was seventeen when I saw It. Just outside of Bedford Falls, there was a drive-in theater, and I was there—well, near it."

"You were in this car, weren't you? Your Dream Machine."

Papaw looked at him, stunned.

"And you were on a date, with a girl named Judy."

"How in the *hell* did you know that?"

"I dreamed it. But how? How could I dream *your* memory? It doesn't make any sense."

"No, it does. It makes perfect sense, son. What else do you know about that night?"

"There was a green light in the sky. The radio started playing that song, 'The Voyager.' I heard this voice in my head—your head, I guess—say, 'I AM MR. FAHRENHEIT.' I thought it was the alien's name. But Mr. Fahrenheit was you?"

"Well, not precisely."

For a moment it seemed that Papaw's breath was hitching in his chest. He turned his head quickly, checking the side-view mirror. They drove on, passing through shades of shadow and light, and when Papaw looked back, his voice was steady.

"Mr. Fahrenheit was some Hollywood bullshit name I made, that's all. I thought it sounded good, like somethin' Brando or James Dean would have—*oh, who gives a damn about that, Lightman!*" Papaw said bitterly.

Benji flinched. He'd never seen Papaw so upset, so angry at himself.

Papaw took a deep, steadying breath. "Point is," he said, "I was practically pissin' myself when I saw the light that night, so I did what I always did when I was scared back then: I told myself I wasn't just Bobby Lightman. I was somebody else. Mr. Fahrenheit.

"So, I get out of the Dream Machi— the Cadillac. Judy is raisin' hell, but she calms down a little when the music stops and the light starts going into the woods a-ways deeper. She wants to go home. I say, 'No, Judy. Let's go see what this was.' She says maybe it's a meteorite, maybe it's a satellite, neither of which sound very appealin' to her. 'I'm not gettin' back in the car, Bob Lightman, unless you *promise* to take me home.' Now, I'm not proud of this, but I just told her, 'Okay, then,' tossed my flashlight to her, and drove off. The actual drive-in was only a five-minute walk down the hill, but she 'bout turned the air blue. I never heard a girl curse like that. Well, Bob Lightman wasn't exactly being gentleman of the year, either, so okay, fair enough."

"Why didn't you want to go home?"

"I have no earthly idea."

"Did you know what the light was?"

"No, I just . . . I seen that light, and I just felt like I was *supposed* to follow it, like if I was brave enough to go after it, then I—"

"You could *become* Mr. Fahrenheit," Benji finished. *Like I thought I could become Benji Blazes.*

"Or some such similar bull," Papaw said brusquely. "I tailed that green light for miles and miles, almost all the way back to Bedford Falls. It started rainin' real heavy, and I had to follow it through the woods on these roads that weren't hardly roads at all. Then there was this lightning flash, and when it ended, the green light wasn't in the sky anymore. I thought I'd lost it. No such luck. It had *landed*.

"I seen the light ahead in this kind of valley. I parked in the woods and walked the last hundred feet or so. I truly did think of goin' back to the car, 'cause I had no notion of where in the world I even was. There were sounds ahead of me, like the earth was being ripped up. Thunder, I reckoned.

"I couldn't quite see the saucer yet—it was farther back in the valley—but I could just see this shape moving in the rain. It had legs but they were not touching the ground. I thought, *It's an angel*. Ha. Maybe the one that lost the War in Heaven.

"I tried to go closer, but It must have seen me. It just flew at me, like It wanted to stop me before I could see what It was doing. I couldn't even move. And I felt something touch my head."

"What happened?" said Benji. "Did you—did It make you see anything?"

"No, because the Beast didn't use Its *hand* to touch me. It was holding this thing." Papaw patted the ray gun strapped in his hip holster.

"It wanted to kill you?"

"Sure seemed that way. But right then, I hear this *BANG*, and there were black cars speedin' up this hill. I guess you know where the boys drivin' the cars drew their paychecks. The Beast turned, like to go back to Its saucer—"

"Why didn't It just kill you? All of you, if It had Its ray gun?"

"I don't know, Benjamin. You're right: It probably could've killed me *and* most of them in a heartbeat. All I know is, the creature saw those cars, and all of a sudden It turns back to me, and then It *did* touch me with its hand. The world kinda went away, like everything was fading. I could feel Its panic, Its fear.

I believe that once It touches you, you have some kind of weak connection to It, maybe one that's activated when It's close to you. And It can't look into your mind without letting you look into Its own. When It touched me, I knew: It had a secret. It had *buried* something there. . . ."

"What did the Voyager bury?"

"I . . . dammit, I couldn't quite see it! But It had come here for a reason, and It didn't want me to remember seeing It at all. I could feel It fogging my mind, Benjamin, making my memory get dimmer. It didn't disappear right away, but it happened soon enough. And I haven't been able to even think about that night for decades, until today."

"Why can you remember all of it now?"

Papaw sighed wearily. "The last few nights, I been having nightmares. I suppose that Beast and I are still connected, and when It came back and sensed me close by, that helped It—and me—remember bits and pieces.

"Anyway, that night, It went back to the saucer and flew away. *Adios* went the cars, too. But It dropped Its gun accidentally, It was so scared. I didn't know this monstrosity was a weapon, a'course. I just put it in my pocket, and you better believe I left skid marks on the road that night goin' home. I locked that gun in a trunk in our attic, and the memories got locked away, too.

"That Beast—that Voyager, that's as good a name as any— did do somethin' to my mind to make me forget. But . . . maybe that's not the whole reason I forgot, Benjamin. Maybe as time passed, I just doubted myself in the light of day. You tell yourself it's not possible, how could you believe such foolishness? And then you start a summer job at the police station, and you push back college for a semester to take 'er easy, and hell, the job you had over the summer is still open, so why not stay until you leave? Then one day, you look up from your desk and realize your job has become your career. It's become your life. I told myself, well, I can be like my own daddy. A real cowboy gunslinger. I don't know if I ever filled those boots. But you don't want to spoil the happiness you've found by lookin' back. God, you don't know how rare happiness is.

"Then this afternoon, the Voyager came to the house. It touched me, unlocked and looked into my memories, and that's when I understood: It was lookin' for *you*."

"I don't understand. Why would It need anyone's memories, let alone mine?"

"Don't you see, son? It's been playin' those damn old songs because It doesn't have any *new* ones to play. Ellie is safe, at least for now, at least I think, because you and your friends have something It *needs*. That Beast was here years ago, It went away, and now It's come back . . . *but It doesn't know why it did any of it*. It had a plan, but can't remember what the reason is! The night you shot It down, you damn near killed It—It took a few days to recover—and you did something to Its mind.

"It doesn't know why It came back, Benjamin . . . *but you do*."

It doesn't know, Benjamin . . . but you do.

The words clanged in Benji's mind like discordant bells.

You know.

There was undeniably a kind of logic to Papaw's theory; it made sense of the mysteries since the Voyager's arrival. But Benji felt no relief—only a kind of vertigo.

Because even if Papaw had just explained everything, on a deeper level Benji didn't *know* anything. He looked at his grandfather's face, which, in the soft radiance of the Cadillac's instrument panel, appeared almost unlined. Benji had recently feared Papaw would die, but now, hurtling through a nightmare in the front seat of a long-lost dream, a new and overwhelming knowledge came to him: His grandfather was *alive.* Papaw existed now, and always had, *independently* of Benji. Papaw had had his own youth and dread and hopes and a heart that beat with the same fierce and chaotic yearning as Benji's own. His grandfather was a *person*, neither more nor less real than Benji. The world of his youth had surely been different, but "different" was a past-tense idea, something that could only be understood by looking back. And Papaw had not lived looking back. He had only lived.

And it was then that Benji understood his own great sin: his blinding, idiotic obsession with obliterating his past. The dreams of childhood were dangerous illusions, things he should have left behind. The true "dark man," the true man in black, was Papaw, for he'd held more mysteries within him than either of them knew. Neither Benji nor Papaw had seen what was really happening around them, because they didn't want to. They hadn't paid attention to reality, but only to their desperate attempts to make it into what they wanted it to be.

I didn't feel like I should spend time with the pod because I was "meant to," Benji realized. *The Voyager was just manipulating me.* It had hidden in the pod, gravely injured and trying to piece everything together in Its scattered mind, only emerging and pursuing Benji when It was about to be turned in to the government.

"I don't know what the Voyager wants, Papaw," Benji said. "When It touched me, It looked through my memory, but I didn't even see anything important. There were flashes from the night we shot it down, but there wasn't anything useful. Some of what I saw wasn't even real. All I felt was Its anger. And that It's lonely. All alone, maybe."

"I think you know more than you realize, son," Papaw said. "Let's talk to Zeeko, okay? Maybe that'll help."

"Sure, I definitely saw something real when It touched me for a second, Mr. Lightman," Zeeko said. It was clear that he kept his voice steady only with tremendous effort.

They'd pulled over to the side of the highway. A sodium lamp buzzed overhead. "I saw it that night at the quarry, when we shot it down," Zeeko said. "Benji, remember I said I saw something else at the bottom of the lake? That's what the alien kept looking at, in here." He tapped his temple.

"Did you get any kind of feelin' about why It wanted to see that?" Papaw asked.

"I just know it's something very important to the Voyager. It buried something there; I don't know what the something is, but I think It was trying to use the tractor beam to pull it out of the lake when we shot the saucer down. It's something *power-ful*." Zeeko shivered. "Mr. Lightman, should we go to the lake and try to stop It?"

Papaw shook his head. "No, that Thing had a head start on us. I imagine It's already got whatever It needed."

"Papaw, when you were young and saw the Voyager burying something, could that have been at the quarry?"

"No, the quarry was just farmland back then. I saw the Voyager in the woods."

"Okay. But if the Voyager needed to get something from the lake, and It already knew that after It touched Zeeko, why would It still need Ellie?"

Zeeko answered. "Because whatever was in the lake was only *part* of what It needs. The Voyager was really relieved when It got my memory, but It also felt angry, or frustrated, like I hadn't given It enough info."

"Zeeko, you're doin' a helluva good job tonight," Papaw said. Zeeko smiled gratefully. "So, it seems like you all—Zeeko, Ellie, Benjamin, and maybe CR, although I'm sure he's safe now, at the game—have bits of information. But none of y'all have the whole puzzle, so It's just tryin' now to put it all together. Benjamin, did Ellie ever say anything unusual, anything *she* saw that nobody else did?"

"N— Wait, yes, she did! She saw something on the ice when we tried to pull the saucer up! There were these blue lights, like patterns the saucer was accidentally projecting. It was the only thing that she recorded before the camera shut off."

"*Recorded*? That's good, son! Where's the tape? Please don't tell me she had it with her tonight."

"No, she didn't want it on her, in case McKedrick came for us. . . ."

Benji trailed off, silently cursing himself. *This is my fault. If I would've just listened to her about the lights, maybe we could have figured it out.*

He'd always envisioned the Voyager's aims as being unimaginable because they were so amazing. There was no use in trying to think like that anymore, no point in trying to fathom the creature as he had before. Benji had no mystery or magic inside himself. In fact, it was pretending that he *had* that let all of this happen in the first place.

I'll do anything; I'll be whoever I need to be. Just let her be safe.

"She hid it someplace where people would find it if something happened to us," he said. "Papaw?"

"Yes?"

"We're going to the carnival."

20

The county fairgrounds waited for them in the eternal quiet of the abandoned farmland dark. The empty carnival climbed the hill like a spider toward the full searchlight moon. There was no ticket required for entry tonight, no lines to wait in for the really good rides. The unoccupied playland was like a kid's ultimate fantasy. But Benji was not on an errand of childhood anymore.

They parked the SUV and Cadillac by the front gate. Zeeko helped remove the Cadillac convertible's soft-top roof. Papaw pulled out his key ring to unlock the gate. Benji took the ray gun and vaporized the lock.

Papaw said, "Attaboy," smiling. Sadly.

Zeeko drove the Cadillac up the carnival midway slowly.

The midway was a wide walking lane covered in cedar chips and sawdust that ran between parallel rows of food trucks and games. Kneeling on the passenger seat, Papaw swept the ray gun back and forth, scanning the carnival. Benji did the same with McKedrick's pistol in the backseat.

There was a brief gap between the attractions, so Benji could see beyond the fences to the area surrounding the fairgrounds. To their right was nothing but cornfields, the cornstalks waving in slow motion like a homecoming queen. To the left were more cornfields, but miles away you could just see the light of the Bedford Falls High School football stadium. The dimmest phantom sounds of the cheering crowd floated to them. It seemed impossible to Benji that there was a place in the world where people still cared about a football game, where they did not know that Ellie had been taken. He had never wanted so badly to let everyone in on a secret. . . . But that was kids' crap again, that was him hoping someone else would step in. *He* was going to fix this, or it wasn't going to be fixed.

"*. . . in Jesus' name we pray,*" Zeeko whispered.

"Zeeko, quiet, this Beast might already be here," Papaw hissed.

Zeeko flinched; the Cadillac jerked to a stop. "I'm sorry, Mr. Lightman. I didn't think anyone could hear me." Zeeko's voice shook. "I'll just do it in my head—"

"Don't even waste your time," Benji interrupted. His voice was low but fierce. Papaw stared at him, taken aback. "If there's a God and He did this, I'm not really sure I want Him on my side."

"Benjamin, easy," Papaw whispered.

Zeeko had been facing forward all this time, and even now he did not look back at Benji. His grip on the wheel turned white. For a second it seemed that for the first time in the history of their friendship, Zeeko would truly and completely lose his meditative cool and erupt. Benji almost wanted him to.

But he didn't. He drove.

Now the midway climbed again. They followed it around a

sharp turn and left the games area behind. A banner stretched above them:

AMAZEMENTS A-WAIT!
(RIDES RIDES RIDES!)

This was the heart of the carnival, jam-packed with rides. The midway grew thinner as the rides pressed in claustrophobically. All Benji's senses seemed to be dialed to their maximum: the wind on the back of his neck claw-sharp, the *pop-pop-pop* of the tires on the cedar chips as loud as distant machine-gun fire. The rides' shadows scrawled the midway wildly, no longer like the neat rectangles of the uniformly shaped food trucks and game booths. The Vomatron unlike the Tilt-A-Whirl unlike the caterpillar roller coaster unlike the mirror mansion unlike the haunted house (its own banner read *YOU'LL HAVE ONE HELL OF A TIME!*) unlike the carousel (*HEY-HEY-HEY GRAB THE GOLD RING TODAY!*). Benji double-checked that the pistol's safety was off.

"We'll walk from here, Zeeko," Papaw said when they had almost reached the top of the hill. Benji peered up at the "Starlight Express" Ferris wheel, whose shadow now webbed them like the work of a spider. In the frozen moonlight, its wires and struts glowed like bones in an X-ray, its dozens of suspended cars swaying, crying softly in the wind.

Because the Ferris wheel required so much power, it had its own diesel generator, which was hidden underneath the raised wooden platform where passengers boarded their carriages. "Zeeko, you know how to turn on a diesel generator?"

"Sure, Mr. Lightman. We use them at the hospital in case the electricity goes out."

"I thought so. Could ya crawl on under the platform and power up the generator, young man? It would be a big help."

Zeeko nodded, looking relieved to have something helpful to do.

Benji followed Papaw up the small wooden staircase to the boarding platform. An operator's control panel sat on a kind of raised metal podium to their left. As they walked to it, Papaw said softly to Benji, "Think you might've been a little tough on your friend?"

"What do you mean?"

"If prayin' helps him through this, where's the harm?"

"I was telling the truth, to grow up, like you always do."

A strange sadness appeared in Papaw's eyes. "Is that what I sound like? Damn. . . ." He peered at the sky, at nothing. "The truth," he said, almost to himself. "Maybe the truth doesn't matter so much, Bob Lightman. What the hell *is* it, anyway?"

The generator sputtered to life under the platform. The lights on the Ferris wheel turned on, clacking and blinking. As Zeeko joined them on the platform, Papaw hit a big green Go button on the control panel, shifted the large emergency brake handle, and with a pneumatic chuff, the Ferris wheel began to revolve. "You said Ellie put it in the top carriage?" Papaw asked.

"Yes, sir," Benji said.

When the top carriage, number five, reached the platform, Papaw pulled the lever to set the brake. The wheel squealed to a stop.

Papaw tucked the ray gun into his waistband and went into the carriage. He found a plastic bag with a note pinned to it (*If you find this, play it & turn it in to the police. The people in this video are Bedford Falls High School students Ellie Holmes, Benji Lightman, CR Noland, and Zeeko Eustice*). The memory card was in a hard plastic case, insulated in several Ziplocs.

"Can we watch this on that fancy phone of yours?" Papaw said.

Benji nodded, popped the back off his phone, and inserted the memory card into the slot. Being several years old, the phone took a while to load.

Finally, a thumbnail image appeared on the screen, previewing the video. The thumbnail showed the quarry, as seen from Ellie's point of view on the cliff. Papaw and Zeeko closed in for a better look at the screen, and Benji, feeling his heartbeat thunder in his thumb, pressed Play.

Ellie hadn't been kidding about how brief the video was: After the mayhem began, it was ten seconds at most. Benji saw himself on the ice, the magnet already lowered into the lake.

Benji-in-the-video said, "You guys, it's working!"

There was a tremendous *THRUMMM!* as the magnet fused with the saucer, and then the magnetic interaction unleashed chaos. (Benji heard Ellie-on-the-video gasp, and could almost literally feel his heart crack.)

From the camera's elevated perspective, it was much clearer that the saucer was going haywire on the bottom of the lake. A dim blue light blazed from the hole in the saucer's hull and struck the underside of the ice. It reminded Benji of the movie light from the projector at the homecoming assembly.

The blue light strobed on and off several times, painting some kind of pattern on the ice, though it just looked like a random series of concentric circles. Then there was a flash of brilliant green from the lake and the video stuttered, pixelated, and went black.

Benji and Zeeko looked at each other, both disappointed. There was nothing useful in the video.

"Can you play that again?" Papaw said. "Real slow this time." He was staring at the screen. Benji didn't know what Papaw could have seen, but played it again in slow motion.

"Slower now, bud. I don't have my specs," Papaw whispered when the video-lake went berserk. He leaned in, squinting intensely. Still bewildered, Benji tapped the video forward frame by frame.

There was a soft scream somewhere very far away. He looked up, expecting to see celebratory pyrotechnics above the football stadium, but just then, Papaw said, *"Stop right there, Benjamin!"*

Benji paused the video, freezing on the moment when the blue light painted the ice. The pattern was just random and meaningless, wasn't it?

"What the ass . . . ," Papaw breathed. Benji was startled to see how very pale he'd become.

"Mr. Lightman, what is it?"

Papaw shook his head and breathed out hard, stunned, like a sucker punch had knocked the wind out of him. Finally, he said, "We didn't have GPS when I was young. If you wanted to get around, you had paper or other people. In high school, I used to sit in my room—your bedroom now, Benjamin—and memorize maps, memorize all the roads in town, and all the elevations. God knows I didn't have a full dance card. Sometimes I'd try to figure out the best way to Hollywood, California."

"Papaw, what are you talking about?"

Papaw tapped a quivering finger on the blue light pattern. "That right there is a *map*, son. A map of someplace in Bedford Falls."

"What? Why would the Voyager have a map?"

"Because that's where It was going to go that night after It left the quarry," Zeeko said, stunned himself.

Papaw nodded, then corrected him: "And where It *still needs* to go tonight. I recognize that spot on the map, I know I do. . . ."

Papaw closed his eyes, trying to think, to remember. . . .

Very distantly, there was that scream again, but Benji didn't pay attention this time.

Papaw's eyes sprang open. He peered at the screen one final time, comparing it to his memory. And when he seemed to confirm the match, he said, "Mary and Joseph. Boys, I know where that Beast is going to go."

"Where?" Benji asked, though he suddenly was terrified to know.

As Papaw answered, Benji heard that faraway scream again, but could not have been less interested, because when Papaw told him and Zeeko the answer—told them where the next piece in the Voyager's secret plan lay—everything inside Benji went cold. . . .

And so that was why it took him so long to realize that the scream on the wind wasn't coming from the stadium, and they weren't alone in the carnival anymore.

21

The scream had gotten louder, and seemed to form a word, but Benji was so thunderstruck by what Papaw had told him that he thought he was only imagining it.

"Benji . . ." said a voice somewhere in the night. He turned numbly toward the midway. The lights from the Ferris wheel glittered across the mirror-like surface of the Cadillac, but otherwise the carnival lay dormant and dark.

"BENJI!" The voice came from somewhere on the midway, and it made Benji's heart leap with both fear and relief.

"That's Ellie!" he said.

The carnival shrieked to life.

It was like a monster being animated by a lightning bolt: a violent resurrection. A thousand lightbulbs along the midway simultaneously sizzled on. Melodies from a dozen calliopes blared like discordant sirens. The merry-go-round revved and then spun at top speed, the faces of the painted horses strained and demoniac as they raced. The doors to the haunted house slammed open, its passenger carts jerking forward and prattling madly toward the prerecorded bellows within the house.

Behind them, the Ferris wheel tried to revolve and strained against the emergency brake.

Benji felt a hand clamp down on his shoulder. He realized he was already halfway down the platform stairs, running toward Ellie's voice.

"Don't you move, honey," said Papaw. His eyes were fixed on the midway. Behind him, Zeeko's glasses flashed with the midway's terrible maniac light. When Ellie screamed again, Zeeko crossed himself. "This is a trick. The Voyager wants you."

"I don't care! This is my fault! I don't care if It kills me, but that Thing is *not* going to hurt her. And I told you: *I don't know anything It could want!*"

"Benjamin, think! If that Thing wanted to kill you, you'd already be dead. We all would be. It knew we would come here, and It still has Its gun. So why isn't It just shooting us? Right now, why isn't It?"

Papaw stepped off the platform, standing in the open air, bringing Benji with him, screaming over the carnival cacophony:

"DRAW YOUR PIECE AND TAKE YOUR SHOT, YOU SON OF A BITCH!"

But nothing happened.

Nothing except Ellie's scream once again piercing the air:
"HELP ME, BENJI!"

Papaw had to drag Benji back up the platform. "Papaw, we can't just let It kill her!"

"I have no intention of that whatsoever. Now listen to me, child. That Thing ain't shooting at you because It still *needs* you. It got what It needed from Zeeko. My guess is It saw something in your mind but didn't quite get to finish the job. Can't you *feel* how much It wants you, son?"

For a moment Benji was silent. Perhaps the Voyager was

trying to block Its emotions from him, but if so, It wasn't quite doing it completely. Yes, Benji thought he felt a dim desperation from the Voyager. But the creature was wrong, just deceived by Its nearly destroyed mind; Benji had *nothing* It needed.

"Benjamin, if you go out there and It touches you again, It might know everything It needs to know, and God help us all then."

"Couldn't It need *you*, though, Mr. Lightman?" said Zeeko.

"No," Papaw said simply. "It's done with me, I believe. Everything I remember from the first time It came, It knows now, too."

"Papaw, dammit, sir, I don't know anything!"

"Benjamin, look at me. Please do that," Papaw said gently. "You love that girl." It wasn't a question.

"Yes," Benji said, confused and caught off guard. "More than anything."

"And you'd walk into the gates of Hell to save her."

Benji nodded. Why was Papaw asking this?

Ellie screamed once more, this time unmistakably a wail of pain. Papaw faced the midway again and said in an oddly calm voice, "It's time. Benjamin, I dropped the ray gun in the Ferris wheel. Fetch it for me."

"We're going to get her?"

Still looking at the midway, Papaw nodded. "I'll see if I can bring down the carriage," he said, for indeed, the wheel had strained against the emergency brakes and rotated a bit since they'd stopped it. There seemed to be something strange and stiff about the way Papaw walked to the control panel at the end of the platform.

The wheel began to revolve as Papaw released the brake. When carriage number five—the one where they'd found the memory card earlier—neared the bottom, Papaw hit a button on the panel. The brakes let loose their pneumatic chuff and the wheel's revolutions stopped, carriages creaking back and forth with leftover momentum.

Papaw's timing had been off: Carriage number five had already swung past the boarding area and risen a few feet into the air, so it was now about as high as Benji's chest. Benji grabbed on to the sides of the carriage and heaved himself up. The carriage swayed underneath him like a buoy. He got onto his knees, checking the dark space under the seats.

"Papaw, it's not in here."

"Zeeko," Papaw said, "how 'bout'cha check number six there?"

And as Zeeko stepped into the carriage below Benji, Papaw reached slowly for the control panel's big green Go button. . . .

"*Zeeko, no!*" Benji screamed, but too late: Zeeko was already in carriage number six when Papaw punched the Go button and released the brake, and the Starlight Express Ferris wheel began to carry Benji into the sky.

The carriage gave an almighty jolt, tossing Benji onto its corrugated metal floor. He struggled to his feet, the tremendous gears of the Ferris wheel clacking and ratcheting. *Jump down! Now! Before you get too high!* he told himself. But already he'd risen twenty feet, and there were dozens of steel beams and struts between him and the earth, just waiting to shatter anyone stupid enough to fall.

There was another lurch; this time, the Ferris wheel stopped. There was one brilliant moment when he allowed himself to hope that Papaw had made a mistake, that he was not sending Benji skyward to protect him.

Then something flew from below, arcing toward Benji like a silver flare. Papaw had thrown the ray gun, and it clanged on the carriage floor between Benji's feet.

"I'll come back for you, Benjamin! But if I don't, you use

that to keep yourself safe!"

"Papaw, don't do this," Benji began, but the gears of the Ferris wheel engaged, and he rose into the windy night, cursing, the light of the carnival world falling away beneath him.

When the wheel had taken Benji's carriage to the highest possible point, it lurched to a final stop.

From here, one hundred feet above the earth, separated by the intricate webbing of beams and gears and lights, Benji could barely make out his grandfather. Papaw was a fragile shape, just the size of a boy. How much Benji hated his grandfather then. And how much he loved him.

Papaw looked heavenward, and Benji had never wished for anything more in his life than to fly through the air between them and vanish into grandfather's arms, and kiss his anciently warm cheek. Papaw called to him, but he was like a man shouting in a dream from another shore. Benji could not quite make out the words. And there they stood for a moment of time that seemed suspended, separated by a hundred feet and a half century of age, and by no space nor time at all. Papaw put two fingers to his lips, kissed them, and lifted them toward Benji. Then he was gone, striding toward the ignited midway, pausing only to retrieve his hat from the Cadillac. For all the world, he looked like a figment gunslinger in a little boy's fantasy, and it was only then, then when it was too late, that Benji realized what his grandfather had been shouting:

Benjamin, you are so loved.

Tears of frustration and anger burned Benji's eyes. Zeeko looked up at him from the carriage below.

"O-oh boy, Benji," he said. "Oh, shit."

"Come out, you ugly pissant!" Papaw shouted as he passed the whirling merry-go-round. *"How 'bout you come out and dance?"*

Benji grabbed the ray gun from the gum-covered floor. He swept the weapon from right to left, scanning the entire glaring panorama of the carnival.

But as Papaw strode past the mirror mansion, the sky made good on its stormy promise, and curtains of snow closed in front of Benji, sealing his view of the fairgrounds.

"Goddammit!" he screamed. "Zeeko, we have to get down there. Do you think we can climb?"

Zeeko leaned over the edge of his carriage, assessing the situation. As soon as Benji had said it, he knew it was impossible: A hundred vertical feet of suicidal jungle gym lay between them and the earth.

Zeeko peered up, his eyes flashing behind his glasses. "Y-yeah, okay. I'm game, sure, sure," he said. "You stay here. Be right back, buddy."

"What?! No, that's not what I meant!"

As if to prove the danger, wind surged into them, making not just the carriages sway but the entire structure of the wheel. Forcing the world's shakiest smile, Zeeko shrugged and said, "Eh. If we both fall, it won't do us any good."

"Then I'll go!"

"No, y . . . *Benji, what is that?*"

Benji followed the trail of his friend's gaze to their right. Although the snow obscured the midway, the storm was weaker in this direction, Benji could see past the carnival's fences, its generators, and beyond them, the cornfields.

It was as if four glowing eyes were approaching through the cornfield, the enormous lit eyes of a monster moving viciously fast and low to the ground less than a mile away. Stalks of corn parted and flew before the monster like the Red Sea.

The four glowing eyes split, becoming separate pairings of two. One pair continued dead ahead toward the carnival, the other turned and sped in the direction of the front gates, corn flying in its wake.

From the hidden midway, Benji heard Ellie scream, *"Sheriff look o—!"* Papaw's pistol fired, then the bright signature green light of the Voyager's ray gun flashed through the snow. Papaw cried out, though Benji couldn't tell if it was in pain or victory.

"Papaw! Papaw, what's happening?"

Benji heard the crack of another gunshot. The gunshot sounded strange, too loud, and it didn't seem to come from the midway.

He felt something like a high-speed needle tug the shoulder of his tuxedo. He whirled toward the cornfield, where the monster eyes had stopped a few hundred feet from the fence. Beside the eyes, he saw a small flash of light, and heard another gunshot—and the sniper's bullet smashed into the side of his carriage with a spark.

"Zeeko, get down!" Benji shouted, diving to the floor.

"It's more agents, I'm pretty sure!" Zeeko said; his carriage screeched as he ducked to shield himself. "They must've tracked the GPS in that dead guy's SUV, Benji!"

A rapid-fire series of bullets, fired from several guns among the corn, stitched into the carriages.

From the front of the carnival came a crash of metal on metal: The other SUV had smashed through the gates. Benji could just see its headlights whipping back and forth as it negotiated the midway.

"Zeeko, if they get to Papaw, they'll kill him! We have to get down there!"

Climbing was not an option. There was no time, and also: snipers. As the snipers' assault paused, Benji dared to look toward the cornfields. Several figures disembarked from the SUV, approaching through the rows. Three glowing circles protruded from their foreheads like eyes on a B-movie Martian: night-vision goggles. The dark men were only a hundred yards away, with nothing but the cornstalks and the thin fence between them and Benji.

Except, no, that wasn't quite right. There were also the generators, just outside the fence.

The *gas* generators.

Benji raised the ray gun over the rim of the car, frozen for a split second by the gravity of what he planned to do.

Gunfire chattered from the other SUV, nearing Papaw's position in the carnival.

Benji fired.

And missed.

The night-vision men were raising their weapons.

He fired again. . . .

FWWWWWOOOOOOOMMMMM!!! The generators roared. A blinding tower punched skyward. Even from this distance, Benji could feel its savage energy. He flinched and closed his eyes against the mushroom cloud.

When he opened them, the blast had begun its terrible harvest: The cornfield had become a red sea, churning with a great and crimson fire that lit more rows every moment. The agents ran back toward the SUV, but already the fire was encircling them.

Benji didn't know whether they'd make it. And he didn't care.

He looked back toward the carnival. The snow abated just long enough for him to see the second SUV speed into the games area, which meant it would soon reach the rides section where Papaw had been. Benji swelled with panic and despair. He peered downward, again contemplating the climb.

The cornfield firelight whipped over the beams of the wheel, tossing wild shadows that made it look like the wheel was revolving. For one insane moment, it reminded him of the way the spokes of his bicycle had flashed as they'd spun through the morning air. . . .

And a stomach-jolting inspiration struck him.

He looked directly under his carriage, at the hub of the Ferris wheel. The hub was the ride's engine, covered with great gears and chains. It was also its most vital means of support; all the wheel's beams originated from it. In other words, if the center couldn't hold, this thing would fall apart.

This idea is insane, Benji thought. Fair enough. It was also the only choice he had.

"Zeeko, hold on to something! I'm going to shoot the middle of the wheel!"

Zeeko's jaw dropped. He seemed like he was about to protest. But after a pause, he just said, "I trust you, Benji."

Benji aimed the ray gun at the hub. Fear threatened to overpower him—he had no idea what would happen next—and despite himself, he said, "Zeeko, pray."

Zeeko laughed an octave higher than normal. "Way ahead of ya, baby."

The ray gun's volley vaporized the hub. The Ferris wheel plummeted, its bottom rim colliding with the ground with a jolt like an earthquake. Tumbling into a seat, Benji bit his tongue; he tasted blood. He braced himself, waiting for the Ferris wheel to move again.

But, surreally, all went still. The only noise came from the trembling of the wheel's steel beams, which sang like a hundred off-pitch tuning forks.

There was the sound of automatic gunfire from the midway.

Benji desperately threw his weight left and right, swinging

the carriage, trying to heave the wheel out of inertia.

And then, with ponderous and unimaginable power, like a tremendous boulder that had been perfectly balanced for a century on the edge of a cliff, the Ferris wheel began to move. To whatever minuscule degree Benji had envisioned this moment, he had assumed the liberated wheel would simply tip to one side and crash to the earth. Down would go Benji, carriage and all.

But the wheel *began to roll.*

Benji's carriage sailed higher into the air, carried by the revolution as the Ferris wheel rolled like thunder through the ride's wooden platform, shattering it into a thousand pieces.

The midway was ahead of them now, and downhill all the way. With every inch it traveled the wheel gained velocity, whirling madly faster and faster, like hands on a haunted grandfather clock.

Its rusting skeleton frame shrieking, the wheel barreled past the Cadillac, missing it by inches. Benji's carriage peaked and then whizzed toward the ground, approaching the bottom of the revolution. He saw several support beams below him bend inward, one of them soaring off like a silver spear. The wheel was coming apart, disintegrating from the weight it had not been designed to carry.

"ZEEKO! WHEN YOUR CAR GETS TO THE BOTTOM, JUMP OFF TO THE SIDE!" Benji bellowed.

The rim of the Ferris wheel began to crimp, its perfect circle collapsing, and so Benji's carriage took him lower than it should have, striking the ground. But this last time, he refused to fall. Ray gun in hand, he hurled himself out of the carriage and as far away from the wild wheel as possible.

He met the ground still on his feet, the momentum carrying him forward for several steps, and then face-planted. Air rushed out of him with a hoarse rasp. He forced himself to stand, looking back just in time to see Zeeko take his own leap of faith. Zeeko almost crash-landed, but Benji was there to catch him before he fell.

They turned together to watch, with great and terrible awe, as the renegade wheel barreled down the remainder of the midway.

And then the awe became less terrible when Benji saw what was at the end of the midway, straight ahead in the wheel's path: the second SUV, which began to reverse too late. The Starlight Express struck the SUV head on, crashing into the grille with an earsplitting scream of metal. The wheel rolled up the hood, shattering the windshield and pulverizing the roof, which caved in like tinfoil. As the wheel rolled off the back of the SUV, gravity finally reclaimed the Starlight Express: Like a slain giant, it listed to one side, tipped to the other, and toppled to the earth, smashing down upon the SUV like an apocalyptic hammer.

For a moment, Benji and Zeeko stood there, panting, shaken, staring at the astonishingly fortunate wreck. "All I prayed for," Zeeko wheezed, "was to not die. But tell ya what, buddy—points for style."

Benji heard someone behind him.

He whipped round, raising the ray gun. As he did, he saw the person behind him draw their own weapon as well. Benji fired automatically before realizing that he was only seeing his own reflection in the entrance of the mirror mansion.

His bolt of light struck the mirror. Rather than blazing a hole through it, the ray *bounced back* off the surface of the mirror, rebounding at him like the beam of a flashlight. Benji shoved Zeeko away and jumped to one side, dodging the rico-chet, which flew by them and vaporized the head of a skeleton outside the haunted house.

Note to self: Never shoot at a mirror again.

"Benjamin . . ." said a soft voice.

Benji's heart leaped: It was Papaw. Benji called out, but got no reply. Ray gun raised, he rushed through the blinding snow, afraid of the Voyager attacking him, but wanting, needing, to find his Papaw. Zeeko followed close behind. Benji sidestepped a hole in the ground: the grated metal cover of an entrance to the sewer. He peered into the sewer. All he saw was a series of ladder rungs descending into trickling darkness.

"Benjamin," he heard again, this time much closer. Benji turned, and as he did, he saw something that sent his heart plummeting: a wet red trail on the snow, scrawled like a violent signature.

He found Papaw propped against the operator's booth beside the whirling merry-go-round. Benji knew the carnival was still glittering and screaming around him, but all of that faded away. Nothing was quite real except for the thing he did not *want* to be real: Papaw sitting there, his hands laced on the side of his stomach, where, it seemed, a poison rose was blooming underneath his shirt. . . .

"No. No, no, Papaw, no." Benji ran to him, kneeled on the ground.

"Benjamin," Papaw said, tears in his eyes. "Oh God, son, I'm sorry. I'm sorry, I'm so sorry."

Blood pulsed between Papaw's fingers. Beyond Papaw, the carousel horses leaped, careening on their endless wheel of fortune toward the unattainable gold ring. There was something Benji should be doing. Something to help Papaw. What?

Zeeko appeared by Benji's side. "Mr. Lightman, I need to apply pressure to this. Sound okay?" He didn't wait for an answer: He took off his letterman jacket, lifted Papaw's hands, and pressed it onto the wound.

Papaw cried out a wordless reckoning of agony and anger and fear that stabbed something inside Benji. Zeeko swayed slightly but looked Papaw straight in the eye and said gently, "I have to, sir. I'm sorry, but I have to."

"Benjamin," Papaw croaked.

"Papaw, you shouldn't talk. You're gonna be okay." He looked at Zeeko, hoping for a confirmation, but Zeeko's eyes were on Papaw.

"Benjam . . . Benji, she's alive." Benji blinked, uncomprehending. "Ellie. I told her to run when I was fighting that Beast. I saw her make it out the front gate, but she can't have gone far."

"She was out in the middle of the midway," Papaw said, "right by the sewer. I knew it was a trap, but I had to save that sweet girl. I thought I could be fast enough, like some damn cowboy, shoot the Beast before It shot me, or at least kill It at the same time It killed me. But . . . Oh God, I am an old fool! Damn me to hell, boy, I am *so sorry!*" He coughed: spittle tinged with blood.

"Mr. Lightman," Zeeko said, "I need you to stop talking."

Papaw shook his head. His breath whistled thinly, like something pierced and going flat and dead. *No. Please, no.*

"It knows now, Benjamin," Papaw said. "The Beast grabbed me, just to make sure there was nothing useful left inside me. It already knew from Ellie that there had been a map on the ice, but It didn't know what place the map was showin'. I did. Now It knows where It needs to go next. If those agents hadn't showed up and started firing at us, It would have killed me right then."

Only a few minutes ago, nothing had seemed more important than unraveling the Voyager's plan. Now nothing was less important. "It—it doesn't matter, Papaw. We're gonna get you to the hospital."

With a grimace of effort, Papaw raised his hand; Benji, feeling tears fill his eyes, reached up and held it. Amid the warm blood, there was something cold and solid in his grip. Benji looked down and saw what Papaw had given him: a single car key attached to a leather fob embroidered with thread stitching: *The Atomic Bobs.*

"Take it, Benjamin. Get in the Cadillac, find Ellie, and *drive.*"

"I'm not leaving you, Papaw."

"*This is not a reques*—" Papaw began sternly, and Benji would have given anything to hear Papaw's strong, reprimanding voice. But something in Papaw's expression cracked, as if he could not summon the strength and certainty that had for so long defined him. He looked exhausted and very old, and frightened and very young.

"Benjamin, please. I tried to pay my debt, and I failed you. I'm sorry with my whole heart. But you have to go. Ellie might still know something you need. You have to find her and go where that Beast is headed."

"No."

"Yes, son."

"Benji," said Zeeko softly, "I can take your grandpa to the hospital. McKedrick's SUV is still at the gates. I'm worried more of those agents might show up, and if I don't take Mr. Lightman now . . ." He trailed off, but the implication was clear: *If I don't do it now, he won't have a chance.*

"Keep pressing my jacket against him, Benji. I'll go get the SUV." Without waiting for a response, Zeeko sprinted toward the front gates.

Benji dropped the Cadillac key and pressed the jacket onto Papaw's wound. Papaw grimaced and closed his eyes against the pain, his Adam's apple bobbing. Benji couldn't watch that. He looked at the key in the snow. The key had once been the same brilliant chromium of the Dream Machine itself. Now it was covered in Papaw's blood. Alongside all his terror and despair, Benji's heart thudded again with impotent and inarticulate rage at himself. If he and Papaw hadn't been possessed by the deadly illusions of their dreams, none of this would have happened.

"Papaw, I . . . I can't fight the Voyager," he said. "I know you think I'm important somehow, but I'm not. I'm really not."

Papaw opened his eyes again, and despite it all, a ghost of a smile tugged at the side of his mouth. "You really are. I always thought I'd be the man who would help you fill in the blanks in this world. Everyone needs someone to do that. But it can't be me, son. It's going to be your friends. Find that girl. There are secrets you can only open together. I can't help you." Again, Papaw's face crumpled into a heartbreaking self-loathing. "What the hell I *ever* done to help?"

"Papaw—"

The SUV swung onto the midway, about fifty feet away.

"I'm no damn good, Benjamin, you deserved so much better—"

"Papaw," Benji said. "I love you, too. Okay? I love you, too."

Many times this night, he had looked at his grandfather and seen a flash of a time when Papaw had been as young and alive as Benji. But it wasn't until right now that Benji understood that he'd only seen the shadowy side of Papaw's youth, the low-lying jungle land of confusion and fear. Now, in the chaotic heart of this carnival, Benji was witness to another kind of time travel: Papaw's pale face lit up with full-hearted happiness, a teenage joy brighter than the merry-go-round could ever dream, and Benji realized, then, that his own tears had begun to spill, too.

Gingerly, Benji and Zeeko helped Papaw stagger to the SUV. As they put him in the passenger seat, Benji almost said "*Good-bye*," but stopped himself.

"I'll see you soon, Papaw."

Papaw nodded frailly. "After 'while, crocodile. . . ."

"Benji, c'mon, I've gotta go," Zeeko said. Benji finally tore his gaze away from Papaw and followed Zeeko to the driver's side.

"I'll get your Papaw to the hospital as fast as I can."

"Thank you so much, Zeeko."

"You can do this. We were meant to do this. All of us were."

Benji disagreed, but he nodded.

"May God bless you, Benji."

Benji waited until the SUV had left the midway. Then he turned the key of the Cadillac and gunned the engine, leaving the carnival behind as the flames of the cornfield finally breached the fairgrounds. Over the building inferno, a thin shout of pleasure rippled across the night, as if phantom carnival-goers had come for one last visit before the fantasy of homecoming burned to ash and memory.

But the shout hadn't come from the carnival, of course.

It had come from the place Papaw had told Benji the Voyager was searching for next.

It had come from the sold-out homecoming crowd at the Bedford Falls High School football stadium.

22

Benji saw Ellie a quarter mile from the fairgrounds, running-limping along the shoulder of the highway. He swung the Cadillac to the roadside behind her and jumped out.

"Ellie, wait!"

She flinched and spun round. She seemed almost miraculously unharmed, physically, just a bruise on her left cheek and thin cuts where the claws had sliced through her jeans at the ankles. But in another way, her condition was nearly as alarming as Papaw's: Her eyes were green glass orbs, unfocused, catching but not seeing the starlight. She smelled not like cinnamon but like rotting sewage, and she was so pale as to look like a ghost.

"Ellie?" Benji said. "Are you okay?" She blinked, but that was all.

He took her by the arm and led her to the Cadillac. She stumbled along with him like a sleepwalker, then sat in the passenger seat.

"Ellie, I need you to talk to me," Benji said as the Cadillac roared back onto the highway. The Cadillac was roofless (they'd left the convertible's soft-top at the gates on the way into the carnival) and the cruel night wind bit into him. As they sped, he thought he heard Ellie say something, as if reinvigorated by the air.

"Ellie!"

Ellie twitched again. Her lips moved.

"Ellie, what did you sa—?"

He saw a curve coming out of the corner of his eye. He heaved the wheel. The Cadillac was like a reluctant boat: He had to turn the wheel far more than he would in any modern car. It was kind of ridiculous. The whitewall tires kissed the edge of the paved road and sprayed gravel as the Cadillac sped past a sign that read *BEDFORD FALLS—3 MILES*.

He didn't look at Ellie again until they were safely back on a straightaway. Though she still didn't seem completely alert, she slowly pushed herself up in her seat, blinking, like someone swimming up from a deep sleep.

"Ellie, can you hear me?"

She looked at him, squinted. And then, quite suddenly, began to scream.

The sound was earsplitting, even over the wind. She kicked back in her seat, clawed at her door handle. Her door began to open. One hand still steering, Benji lunged, grabbing her arm, wrenching her away from her door. She flailed, fighting him.

"Ellie, that Thing doesn't have you anymore! Everything is okay!" he lied.

It took several seconds for her to calm down, and in every one of those seconds, the Cadillac boated crazily in both lanes of the lonesome highway. Benji let go when she stopped screaming. She slid down in her seat, panting as the wind hauled her hair in all directions.

A sign flashed by: *BEDFORD FALLS—2 MILES*.

"I need your help, Ellie," Benji shouted. "There isn't much

time and I need you to talk to me. Okay?"

Dimly, still looking shell-shocked, Ellie nodded.

"Good! What did you see when the Voyager touched you? Did It make you remember anything?"

Softly, like a little girl reduced to tears, Ellie said, "The shapes. On the ice. It knew the memory card was at the carnival. And It knew you would come for me. It . . . It wanted you, too."

Why? "That's all you saw?"

"Yeah. Well, the only memories."

"Did It take you anywhere?"

She closed her eyes, as if trying to remember. "The quarry. I didn't really understand why, because I don't think *It* really understood why. There was something . . . something buried at the bottom of the lake."

"What was down there?"

"It was a . . . some kind of an engine. This glowing engine. It was small, but you could *feel* how powerful it is."

"An engine for what?"

"A machine, but I don't . . . I don't really know what kind of machine. *The Voyager* doesn't know what kind. Its mind felt like it was breaking down, like It's losing control of Itself. But I think It's almost pieced everything together. Once It blasted to the bottom of the lake—like, *pew-pew*—It remembered It buried the engine there a long time ago. And It knows the machine is somewhere else. It buried them apart from each other, in case anybody ever found one of them."

"God," Benji said, gooseflesh spreading across his body. "The machine is under the football field, Ellie."

Decades ago, Papaw had seen the Voyager burying something. Could that have happened at the football field? Yet that didn't make sense. Papaw had been outside of Bedford Falls, then, and the football field was in town. How many more pieces remained of the Voyager's plan?

If It's going to the field, It might try to grab CR and find out what he knows, too.

23

The Dream Machine rocketed into the football field parking lot.

"The pass by Bedford Falls is ruled incomplete," boomed the referee's amplified voice over the stadium speakers, eliciting shouts of disapproval and joy. *"The clock will be reset at seven seconds. Fourth down and twelve for Bedford Falls. Ball is on their forty-yard line."*

Benji stomped the brakes and skidded to a stop beside the stadium entrance. Security guards weren't stationed here, as they normally would be: They stood on the other side of the turnstiles, faces angled toward the light of the field, hypnotized by the gridiron clash.

"Stay with the car, Ellie, don't let anyone move it."

She tried to stand, but couldn't quite do it. "What are you going to do?" she asked.

Benji said the honest thing. "I've got no idea."

He hid the ray gun inside his tuxedo and hurdled the turn-stiles into Bedford Falls High School football field.

To him, everything inside the stadium looked like a highly

colored movie dream, a reality drenched in rainbow.

The Jumbotron: a live, video-feed close-up of CR shouting bright steam at the line of scrimmage, about to begin the play, the red numbers displaying the time clock glowing like sticks of fire.

The bleachers: full to bursting with fans, thrashing their pennants like flags of war.

The crowd standing at the fence that ringed the field: ten people deep, swelling against the chain-link for a better view, shouting at Benji as he shoved through them.

And despite all the insanity, as Benji finally reached the chest-high fence, a tiny piece of his heart broke for his best friend. The score was 21–17, and Bedford Falls was losing.

Benji tried to climb the fence. Someone cursed, yanking him back.

CR screamed, *"HIKE!"*

A series of machine-gun pops: The shoulder pads of the offensive and defensive lines collided, powered by all the fury and hope of their two towns. Ball in hand, CR faded back, back, and perhaps it was the snow that did it, but CR suddenly stumbled. For one electrifying instant it seemed that he would fall, fumble, and end the game and his fans' world.

He caught himself and scrambled up again, head whipping left and right, left, right, searching frantically for a receiver.

And so that was why CR didn't see the impossible thing occur: A seam opened in the vaunted Bedford Falls offensive line, and a Newporte defender surged through. CR was looking left, the defender barreling in from the right, and as the game clock hit *0.0* and the stadium's buzzer blared, the Newporte defender dove at CR, going airborne, a lunatic missile aimed directly at CR's knees.

AND CR LEAPED OVER HIM.

But it was not just a leap: It was art, a miracle on Earth. The defender sailed under CR harmlessly and the hometown crowd let loose a shout like a beat of their single collective heart.

Returning to the ground, CR spotted a receiver downfield, cocked back his arm.

And there it went, *zoom*, the long bomb, the Hail Mary, the most important throw of his life. The spiral split the snow like an asteroid ascendent, soaring, ten thousand necks craning to follow the leather rocket, and whether they wanted the quarterback to win or lose, there could be no doubt: This was what destiny looked like.

Amid all the other noise, there came a low quivering shriek of metal being rent apart. At the same moment, the shadows of every football player were thrown in a new direction. Benji looked up and saw with a surge of terror and awe that the great silver poles of the field lights were *bending forward* toward the field, like divining rods pointing to something secret in the earth.

The sky overhead looked as if it had been lit on fire. The blizzard above the field had become something like a hellish vision of the northern lights. But the northern lights, which Benji had watched longingly on YouTube a hundred times, were caused by a wondrous conspiracy of nature. Whatever was up there was not natural.

The announcer's voice came over the speakers: "Oh, Christ almighty, boys, look out, get off the field!"

A black helicopter tumbled out of the clouds, its blinding searchlight whirling. Its blades cut CR's football cleanly in two. The helicopter slammed straight down on the fifty-yard line.

Touchdown.

The field lights, still bowing magnetically, exploded all at once, throwing glass and sparks, burning an afterimage of the stadium on Benji's eyes. As the crowd and players began to scream, he climbed over the fence and sprinted through the darkness.

Get CR before the Voyager does!

Benji shouted for CR, but the air was a chaos of voices. He was almost knocked off his feet as he collided with another player. He checked that the ray gun was still in his jacket and barreled on.

Now he could just make out the stampeding shapes in the moonlight. He wove through them, calling *"CR!"* again and again. He felt the earth begin to quake underneath him and tried to tell himself it was only because so many people were running from the stadium at once.

After a minute of fruitless searching, Benji seemed to be the only person left on the field. Just as he was about to leave the field, he spotted one of the players standing a few feet from the helicopter wreckage, staring at it. Benji's heart leaped when he saw *NOLAND* on the back of his jersey. Benji reached out for him—

The field gave a roaring seismic lurch, as if the whole planet had been rocked off its axis. Benji was knocked off balance, staggering into CR. They fell together onto the trembling ground, Benji landing on top, CR crying out beneath him.

As Benji rolled off him, a tower of light suddenly erupted upward from the place where the helicopter had been. A hole had opened in the earth and was expanding every moment, threatening to take Benji and CR down to whatever lay buried beneath them.

Benji pulled a strangely wooden CR to his feet and away from the hole, no longer caring about the Voyager mystery, only that he get his friend to safety.

They had gone only a few steps when they had to stop: Without warning, a wall of flames jetted straight up from the ground before them, as if the awakening of the Voyager's subterranean machine had ignited a long-lost pocket of Bedford Falls's natural gas. As the earthquake grew stronger, so did the inferno: The fire raced around nearly the entire field, a ring of flame encircling them on all sides. The terrible memory of being stranded in the House flashed through Benji's mind.

"We have to get out of here!" he shouted over the flames, spinning toward CR. "The Voyager wants y—"

CR grabbed Benji by the collar of his tuxedo. "You did this!" he screamed. "Look what you did, you sack of selfish shit! Is this what you WANTED?!"

Benji knew he deserved every bit of CR's rage, but the great hole in the ground was still widening as more and more of the earth collapsed. It would reach them in just a few moments.

Benji tried to conjure Papaw's steady, grown-up calmness. "I'm sorry, CR! I'm sorry for everything! *I'm* the stupid one, okay? I know I screwed up, I know I've done nothing but screw everything up since you pulled me and Ellie out of the House, and I'm sor—"

CR released Benji and shoved him away. "Stop lying!"

"I'm not."

"I didn't pull you out of the House!"

Despite the madness all around them, Benji blinked, stunned, confused. "Yes, you did. I passed out inside and you came in."

"That is not what happened, and you know it!" CR screamed. "You found Ellie and brought her out, and *then* you passed out, on the porch! All I did was drag you into the damn yard!"

Benji didn't hear whatever CR said next. He couldn't hear anything at all except for a kind of dizzied ringing in his head.

I didn't pass out until I got outside, he thought, and the idea seemed inconsequential, so why did it hit him like a depth charge? *I didn't pass out by the door to the cellar.* He felt something enormous hauling itself up and up into the light of his mind, like the bogeyman mounting the stairs.

The dark man in the cellar. I saw something in the cellar when the House was burning. It was coming out of that huge hole in the ground where the gas exploded.

He'd assumed it was just a hallucination. After all, he'd thought he was passing out.

But if he *hadn't* been passing out, then . . . then . . .

"Benji, look out!" CR shouted, his face transported with horror by something he saw behind Benji.

The ledge of the pit had reached them at last. Benji had enough time to look down and see a huge metallic saucer rising from the earth. The Voyager stood atop it. Benji reached for the ray gun within his jacket at the same moment the Voyager's claws flew up and clasped his head like a vise.

It felt as if the inferno had breached his skull. As agony consumed him, Benji again flew gravityless down the memory corridor of mirrors, and he understood why both Papaw and Ellie believed the Voyager's mangled mind was shattering: The corridor was now filled with the smoke and the sound of sizzling snow from the football field. It was as if the Voyager could no longer tell the difference between the past it sought and the present by which it was surrounded.

Still, the creature pressed on through the corridor, piercing more deeply into Benji's mind. At the end of the corridor, growing brighter and nearer, Benji could see the image of "the dark man" in the cellar. An overpowering feeling of longing and loss suffused the Voyager: *This* was what It wanted! Where was this place, where was this House? It needed to find out—

But then, through the memory, light erupted: three brilliant ovals, atomically green, crashing through the mirror and shattering it into a thousand pieces. The Voyager's physical and psychic grips on Benji loosened.

Benji was back on the football field, lying in the snow. CR stood beside him, aiming the ray gun past Benji.

"I don't think I killed It, but I hit It," CR said. "This gun kicks like a *mother!*"

Benji saw something strange behind CR: A collection of sod, soil, and snow had floated from the ground and formed an odd ghost shape, a shape that resembled Benji-as-a-boy. It was like when the Voyager had telekinetically used snow at the drive-in to reenact the saucer explosion.

Before Benji could fully process this, the shape collapsed and CR yanked him to his feet.

The secret machine, buried so long ago beneath Bedford Falls, had finally risen.

Stumbling backward from the pit, Benji thought, *It's another saucer.* But that wasn't true. It had the same basic shape as the original saucer they'd shot out of the heavens, but this looked like a vehicle from hell. The new saucer was not silver but black, marred by clots of the sediment and stone in which it had hidden. Savage arcs of electricity hissed across its surface, filling the air with a wild ionic charge. Ten times the size of the original saucer, it seemed to take an eternity to escape the ground.

"Shoot it, CR!" Benji shouted. But CR just gaped at the ship like a terrified kid.

Benji grabbed the ray gun from him and aimed at the ship.

Just before he fired, without warning or explanation, the saucer tilted backward, as if reeling from a devastating impact. For an insane moment soaked in adrenaline and hope, Benji thought he had inadvertently dealt the death blow.

The portal on the underside of the ship opened, like a poisonous and omnipotent eye.

The tractor beam blazed into CR like a searchlight. Benji

dove for him, but he wasn't the athlete in the friendship.

CR tumbled upward, screaming, abducted from the only place he'd ever felt at home. He vanished into the portal, which sealed shut as the ship began to rise. Benji raised the ray gun and almost pulled the trigger, but he had to stop himself: Hitting the ship might mean killing CR. He could only stand there on the football field, watching helplessly as the Voyager's unholy ship ascended into the storming sky.

24

No. Please, no. Please let it not have happened.

Benji might have stayed there forever, but slowly he became aware of the world around him mirroring the way he felt: It began to shred and fall into the fathomless sky.

Several long, ragged objects whizzed past his head. Great sections of turf flew from the field, strips of flesh being gashed by invisible claws. They soared into the sky as if drawn by a black hole, and as the saucer climbed out of sight, Benji saw the pieces of debris coming together to form some larger shape as the Voyager's malfunctioning mind explored CR's own brain.

Where was the saucer going? *I don't know—we have to follow it!*

He turned, facing the flames, which still burned hot and were as tall as he was. He ripped off his tuxedo jacket, yanking the strings on the shoulders to make the full-length cape unfurl. He smashed snow onto the fabric until every inch of the cloth was soaked. Then he wrapped the cape around himself like a fireproof tarp, sprinted to the firewall, and leaped. *Ladies and gentlemen*, he thought madly, *Mr. Benji Blazes!*

Flames licked his exposed ankles and the cloak hissed viciously, but he landed on the other side, unburned. He detached the steaming cape from the jacket and tossed it to the ground, whipping his jacket back on as he sprinted across the field.

The fire illuminated the stadium. Benji was alone, the bleachers and sidelines deserted. The snowstorm and smoke had formed a visually impenetrable seal around the field, and he had to use the distant sounds of chaos from the parking lot to orient himself. The stadium destroyed itself around him as he ran, the light poles and goalposts spearing into the sky. To his relief, the objects were at least flying away from the parking lot; the saucer was retreating in that direction.

The Cadillac was where he had left it, just past the turnstiles, a reflection of the firelight dancing across its hood. All across the parking lot was a roiling, shouting mass of people and cars. From the sound of the sirens wailing across the night, it seemed every last fire truck, ambulance, and police cruiser in town was on its way. But how would they even get into the parking lot? How would Benji leave? The main exit of the lot was blocked by a several-car pileup, all the drivers fighting frantically about who needed to move and where. . . .

Benji slid over the Cadillac's hood. Only when he opened the door did he realize the driver's seat was already occupied.

"Ellie, move over, we've gotta go."

"Go where?"

"I don't even know. We have to follow the— Listen, you don't have to come, okay? This is my fault—"

"We will leave," Ellie said firmly, "after you tell me what happened."

When Benji had left her in the car a few minutes ago, she had been shattered, and so it was a shock to him to hear the dark steel in her voice. Her jaw was set, her knuckles whitening as she grasped the steering wheel. She was Ellie, undeniably, but she didn't quite look like the girl he loved. Sitting before him was a *woman*, a fierce woman with green eyes ablaze with determination.

"I want that asshat dead as much as you do," she said. "And you can't kill It by yourself. If you could, you already would have. So tell me. Tell me where we are going to go."

A dozen different emotions whirled in Benji. It took him a moment to find his voice. "We have to follow the saucer."

"What saucer?"

"One the Voyager buried under the field. I don't know where It's going, but It has CR."

Ellie's eyes may have widened, but their spark never wavered.

"Get in," she said.

"Huh?"

"Benji Lightman, if we live through tonight, I imagine that we'll have a lot to talk about. And whatever happens, I want you to know that I care about you very, very much, and you have many brave and beautiful qualities, so please don't take offense when I say this: You drive like both an old man and a little girl. *Now get in.*"

The Cadillac exited the parking lot faster than Benji would have thought possible. As the fire crept closer to the lot, someone had taken charge and cleared the pileup that had been blocking the exit. Now the emergency vehicles were arriving, and when the crowd parted, Ellie threaded through oncoming ambulances and fire trucks like a needle. She ignited the high beams and floored the accelerator as they reached the street, the g-force pushing Benji into his seat's soft leather embrace. Snow zoomed into the open-air Cadillac, making it feel as if they were piloting through a meteor storm.

Soon they had the roads mostly to themselves. Benji was navigator, and he peered upward, trying to spot the ship. The storm seemed to be weakening, but it still obscured the sky. He caught only a glimpse of the saucer, miles to the east.

"Ellie, it's heading out of town!" he shouted over the wind. "Go left!" As they raced in the direction of the saucer, his heart thudded sickeningly. He wondered what was happening up there, and whether the Voyager had finished with CR. . . .

Miles later, the road beneath them transformed: Bedford Falls's streets had their share of potholes, but this route into farm country was wild and unpaved. Ellie sped through switchbacks, passing rows of corn and rusting natural gas mining equipment. Once more the storm momentarily slackened. Benji spotted the silhouetted treeline of a forest about a mile ahead.

That's . . . that's the forest where the House was.

"It's taking us to the House," Benji said.

"What house?"

"The one I burned down."

"Why?"

His thoughts returned to what CR had told him. *I wasn't passing out when I opened the cellar door. That Thing in the cellar wasn't a hallucination.*

As a teenager, when Papaw had watched the Voyager bury something outside Bedford Falls, the creature had fled, frightened not for Itself, perhaps, but for something far more vulnerable. . . . And when the Voyager had seen Benji's memory of that moment, It had filled with loss and longing. . . .

Papaw had been right: Benji did have a secret the Voyager needed, after all. It just wasn't a secret he'd learned the night he'd shot down the saucer.

The secret came from the sunset of his childhood's last

summer, a moment he'd tried so desperately to forget but could instead only misremember.

"Oh my God, Ellie. I know what It wants. It left Its— *Hey!*"

Ellie nearly drove off the road: Her gaze had been drawn to something to their left. She cursed and jerked the wheel, righting the car.

He saw why she'd been distracted. The Indiana countryside looked like a war zone. The cornfields had been ravaged flat, the roof ripped from a corn silo, the bell tower torn from an old church by the forest. Even as he and Ellie watched, the destruction continued. Headstones from the church's cemetery were wrenched out of the ground and flew toward the forest ahead, stolen telekinetically by the Voyager's malfunctioning mind. A brilliant green light surged from deep within the heart of the woods, making the trees appear to be gaunt, gigantic guardians from a fairy tale.

Now the road thinned, becoming little more than a path snarled with roots that rocked the Cadillac back and forth. As they drove into the forest, tree limbs scratched along the sides of the car like hands begging them to go back. The green light ahead grew brighter and closer. The hair on the back of Benji's neck stiffened, the air humming with that ionic charge.

They heard the thunderous sound of earth being torn apart ahead. "What is that?" Ellie shouted.

"I think the Voyager's using the tractor beam to dig!" Preparing to leave the car, Benji secured the ray gun firmly in his waistband.

"Dig *what?*" Ellie said.

Before he could answer, the Cadillac emerged from the forest and reached the field where the House had been. Benji had not visited this place since the day the House had burned. The forest had grown and shrunk the field, and the witchgrass of summer was smothered underneath the snow. The passage of years had changed everything on this storied plot of land.

But the sky? The sky was a time machine.

Benji and Ellie stumbled out of the car, and there it was, aloft above the earth on the borderland of the only town he'd ever known; there it was, a memory beside the mothership in silhouette before the starlight; there it was, the final resting place of a billion ghosts of make-believe and their own mythic childhood.

There was the House, resurrected and floating in the sky a hundred feet overhead, in all its great and terrible glory.

"Oh, Ellie," Benji breathed. Awe and terror of holy intensity flooded him. "Oh, look at it."

"I can't believe . . ." Ellie said. "It's real, isn't it?"

It was, and wasn't. This new House was the progeny of memory and madness. The detritus of Bedford Falls—stoplights and swing sets, bicycles and gravestones—had fused together in the shape of the House. More shattered tree limbs missiled out of the forest every moment, uniting to form all the porch steps, all the spires and turrets. If this House differed some from Benji's memory (and it did), it was because this House was not Benji's memory: It was CR's.

Beside and above the House, the saucer's tractor beam blazed into the pit that once had been the House's cellar. Endless tons of earth rose in that poison light, and so did shadows in the shapes of pods.

"What are those things, Benji?"

"They're the Voyager's children," he said, goose bumps going all the way to his heart. "It left them here to grow, when Papaw was young. He saw the Voyager bury them. Now they're ready to be born."

From somewhere within the floating skeleton of the House

came a scream of shock or pain.

"That's CR!" Benji said. "We have to get him!"

"How do we get up there?"

"I don't know, I'm making this up as I go."

He couldn't bring himself to move. He felt small.

"I can't do this," he said.

"I can't, either," she said.

And so they found each other's hands, and ran together.

With every step, the chaos climbed.

Whips made of torn tree bark whizzed by them. The earth erupted in all directions, as if struck by invisible cannonballs. Benji and Ellie hurtled onward.

In the great tower of light ahead, the shapes became clearer: the children of the Voyager clawing free from the pods that had been their hidden wombs. They emerged writhing and glistening, shrieking heart-chilling wails.

"Ellie, whatever happens," Benji shouted, tightening his hand just before they leaped into the tractor beam, "hold on to me!"

But no sooner had they entered the beam than holding on became nearly impossible. It was as if he'd been wrenched upward by a chain wrapped around his waist. His head snapped back. They spiraled upward, the beam a whirlpool teeming with newborn cries and chaotic earth. He felt Ellie's fingers slipping away, and he held on tighter than he had ever held anything, knowing only that he must not let go of the hand tethering him to this woman he loved.

They were getting closer to the portal, fifty feet away now. The House, which was outside of the beam and slightly lower than the ship, was just above them. More cocoons split, and creatures soaked in green slime emerged. With his free hand,

Benji pulled the ray gun from his waistband.

Around the rim of the portal, an enormous silhouetted head appeared: the Voyager. Everything inside Benji longed to fire at the creature.

No, not yet, not yet.

Now Benji and Ellie were approaching the porch steps of the House. "Get ready, Ellie!" he shouted, her grip tightening.

They were even with the porch.

"NOW!" Benji roared, and pulled the trigger.

But he did not shoot at the Voyager. He fired the ray gun straight past his shoes, so that the blast was parallel with the ground.

Just as the blast of "the Question" had propelled the Rust-Rocket when it became their unexpected afterburner on Prank Night, the ray gun's blast now sent Benji and Ellie soaring backward through the tractor beam. Benji heard a shriek of pain from one of the creatures—he'd hit one of the cocoons, which was a wonderful accident—and then he and Ellie broke free of the light. They screamed as gravity reclaimed them, but they did not have far to fall: They crashed together onto the porch and rolled through the doorway of the House.

This entrance hall was an echo of an echo, differing in small ways from the hall from his memory and dreams. The staircase to upstairs was on his right instead of his left. The deer head mounted on the wall had become a moose. The replica of the once broken grandfather clock was "working," the tricycle wheel that served as its face rotating slowly to keep time. Most of all, the hall was much shorter than he remembered it.

It took Benji several moments to see CR, still in his football uniform, lying in a heap at the end of the hall. Benji and Ellie ran to him. Benji grabbed him by the collar. "C'mon, buddy, wake up!"

CR twitched, his eyes opening groggily. He seemed to nod. Benji and Ellie lifted him to his feet—

Someone struck Benji from behind, knocking him to the floor, the ray gun flying out of his hands.

It was Shaun Spinney.

Or rather, it was the manifested memory of Shaun Spinney, the eighth-grade version of Spinney, remade from stone and earth and recollection. Benji peered up at this echo of his past, thunderstruck as the phantom bully marched down the hall, reenacting CR's memory of the event.

Ellie gasped, looking down the hall, for Shaun Spinney wasn't the only ghost here.

Near the front door stood four child-size forms: Benji, Ellie, CR, and Zeeko. The reincarnations of Spinney's buddies, who were blocking the front door, were all blurry-faced; apparently, CR didn't remember them well.

But the ghost forms of Benji and his friends were detailed sculptures of snow and dust, their faces achingly familiar as they argued silently with Spinney to let them go. In a few seconds, Benji knew, the ghost form of CR would hurl a stone at Spinney's phone.

And yet there was one clear detail where CR's memory differed from Benji's.

In CR's memory, Benji was much taller than CR.

That wasn't the way it really was. I was way shorter, Benji thought, but seeing the event through CR's eyes only drove home the point Benji had been learning all night: Envisioning the future is an act of imagination, but so is remembering the past.

"Let's go," the real CR said weakly, snapping Benji back to his senses. Benji nodded, looked around for the ray gun. It had landed inside the living room a few feet away. He ran for it—

Suddenly, the living room wall blasted apart, sending him stumbling backward.

Holding a ray gun in Its claw, the Voyager floated in the storming air outside the House. It soared into the room and was upon Benji instantly, placing Its claw against his forehead.

The familiar agony consumed Benji. As their minds fused and the Voyager began to search his memory one final time, Benji saw something he did not think the Voyager intended him to see: a message transmitted psychically to Its children.

The Voyager removed Its claw from his head. As the creature had done with McKedrick, It began to thrust the barrel of the ray gun into Benji's chest, plunging it in like a dagger, as if to maximize the pain before death.

"Hey, asshat," Ellie said. "You're in our House."

Ellie's ray gun blast hit the Voyager square in the chest. Like magic, a hole appeared. The Voyager's claws released Benji and the creature flew backward into the night, for one moment seeming to float out there like the Wicked Witch of the West. Then It fell out of sight and was gone.

"Holy crap, Ellie," Benji said, stupefied and weak with relief, "that was *awesome*."

The House lurched beneath them, dropping closer to the ground and pitching back and forth like a fragile ship ill equipped for the storm. Large holes began to appear in the walls and floor: With the Voyager dead, the House was falling apart.

"Banjo and Eleanor," CR said, "let's get the hell outta here."

"I never liked this place anyway," Benji said shakily.

At the end of the entry hall, just outside the front door to the porch, Benji saw something that made his heart almost burst: It was the shades of the three children they had been, helping one another to safety. The emotions Benji felt were overwhelming and unnameable, all terror and ache and revelation and hope, but together they formed the shape of a fierce love.

He ran with his best friend and the love of his life toward the front door, and as they leaped off the crumbling porch together, the three of them physically merged for one fleeting fragment of time with the children they had been. The dust enveloped them, and Benji knew that their childhood had never truly ended. They were still twelve years old, but they were also thirteen and fifteen and thirty and ninety-nine, their selves composed of all the ways they had imagined their past and remembered their future. Then Benji, Ellie, and CR burst free from the bounds of those children of dust, tumbled through space, and landed side by side on the earth.

Benji rolled onto his back. The last of the pods had ascended, though the tractor beam still burned bright.

"We have to stop them from leaving," he said. "We have to stop them all." When the Voyager had touched him, Benji had seen something: In Its first and final moments with Its newborn children, the Voyager had psychically passed all Its knowledge to Its offspring. It had no past to guide It, and could only give Its children a bleak rage, and the knowledge that humans from Bedford Falls had hurt It. If the creature had originally come to Earth for anything resembling a peaceful purpose, Benji had made that peace impossible. The Voyager's only legacy would be destruction.

Benji spotted the ray gun, which Ellie had dropped during their fall, a few feet away. He scooped it up and fired directly at hull of the saucer.

But when the rays were a few feet from impact, a semitransparent shell of white light appeared around the ship, a force field protecting the ship from the blast. Benji fired at the still-open portal; again his assault was blocked.

The ship was coming for them now, the tractor beam nearing them and ripping the earth apart, a mere hundred feet away.

What do I do? What the hell do I do, Papaw?

"Come on, Benji, we have to get out of here!" Ellie said, pulling him back toward the Dream Machine.

Benji tried to shake her off. He looked back and saw Papaw's Cadillac, saw the reflection of the mothership clearly on the mirror-like hood of the car.

The carnival, he thought. *The mirror mansion. The ray gun bounced off a mirror. What if the tractor beam will, too?*

"I've got an idea!" Benji said, leading them toward the car. "I need your help! I'm going to drive into the tractor beam!"

"What?" Ellie said.

"I'll jump out right before I reach it! And CR, when I do, I need you to shoot the car."

"You want to blow up your grandpa's car?"

The tractor beam was gaining on them, seventy-five feet distant now. "Trust me," Benji said, "this is the only chance we've got."

"In that case, Benji," Ellie said, "*I* better drive."

And before he could object, she was in the car, driving straight toward the beam. As Ellie roared toward the beam, the Dream Machine glowed like a comet.

"Now, Ellie!" Benji shouted. "Jump out!"

She did, opening the door and barrel-rolling through the snow. The Dream Machine's momentum carried it forward. Benji raised the ray gun, but right before he pulled the trigger, CR grabbed his wrist and steered his aim.

"Banjo, I told you, aim for where it's going to be!"

And he did.

The atomic ray gun light hit the Dream Machine just as it entered the beam. The car detonated, bursting into a hundred pieces, the brilliant chrome transforming into a hundred mirrors flying through the air. And those pieces did something that would not have been possible if Papaw's teenage dream had remained a single intact piece: They reflected the tractor beam in a hundred directions, back at the saucer. The beams tore the ship apart. Its own power, turned in on itself, was the only thing that could have stopped it, because it was the only thing against which it did not know how to defend itself.

Benji felt someone take his hand.

It was CR.

Ellie ran to them and took Benji's other hand. And the three of them stood together, watching as the ship destroyed itself and crashed to the earth, a constellation they had ripped out of the sky.

EPILOGUE

BOY WONDER

The more he knows, the more he will find
to wonder at.
—Harry Houdini

From the Bedford Falls *Exponent-Telegram:*

AN UNFORGETTABLE HOMECOMING
BY THE EXPONENT-TELEGRAM STAFF

It has been five days since the most bizarre homecoming in memory shook Bedford Falls.

For the crowd gathered at Bedford Falls High football field, the homecoming game was meant to be a battle for the ages, not a battle for their lives. It may be weeks or months before the whole story becomes clear, but here are the facts as we currently know them.

At 8:49 p.m., moments before the end of the homecoming game, a small aircraft plummeted from the sky and crashed onto the middle of the football field. Initially described by some witnesses as a darkly colored helicopter, it has since been identified by the National Weather Service as an unmanned, "drone"-type craft.

Said National Weather Service Regional Director Donald Bray: "These are relatively new aircraft, outfitted with sensitive measuring instruments. They can be inserted directly into extreme weather conditions; they're more accurate and less expensive than Doppler radar; and unlike most Doppler systems, these crafts are manufactured in America. It's a win-win-win." When asked to elaborate on how an aircraft that crashed in a populated stadium could be described as a win, Mr. Bray paused before answering, "Well, as I say, these are relatively new. But we hope to amp up production soon, and our department is currently assessing whether Bedford Falls is a viable location for a manufacturing facility."

Mr. Bray declined to comment on whether this proposed facility should be viewed as the government's mea culpa for the crash.

Whatever the case, it is clear that the drone had been dispatched earlier that night due to the National Weather Service's detection of a small tornado in the vicinity of Bedford Falls. It was this tornado that would destroy the county fairgrounds, devastate much of the outlying farmland, and seemingly cause the explosion of an undiscovered natural gas deposit beneath the football field.

The tornado would also be indirectly responsible for sending one beloved local lawman to Bedford Falls Community Hospital with grave injuries.

[CONTINUED ON PAGE 2]

Benji Lightman wore a tuxedo and goose bumps, performing there in the footlights on the celebrated Magic Lantern Theatre stage. His nerves showed only once—he dropped a Ping-Pong ball during a technically difficult sleight—but that was understandable: He'd only been in Chicago a few months, since right after graduating from high school, and he was still growing accustomed to the genuinely unexpected fact that his dreams seemed to be coming true.

When he finished the act he'd spent several weeks designing, he turned to face the audience, taking a deep bow. Out in the great cavern of the theater, one person—and only one person, for he was the only one there—applauded.

"That was real nice, Benjamin," Papaw said. "How 'bout I become your agent? I deserve a cut, don't ya think, since you got all your talent from me?"

["AN UNFORGETTABLE HOMECOMING" continued]

From his hospital room, Sheriff Robert Lightman, 73, told the Exponent-Telegram staff his story. "I was sitting on the porch, cleaning my old six-shooter. When I heard that commotion at the field, I sprung right up, and I guess I just fumbled my gun. It fell, it fired, and boy did I get one heck of a bellyache. I just thank the good Lord that Zeeko was there."

Zeeko Eustice, a senior at Bedford Falls High School, is the football team's trainer and a neighbor of Lightman's. Eustice had contracted a stomach bug that afternoon and was unable to attend the game. Hearing the gunshot, he rushed to Lightman, but was unable to reach 911, as operators were overwhelmed with calls from the football stadium.

After administering first aid, Eustice drove Lightman to the hospital, where Dr. Elroy Eustice, Zeeko's father, was able to stabilize Lightman during emergency surgery.

Lightman said, "What do you call a policeman who never took a bullet except the one he shot himself with? 'Ready to retire.' I always planned to slow down someday when the conditions were right. Well, I'm done waitin'. Sometimes you just got to cast the die and then make the best of whatever comes."

Given that he has been sheriff for decades, is Lightman concerned about who will be able to fill his shoes, the Exponent-Telegram asked.

"Not in the least," Lightman said. "I've got some fine deputies. And this generation coming up, they'll surprise you with how good and smart some of 'em are. Heck, look at what happened with Spinney the other night. . . ."

[For more information on Shaun Spinney, please see "FORMER BFHS QUARTERBACK BECOMES HOMECOMING HERO ONCE MORE" on page 5.]

It was the last afternoon of Papaw's two-day visit, which was why Benji's manager had let them into the theater. Usually, Benji just spent his day as the grunt-worker-slash-custodian for the Magic Lantern's front shop, but he didn't mind the work. Even scrubbing toilets is kind of appealing when you get to the bathroom via a passageway hidden behind a bookshelf. And he knew how absurdly lucky he was to have gotten the apprenticeship. It wouldn't have been possible without the audition video Ellie had made for him.

It had been months since he'd seen Papaw. Papaw moved slower these days, but also looked younger somehow, and retirement seemed to suit him. Even when he complained about how expensive everything in the city was, he did so with a kind of delight.

Benji felt a wonderfully strange sort of pride as he showed Papaw the city, like he'd built Chicago with his own two hands. In a way, maybe he had. He was creating *his* Chicago here. His Chicago had a studio apartment with uneven floors and perhaps the world's most unreliable toilet.

But it was *his*.

FORMER BFHS QUARTERBACK BECOMES HOME-COMING HERO ONCE MORE
BY THE EXPONENT-TELEGRAM STAFF

Bedford Falls owes a debt of gratitude to BFHS alumnus Shaun Spinney. Spinney, 21, was in the football field's parking lot during the chaos that erupted following the drone's crash.

When the entrance to the lot became blocked by a multi-car collision, it was Spinney who took action and directed the frantic drivers and cleared the pileup to make way for the arrival of emergency workers.

How can Spinney explain his heroic actions?

"I'm super good at telling people what to do, and I like being in charge," said a somber Spinney in a telephone interview. "I'll be real truthful, okay? I could be a real cocky son of a [gun] sometimes. Then I hurt my knee in college, and all of a sudden, bam, I couldn't see a future for myself anymore. When those people crashed in the parking lot, and everyone was losing their [minds], I thought, 'Somebody better step up, right in this moment.'

"And I'll tell you what," said Spinney, with obvious emotion, "that was the first time I felt proud of myself in a [darn] long time."

When asked if he would be interested in pursuing a career in local law enforcement, owing to the looming personnel changes, Spinney said, "I'm thinking about it. I'm thinking about it a lot. . . ."

As night came, they headed to the restaurant Benji had chosen for dinner: Rita's Retro Café, which was modeled after 1950s diners, all chrome stools and tabletop jukeboxes.

"This is quite a home ya got here, bud," Papaw said after they ordered.

"It's nice," Benji said. "Well, not always 'nice,' but exciting, I guess."

Papaw nodded. "Sure, every place'll have its good and its bad." It came so easily, the way he agreed with Benji, supported him, even though Benji knew Papaw would have liked for him to stay at home.

"Zeeko's been askin' after ya," Papaw said.

"How is he?"

"Doin' real good. Taking EMT classes at the community college. I'm sure he'd love to hear from you. Have y'all talked at all since graduation?"

"No."

"How 'bout CR?"

Benji smiled a little. "He sends me the same text once a week: 'What are you wearing?'"

Papaw laughed. "That boy's got too much time on his hands, I'd reckon. Doin' a lot of bench-warmin' this year. But Notre Dame's a competitive program. He'll get his day. So what do you say back to him?"

"Not much. He asked me if I wanted to come back for homecoming next week. I never answered, though."

"Benjamin, y'know, I've gotta ask. . . . I appreciate you callin' me every once in a while. But don't you ever get lonely, son?"

"Yeah. I do. But I wanted to be lonely, honestly."

That loneliness, the leaving behind of all the people and places that had defined him, was a big part of why he had wanted to come. Of course, he knew he hadn't really left everything: He and his hometown and friends were so intertwined that it was hard to tell where they ended and he began. The real magic wasn't making his past vanish from him; it was becoming big enough to accommodate other things, too.

There was another reason Benji didn't talk to them regularly: He worried that their phone calls and texts would be monitored. None of them had been "disappeared," and he assumed this was because the government wasn't sure they had been involved. He had seen Agent McKedrick's memory; he knew the man in black had never told his superiors the names of the high school seniors he believed might have been involved with the alien incident. Even if any agents had survived the Battle of the Bedford Falls Homecoming Carnival (and Benji had no clue if they had), they apparently hadn't gotten close enough to positively identify Benji, Papaw, Ellie, or Zeeko. In other words, it was possible that no living person knew for sure what Benji and his friends had done.

Which wasn't to say Benji didn't sleep with the ray gun on his nightstand, and carry it with him everywhere he went.

The door of the café opened behind Benji, the city's ambient symphony of honks and shouts and famous wind filtering in. Papaw's face lit up as he saw the one person Benji had *not* gotten away from since moving to Chicago.

"Ellie, honey, how are you?" Papaw said, standing to give Ellie a hug.

"Better now that I've got my two handsome Lightmans with me, Sheriff," she said. She took off her winter hat and shook out her hair, which she'd recently pixie-cut after years of wearing it long.

"Ellie, somethin' happened to your head."

"I got my hair cut."

"On purpose?"

"How I've missed you, Atomic Bob," Ellie grinned.

She slid into the booth beside Benji. "Sorry I'm late, sweets," she said. "Cinema History ran over." She kissed him on the cheek. No apology necessary.

It was all pretty new, him and Ellie, still the first tentative steps. But it was a wonderful mystery.

Papaw and Ellie talked awhile, just catching up, just a normal conversation. *This is so nice*, Benji thought. He'd once been so certain that life was only and always measured by huge, grand moments. He'd thought that people who chose not to chase those moments were somehow less significant, somehow less alive.

He'd learned better when he went to the emergency room after they'd destroyed the saucer. Many of the normally reserved people of Bedford Falls wept in relief and joy as they found their loved ones safe. All those people had their own stories, ones as complex as Benji's own. On the surface, it might seem that people in small towns all made the same cookie-cutter life choices. But it was like old rock 'n' roll. If you weren't paying attention, you might think, *These songs are all the same. They're just playing the same chord progressions over and over.*

But within those similar progressions, you could make masterpieces.

Ellie walked with them to the train station. She gave Benji a kiss and Papaw a hug before catching the "L" train back to her dorm at Northwestern University.

Benji and Papaw stayed outside on the open-air platform; Papaw's train back to Indiana would depart in a couple of minutes.

An announcer came over the speakers. *"Ladies and gentlemen, the train scheduled for Indianapolis has been delayed. The delay is anticipated to be no more than ten minutes. We thank you for your understanding."*

Papaw rolled his eyes. "Your tax dollars at work," he muttered. He didn't sound lighter, like he had all day; he sounded genuinely bitter about the government, as he had for most of Benji's life.

Same old Papaw, Benji thought.

And almost before he realized what he was doing, he stepped closer and pulled Papaw into a hug, feeling a fierce wave of love. He loved his grandfather: all his kindness and crankiness and generosity and stinginess, all the imperfections that made up the mystery of him.

After a moment of surprised stiffness, Papaw eased, hugging Benji back.

"Oh, thank you so much, Benjamin," Papaw said. "I keep thinking, 'You're a good boy, Benjamin.' But you're not. You're a good man, Benji."

"So are you, Papaw."

They sat on a bench until the train came. There was not much to say, and they no longer needed to fill silence to enjoy it.

As boarding began, Papaw said, "You sure I can't talk ya into comin' with me for a couple days? I mean, look at this old man before you, Benji. Do you really trust him to be okay on his own?"

"I'll be home for Thanksgiving."

"Good. With something to look forward to, I'll almost certainly not die before then."

"Papaw!" Benji laughed.

They were almost to the train, small red lights blinking on it to indicate its imminent departure, but Papaw stopped in his tracks. He peered upward, into the gap between the roof and the open air. "Will ya look at that, bud," he said.

"What?"

"You can see some of the stars comin' out."

Benji stood there on the platform while the train pulled out, stood in the city wind and the silver billowing steam. He felt a pang deep down in his chest as the train carried Papaw toward the horizon, and for one moment part of Benji thought, *Maybe I should move back to Indiana.* And maybe he would.

Or maybe he would stay in Chicago forever. Or maybe he would move to L.A. or New York. He wasn't in the business of predicting the future anymore.

He stood there until the red lights on the train reached the horizon and blended with the other lights: the blue stars and the white city. And for some reason, the merging of those things struck him as almost impossibly beautiful. He was awash in the middle of his *maybes*. He was happy. And what greater magic was there than that?

ACKNOWLEDGMENTS

It took two and a half years for this flying saucer novel to achieve liftoff. Thank goodness I was blessed with so many extraordinary copilots.

My gratitude to the Nerdfighter and YouTube communities, who have taught me the beautiful flexibility of the concept of "home." Some of those people include Craig Benzine, Bryarly Bishop, Ryder Burgin, Sabrina Cruz, Lindsey Doe, Bertie Gilbert, Emily Graslie, Caitlin Hofmeister, Akilah Hughes, Nick Jenkins, Alan Lastufka, Ashley Mardell, Peter Musser, Link Neal & Rhett McLaughlin, Tyler Oakley, Josh Sundquist, and Nathan Zed.

Many fellow storytellers were also instrumental in guiding and sustaining me through the making of *Mr. Fahrenheit*. Many thanks to Scott Derrickson, Sara Zarr, Paolo Bacigalupi, Emily Wing Smith, and the Glen West 2012 Workshop, perhaps especially Jennifer Baker.

And special thanks to . . .

My wonderful "IRL" friends, including Scott Faris, Eric Cooney, Nathan Talbott, Kelsey Roach, Caleb and Emily Masters, and Chris and Kerri Waild.

The incredible magicians who inspired me to write about "the business of wonder," especially David Copperfield (!!!), Nate Staniforth, and Christian Painter and Katalina Absolon.

My *How to Adult* comrades Emma Mills, Hank Green, and John Green. Emma, you're one of my best buds, and I'm so lucky to get to make things with you. Hank and John, aside from the people who 1) created me, 2) married me, 3) agent me, or 4) edit me, you are responsible for more of the best things in my life than anyone else. Not to be mushy or anything, but, look, I mean, it's just, I like you. Thanks for being my fairy godbrothers.

The amazing team at HarperCollins, especially Alessandra Balzer, Viana Siniscalchi, Jon Smith, and Margot Wood.

The New Leaf Literary crew, including the amazing Pouya Shahbazian, Christopher McEwen, Kathleen Ortiz, Suzie Townsend, and Danielle Barthel. Also, super-special shout-outs to my awesome VidCon buddy Jackie Lindert, and Jaida Temperly, who is not only the most delightfully helpful person I've never met but also stepped in to help edit a pivotal draft of the book when I had lost the forest for the trees. Thanks so much, guys!

My agent, Joanna Volpe. People of Earth, would you like to know the great thing about Jo? That's a trick question, because the answer is "everything." Jo, I knew from the beginning that you would be a fantastic agent, first reader, and business partner. What I did not know was that you would also be such a generous, kind, and amazing friend. I wish I could find the words to express how much you mean to me and Sarah. All I can say is, we love you. Thank you so much for everything, Jo. Let's keep doing this thing, okay?

Donna Bray! You had faith in me and this book when I had faith in neither. Many times, you had every right in the world to tell me to hurry up already with my flying saucer manuscript. Instead, you told me, "I trust you," and without your faith and caring patience, I would not have had the heart to brave the fallow months when Benji Lightman & Co. felt like ungraspable vapors. I love this book, and that is largely because you and I worked on it together, which is another thing I love. I said it in *The End Games*, but I'll say it again: I think you're ingenious, Donna, and I'm forever grateful to be one of your authors.

My family, including extended family and the Laynes and Prindles, but especially my siblings (Matt, Molly, Patrick, and "outlaws" Adriane Martin and Dave Butler) and parents, Mike and Kim. Mom and Dad, you have saved me again and again. Whatever is best in me, I owe to you guys. I hope to be half the parents you are one day.

My grandparents, especially Grandma "Bobbie" and Papaw Crouse, and Nonnie and Papaw Martin. Bobbie is, no joke, one of my best friends ever, and by far the strongest woman I know. Talking with Papaw Crouse, on the front porch in the evening time, taught me so much about people, goodness, and life in the past. Without those conversations, *Mr. Fahrenheit* wouldn't exist, because it never would have occurred to me to write it.

Thank you to Nonnie and Papaw Martin for helping teach me by example how to live a good and decent life. You've both worked so hard to make the world a more comforting, promising, and loving place. Talk about magic.

And of course the biggest thanks goes to my wife, Sarah Martin. Our lives changed so much during the writing of this book, and you, Sarah, were with me through the tears of pain and tears of joy. I will tell you a secret: For all my life, I often felt like a spiritual twin of the narrator in Marty Robbins's 1959 song "El Paso," who sang of saddling up and riding alone through the dark. But recently I've realized the comparison no longer rings true. The greatest gift of my life is that you have traveled with me through the cold of all the lightless nights, with the faith that dawn would gather soon on the horizon ahead. In the Chordettes' 1954 song "Mr. Sandman," the singers asked the magic man to assure their beloved that his lonesome nights are over. Sarah, thank you so much for bringing my lonesome nights to an end.